T0271524

THE WIDOW

Also by Helene Flood in English translation

The Therapist
The Lover

Helene Flood

THE WIDOW

*Translated from the Norwegian
by Alison McCullough*

MACLEHOSE PRESS
QUERCUS·LONDON

First published in the Norwegian language as *Enken*
by H. Aschehoug & Co, Oslo, in 2023
First published in Great Britain in 2024 by

MacLehose Press
An imprint of Quercus Editions Ltd
Carmelite House
50 Victoria Embankment
London EC4Y 0DZ

An Hachette UK company

This translation has been published with the financial support of NORLA

A CIP catalogue record for this book is available from the British Library.

ISBN (HB) 978 1 52940 607 8
ISBN (TPB) 978 1 52940 606 1
ISBN (Ebook) 978 1 52940 609 2

10 9 8 7 6 5 4 3 2 1

Typeset by Jouve (UK), Milton Keynes
Printed and bound in Great Britain by Clays Ltd, Elcograf S.p.A.

Papers used by Quercus are from well-managed forests and other responsible sources.

But the line dividing good and evil cuts through the heart of every human being. And who is willing to destroy a piece of his own heart?
Aleksandr Solzhenitsyn

Fuck you, I won't do what you tell me
Rage Against the Machine

TWENTY-FIVE DAYS AFTER

Just before they arrive, I light all the candles. The ones on the dining table; those on the sideboard and on the shelves. I take great pains with it, really go to town. Apparently wanting to show them something with all these open flames, in spite of the bright June evening. That I'm not afraid, perhaps.

But is that true? The naked candle flames flicker on the table. Behind me, from the living room, I hear the ticking of the grandfather clock, its long, slow sighs. Yes, I think so. I'm excited – I am. A little nervous, maybe. But above all, I am prepared.

Outside, the weather is overcast, foggy. I open the double doors to the hallway, and the burnt smell immediately hits me. It is acrid and unpleasant, an odour of bitter ash and spoiled milk. This is the stench the flames leave in their wake – it's unlike anything else. It sticks in your nose, a smell you never forget.

On the stairs, the banister is black in places, and the wall's wooden panelling is damaged. The door to Erling's study stands half open. Everything in there has been destroyed. I walk past the doorway without looking in.

From the hallway window, I have a view of the road. In fact, you can look out across the neighbourhood and all the way down to the fjord from here. The water, which can usually be glimpsed between the treetops, has vanished in the mist this evening, but no matter.

My eyes are fixed on the road, on the lookout for cars. For headlights making their way towards the house.

Their arrival is imminent. They're on their way, and soon they'll be here. And I'm not afraid. I'm ready.

FOUR DAYS AFTER

There's an echoing in my ears, even though there is only silence. As if someone has just turned off a loudspeaker that had been playing at full blast for several hours and the sound still lingers. I sit on the sofa, straining to hear. My hands are shaking. I could do with something to calm my nerves, but I resist. I sit here and listen to the only audible sound in the house: the ticking of the grandfather clock.

The intention is that I'm not left alone. I haven't been told this in these exact words, or at least I don't think so, but I must admit that these days I have a tendency to zone out of conversations. The doctor who spoke to us at the hospital That Day asked if she could have a word with me, and I remember precious little of what she said. She was around fifty, perhaps, and she had these lines on either side of her mouth, indentations in the skin that decades upon decades of smiles and laughter and screaming and shouting had rendered permanent. I considered them, and wondered when the ones on my own face had arisen. Was I older or younger than her at the time? I never noticed their arrival. Once they had appeared, it was as if they had always been there. This is what I was thinking about as the doctor spoke to me. She had set aside time in her busy day for our conversation. One has to assume that what she said was important.

It was my children who decided that I can't be left alone. I overheard my daughters talking about it. One of these past few days – yesterday, or maybe the day before that. They were in Erling's study, and I was listening from out in the hallway. It was Hanne who spoke, in her insistent voice. Hanne always does most of the talking.

"That's going to be a hell of a job," she said. "Pappa must have five boxes full of them."

Silje didn't answer. Or maybe I simply didn't hear her reply. Regardless, Hanne went on and on about all Erling's things. She felt responsible for them, is what I gathered. She wanted to ensure they were taken care of, or sorted out – even thrown away. This was news to me. Erling's possessions are scattered through every room, and why shouldn't they be? It's our house.

And now it was vital they keep a close eye on me, Hanne said. Silje made an approving sound, and Hanne went on: it must be so hard, Mamma shouldn't be left alone. Huh, I thought – shouldn't I? I've always liked being alone.

The door was half open, and I peered into the room. They were standing at the desk, sorting through some papers. Erling's appointment book lay open, presumably full of appointments that would never amount to anything now. My daughters had their backs to the hallway where I stood, and neither of them saw me.

Today it's Bård's turn to visit me. He called a little while ago to tell me he was on his way. He said he just had to drop in on a client first, I can't remember where – was it Drammen? Tønsberg, perhaps? I had another one of those moments, where I simply dropped out of the conversation. It's happened several times over the past few days. Is it a consequence of what's happened, a side effect of the shock? I've been spared major losses until now, though I lost my father many years ago. And you hear things, of course. About other people, their losses. Has anyone ever mentioned it? This inability to keep the thread of a conversation. The way the attention simply slips away and attaches itself to whatever the eyes happen to fall upon, the first thing they see. As if the mind is no longer able to prioritise effectively.

Outside, the terrace lies bare. If I close my eyes, I see flashes from That Day: Maria Berger as she comes running up Nordheimbakken, calling out to me. The plastic clip that fastens the strap of the bicycle helmet under Erling's chin, the white strip of eyeball just visible beneath his upper eyelids. The hand with his wedding ring on one finger, as familiar to me as my own, lying there on the tarmac. The surprisingly uncomfortable chairs in the hospital waiting room, the clicking of Hanne's heels along the corridor as she came running. The lines around the doctor's mouth. The song that was playing on the radio when Bård drove me home afterwards, *oh, baby, baby, it's a wild world*. Letting myself into this house, alone. The fact that I didn't take a sleeping pill, because what if Erling came home after all – I'd need to be able to wake up, to go and unlock the door for him. Of course, I knew he wasn't coming – I hadn't completely lost my mind. He's no longer here, and the knowledge rattles my body, crackles all the way down to my fingertips: *Erling is dead*.

Of course I know this. I knew it then, too. But I lay there all the same, alone in the bed, and thought: If he comes home, I want to be able to hear him.

I catch sight of the tip of the grey paper wrapping of the bouquet of flowers that's leaning against the dining-room wall. When did I put it there? Could it have been just before I sat down? I'm not sure, I'm uncertain as to how long I've been sitting here. The bouquet was left propped against the front door when I got home from the supermarket earlier today. I haven't done anything with it. I haven't even opened it to see who it's from. For a long while I just sat at the dining table, staring at it.

There's something peculiar about all the demands made of the recipient, I thought as I stared – all these tasks that accompany a bouquet of flowers. First, it has to be unwrapped. The paper has to be thrown away and the stalks cut; a vase has to be dug from the depths of a kitchen cabinet and filled with water and plant food. Then the flowers need constant attention: the water has to be changed, any dead ones need to be taken out and those remaining rearranged. Eventually they all die, of course, and then the whole lot have to be thrown away, the vase washed and dried, the rubbish taken out. What an idea: your husband died, so here you go – now you have twenty individual plants, lopped off at the root and therefore at death's door, and now it's your job to take care of them, to do what you can to delay the inevitable, before you finally have to accept your own inadequacy as they wilt and die. On the other hand, it's just a custom, so perhaps it's sensible not to think too much about it. Erling was very concerned with common sense. *She's a sensible woman*, he might say about someone, or *he acted very sensibly*. This was the greatest compliment he could bestow. The opposite was his ultimate condemnation.

The grandfather clock strikes the hour. Then the ticking resumes, tick, tock, the very pulse of the house. I sit on the sofa and consider the still-wrapped flowers. A sensible woman would unwrap them. In my mind I leave the bouquet leaning against the living-room wall, get up and turn and saunter upstairs, into the bathroom, and open our little medicine cabinet. Find the box with its brand name, its label with my name printed on it in neat, black letters: EVY KROGH. FOR THE TREATMENT OF SLEEPLESSNESS AND ANXIETY. How long can it be since I last took one?

But what I'm feeling isn't really anxiety. I don't know what it is. I just wish I could be spared having to deal with all this.

*

Earlier today, a young man from the environmental non-profit came to the door. He offered his condolences, and he had brought me a plant. Jesus, it's just tragic, he said, then he moderated his words: or, I mean, it's terribly sad. Afterwards, I thought about this downgrading. Erling is sixty-eight. Was. Probably a good deal older than this boy's parents. I didn't say anything. At least he brought a pot plant rather than cut flowers.

Synne came yesterday. Olav came over the day after it happened, as did Erling's sister, who made a brief trip from Bergen. I sit here, trying to keep count, to keep track of them all. Erling and I live a fairly quiet life. We don't have many visitors. Generally it's just the two of us here, but over the past few days there's been a non-stop barrage.

A harsh noise cuts through the room. The doorbell is like an air raid siren – it slashes through the silence, demanding action. It's been this way ever since we took over the house from Erling's parents. It was probably my father-in-law who installed it, it would have been just like him. There's nothing inviting about it, it orders you to stand to attention, and on each and every day of the thirty-odd years I've lived in this house, I've hated its strictness. Now, though, I find it reassuring. On your feet, it says, and my legs, which I don't otherwise seem to be entirely able to control, obey.

"Mamma?" Bård calls.

I'm clearly not moving fast enough for him, and he's let himself in. He hasn't taken off his shoes. He was like that as a child, too – always forgetting himself and stomping in with his boots on. When I notice this, my heart gives a little squeeze.

Now he's taller than me. And not really young anymore, either. He hugs me, and I see that his hair is thinning at the back of his head, that his pale brown curls are in the process of disappearing. His hair is the same colour mine was when I was younger, the same as Hanne's, too, but his curls are beginning to grey. Hanne has retained her colour – presumably with a little help from regular trips to the hairdresser, which cost a fortune. Bård smells of his car and of coffee, and he's wearing a pale blue shirt with fine stitching. I release him, look at him. The skin around his eyes is grey and twitchy.

"How are you?" he asks, and I refrain from mentioning his shoes.

"Oh, you know," I say. "And you?"

He wipes a hand across his forehead, as if to wipe away the exhaustion. Gives a weak smile.

"Oh, you know."

Bård is my firstborn. He came into the world the year I turned thirty-three, all red-faced and thrashing. He was a sensitive child. Timid, good-humoured, for the most part, but when provoked he could fly into a rage. You shouldn't rank your children, and I love all mine equally – I do. But I'm closest to Bård. I can read him more easily than I can the girls. I have a special fondness for him, too. Now we're eating in silence, and I realise that I've forgotten to get out the placemats. The old mahogany dining table belonged to Erling's parents – it scratches if you so much as look at it. And now I've just put the greasy tub of chicken stir-fry Bård brought straight onto the bare wood.

Bård stares into space, glassy-eyed – he's far away. Is he thinking about his father? Is the sudden loss causing him pain? But no, it isn't that. Or at least, not only that. Part of him is still at work, I think, contemplating his last meeting.

He looks up and sees that I'm watching him. He smiles. He's handsome, too, my boy. Grew up to be tall and slim, with fine, symmetrical features. "So what have you been up to today, Mamma?" he asks.

"Nothing," I say. "I've just been sitting here."

This surprises him. He probably can't remember when he last had a day free of demands on his time. He and his wife live in an old house they're currently renovating, and they have two boys who participate in all kinds of sports. Every single weekend the family attends a rally or a match or a race; they sell waffles to raise money, they wax skis and cheer on the team. And when they're not doing that, they're painting skirting boards or working in the garden.

"All day?"

"What else was I supposed to do?" I ask.

He looks taken aback. Then a small smile breaks across his lips.

"Pfft, who knows."

As he reaches for the tub of takeaway, lifting it to reveal the puddle of oil on the tabletop's mirror-like surface, he asks about the package wrapped in grey paper lying on the floor next to the sideboard.

"Some flowers were delivered to the door," I say. "I didn't have a chance to unwrap them."

"You didn't have a chance?"

He frowns, and his smile disappears.

"I'll do it," he says.

The scissors are in the study. The huge desk belonged to Erling's father – Professor of Law and Supreme Court Justice Krogh. It's made of solid, dark oak, with elaborately carved ornamentations that collect dust it's almost impossible to get rid of. I've never liked it. We inherited a great deal of furniture when we took over the house, this brown-stained detached property atop a rocky knoll in Montebello. It was part of the deal. All Erling's books are arranged on the shelves that line the walls. The desktop lies open and empty, ready for work.

But something in here is different. Isn't it? I can't quite put my finger on what. The smooth desktop, the high-backed chair tucked under it. I grab the scissors from the desk tidy. In the doorway I turn and look about me. Yes – something in here isn't right.

But perhaps this is only natural. *He's* missing, of course, and maybe it's just that.

"Here," Bård says once he's managed to tear the first layer of paper off the bouquet. He hands me the card.

The envelope is bright white, pristine, unsullied; the note inside written on creamy, textured paper. *Dear Evy*, it says. *I'm so sorry for your loss. Erling was a dear friend to me, as are you. With best wishes, Edvard Weimer.*

Beneath the grey paper there's a layer of plastic. Bård sighs – all this packaging. I say nothing. Read the card again. *A dear friend.*

"Is it really necessary to wrap so much rubbish around a single bunch of flowers?" Bård mumbles. "Dad would have hit the roof."

As are you.

Wrapped in the plastic is a bouquet of twenty long-stalked white roses. Mother used to sing a ditty that explained the meaning of various colours of rose. *Red is for a lover, yellow for a friend. White is for* . . . I don't remember. It's decades since I last spoke to Edvard Weimer, but something tells me he's a man who knows these kinds of things.

"Who are they from?" Bård asks.

"Someone called Edvard," I say. "He's an old friend of Pappa's."

Bård glances at the card and frowns.

"Never heard of him."

Once again, I refrain from taking a sleeping pill, so I lie awake, tossing and turning in bed. At around two in the morning I get up and go downstairs.

The hallway is dark, but for the faint light from outside, which streams into Erling's study through the window and seeps out here through the open door. I stand in shadow. My feet bare, I walk over to the doorway and peer into the room.

Something is wrong in here. Something has been moved. Something that should be here is missing.

But so what? Objects get moved – that kind of thing happens all the time. The night muddles one's thoughts. The darkness and silence give the surroundings alternate meanings. Make little things into warnings, trifles into sombre premonitions. I should go back upstairs, get back into bed, snatch a few hours' sleep.

But I stand there all the same. Counting the seconds, looking about me.

FIVE DAYS AFTER

They are standing on the front step when I open the door – a man and a woman. The man is tall and sinewy, with a bushy moustache. I've never liked beards or moustaches – I get that from Mother, who found facial hair unseemly. The woman next to him is wearing a leather jacket, her reddish-brown hair gathered into a ponytail. The lanky moustachioed man is wearing jeans and a windcheater. He appears to be the one who rang the bell.

"Krogh?" he asks. "Evy Krogh?"

"Yes?"

"Gundersen here, with the police. This is my colleague, Ingvild Fredly. I'm very sorry to hear of your husband's recent passing."

I nod, not entirely sure how I'm supposed to respond.

"We have a few questions in connection with that," he says. "May we come in?"

The man who calls himself Gundersen dominates my living room. Erling was tall, too, but his shoulders became increasingly stooped as the years passed. Gundersen's back and shoulders are immodestly erect, his body leaning forward slightly, as if he can't wait to make a start on what's coming. He's quick, is the impression I get. Already several steps ahead of the rest of us.

"Is it okay if I take a look around?" Ingvild Fredly asks.

I only look at her. Is it okay? I don't want her snooping through our things, I really don't, but you don't say no to the police. At least, not if you're from a decent home and grew up with law-abiding parents who did their duty, paid their taxes and never got so much as a speeding ticket.

"Of course," I say.

She has strong features – large eyebrows, a heavyset jaw. But her eyes are kind.

I show her into the hallway. Open the heavy double doors that have always been here. They were my mother-in-law's idea, I imagine. When closed – as they always are – they separate the more public parts of the house from the private: the upstairs with its bedrooms; the study and the cellar door. Before we moved in, I had thought this an old-fashioned arrangement, but somehow, we ended up living the same way.

Whenever we have guests – even if it's our own children – we close the double doors. What lies beyond them is for Erling and me alone. But in just a matter of days everything has been turned on its head – my daughters now walk through the double doors and into the study, thinking nothing of it. I let Fredly through, too. Perhaps it's outdated to believe that certain things are private and must be hidden, I think, as I watch the policewoman stride towards the stairs.

When I return, Gundersen is standing there looking about him.

"Is there somewhere we might take a seat?" he asks.

He settles his weight over his heels now, observing. It might look as if he's simply taking his time over things, but I watch his gaze – it hops from one place to the next at lightning speed, taking everything in.

We sit in the living room. I take the sofa, and he chooses the armchair. He rests his elbows on his knees, leans forward.

"So," he says. "I suppose you must be wondering why we're here?"

I nod.

"As you'll be aware, a post-mortem was just performed on your husband."

Was it? The doctor with the laugh lines. The things she said, and which I didn't pay attention to. My hands tremble slightly against my thighs, and I gather them in my lap, hiding them. The policeman must notice my hesitation, because he flicks through some papers, says something about information I should have received at the hospital.

"It was, you know . . . That Day," I say. "There are things I don't quite remember."

"That's perfectly understandable."

There's compassion in his eyes – but not too much, and I like that. Now I see that, like Fredly, he too has kind eyes.

"The thing is," he says, "certain irregularities were discovered. So we thought it worth looking into them."

He leafs through the papers again.

"Erling's medical records state that he was taking certain medications. For his heart, things of that nature. Is that correct?"

"Yes," I say. "Daily."

Gundersen rattles them off: Digoxin, Metoprolol, Simvastatin and so on and so forth, prescribed by the doctor after Erling's heart problems were diagnosed some years ago. I nod obediently. I recognise the names from the boxes and the bottle in the bathroom cabinet, but I don't remember what was prescribed when or for what purpose.

"One thing that surprised the pathologist," Gundersen says, "is that no traces of these medications were found in Erling's body."

It feels as if I only partly hear him. This feeling again, as if I've been listening to deafening music for hours and someone has only just turned it off.

"That is, it appears he hadn't been taking his pills," the policeman says. "Not for weeks."

"That's strange."

"He never said anything about stopping taking them? That he was worried about potential side effects, or that he'd started exercising instead? Eating more healthily, consulting a homeopath, those kinds of things?"

I snigger. The sound is inappropriate, and it surprises both him and me.

"You didn't know Erling," I say. "If the doctor told him to do something, he did it. Had she asked him to run a marathon by next summer, he'd have started training. And he despised alternative medicine."

Gundersen smiles.

"I know the type," he says. "Which makes it even more strange. Do you know where he kept his medicines?"

"Of course. In the medicine cabinet, in the bathroom upstairs."

I imagine Fredly's hands in the cabinet. And my own box of pills: *for the treatment of sleeplessness and anxiety.*

"Good," he says, but he makes no move to get up. Instead, he leans on his forearms, which rest on his thighs, and looks at me.

"So how do you make sense of this, Evy? Erling follows his doctor's orders to the letter, his doctor has prescribed him medications for his heart and to lower his cholesterol, and yet we found no trace of these in his body."

"I don't know," I say. "I don't know how to make sense of it."

I hear my voice as an echo. I'm so lethargic, so listless, despite not having taken a pill yesterday. It's as if I'm watching us from a distance. As if none of this really concerns me. As if it's all a dream. Erling is dead, and now a policeman is sitting in our living room.

"Gundersen," the policewoman shouts from upstairs.

"Excuse me for just a moment," he says, and gets up.

The grandfather clock ticks its way through the viscous seconds until he comes back. I count two hundred and seventy-nine of them.

"There are no medicines in the bathroom cabinet," he says when he returns.

"That's where he keeps them," I say. "In the cabinet on the wall beside the mirror."

"We've searched the shelves," Gundersen says. "There are ordinary painkillers, two boxes of pills with your name on them, and a bottle of cod liver oil capsules. Nothing belonging to Erling."

And I'm still far away, as if I'm watching us through the wrong end of a telescope. I feel an uneasy gnawing at the back of my mind: haven't I seen the boxes of pills there, only recently?

It must be around three years since he was given the first prescription. He'd started complaining that he was getting out of breath, so I told him to go to the doctor. Pfft, he said – was that really necessary? Weeks passed. I complained to Hanne. Hanne called the GP and booked an appointment, then called Erling and said: you have an appointment on Wednesday, could you please make sure you go?

The doctor had a listen, did some tests, and was concerned. Erling was referred for further tests at the hospital, then sent home with some prescriptions. The pharmacy gave him two boxes containing blister packs, along with a glass bottle. In the living room, he spread them across the coffee table's worn surface.

"My daily dose," he said, looking a little pale. "From now on, I'll be on medication for life."

We looked at them, the boxes and the bottle. Erling glanced up at me, his mouth twisted into the lopsided smile he sometimes wore.

"No-one can live forever, Evy."

I blinked a couple of times, feeling strangely moved. And so it begins, I thought – old age. I think I'd had a glass of wine with lunch that day, so I have to ask myself: were those his exact words? That he'd be on medication for life?

Gundersen sits down again. The armchair seems a little too low for him. His long legs splay out on either side of his body, his knees sticking up like mountaintops.

"How was your marriage?" he asks.

"Good," I say.

There's a tickling in my throat again, because isn't this absurd? Part of me thinks: Erling is going to be so surprised when I tell him about this. As it dawns on me that this will never happen – that I'll never tell him anything ever again – something heavy settles over my chest and squeezes, pushing my lungs together. For a split second I'm completely breathless. My windpipe empty, my throat stiff and freezing cold, *oh, this loss – the magnitude of it*, to lose Erling along with everything that will disappear with him – it's so overwhelming that I can neither see nor hear. Then the sensation eases, my sight and hearing return, and it's as if nothing has happened. It occurs so quickly that I don't think the policeman can have noticed.

"And family life in general," he says. "You have children, don't you?"

"Yes," I say. "Three of them. All grown."

"And they're married, with children of their own?"

"The oldest two are married with children, yes. I have three grandchildren."

"And how do you get along with your children? Any friction or feuds, anything like that?"

"No."

"I'm not necessarily thinking of major conflicts, but, you know, the usual kinds of tensions that can arise now and then."

"There's nothing," I say, slowly, distantly. "We get on well."

"Of course," Gundersen says with a nod. "Well, every family is different. How about your extended family?"

"The same. Erling's parents are dead, my sister-in-law lives in

Bergen. We see my brother and his family now and then. And my mother is in a home, I visit her a couple of times a week."

He nods. In my head, I do the maths: how often do I see my mother? Is it really every week?

"Who has access to the house?" he asks.

"Access?"

"I mean, who's been here? During, let's say, the four weeks prior to Erling's death?"

"Four weeks? Let's see . . ."

My brain is like thick porridge, everything's moving so incredibly slowly in there.

"Erling and me. Our children, perhaps. I mean – they visited us. When might that have been . . ."

But it's so hard to remember. Can the dinner party at Easter really have been the last time?

"I'm sorry," I say, my voice hoarse. "I'm not usually like this. There's something in my head that . . ."

I clear my throat; the sound emerges as a sob. Gundersen remains silent, allowing me to pull myself together, and I take a deep breath, drawing the air into my belly.

"The family came to dinner on Easter Saturday. That must be around three weeks ago. The weather was good, we had drinks out on the terrace first, then ate roast lamb in the dining room."

"And who is 'the family'? Your children, their partners, your grandchildren?"

"My son Bård and his wife, and their two boys. Hanne and her husband, with their five-year-old. And then Silje, my youngest daughter. And Olav was here – Olav's my brother. His wife came along, and they brought my mother. So yes, the entire extended family."

He writes nothing down, but I can see how he takes note of this, appears to store it in his memory.

"And who has been here since Erling died?" he asks.

"Well. The children. Olav and his wife. Erling's sister. Immediate family – and yes, my friend Synne has been over, she lives close by, in Røa."

I think a little more, and as he takes a breath to say something, I add:

"And the manager from Green Agents – that's the environmental non-profit Erling worked for until May last year, when he retired. He was here, let's see, I think it was yesterday. What was his name again? Kalle, or, no – I don't remember."

Gundersen raises an eyebrow. He glances quickly at his papers. I think of the young man with the pot plant. *Tragic . . . or, I mean, it's terribly sad.* I remember how he stood there, leaning against the study door frame. The policeman makes a note in the margin of one of his documents and closes the folder before I can read what he wrote.

"And other than that," he says. "Who might have had the opportunity to enter the house? If you were out running errands, say. Do you lock the door? Is there anyone who has a key?"

"Our children do," I say. "And we have a spare key hidden in the garage."

Footsteps can be heard above us. The woman up there must be going through our things, casting a professional eye over them. Erling's toiletries, and mine, too. She's probably found his pyjamas, folded on his side of the bed, which I haven't been able to bring myself to put away. The languishing plants. The photograph on the chest of drawers, of the children when they were small: Silje on Hanne's lap, Bård standing behind them and wearing a serious expression. The dust on the frame. The dirty laundry, which I haven't touched since last week. Perhaps she's digging through my underwear drawer, finding the boxes of pills I keep in reserve, hidden behind the knickers and bras. Trying to piece together a life.

Now she walks onto the landing. They're rhythmic, her footsteps – they create a peculiarly even beat.

"And just one more thing," Gundersen says. "I understand there was another cycling accident? And that it happened a few months ago?"

"What?" I ask. "Oh – you mean when he fell? Well. He was on his way to a meeting at Green Agents. He's retired now, of course, but he still goes into the office a few times a week. He was on his bike, just heading down Nordheimbakken, when he braked because he realised he'd forgotten some paperwork. The brakes didn't work, he couldn't stop, and so he ended up in a ditch. He wasn't injured or anything like that, just a few cuts and scrapes, grazed palms. But it was lucky he stopped there. If he hadn't remembered the paperwork, he wouldn't have braked until he reached Husebybakken, and then it could have been much worse."

"Yes," Gundersen says. "That was lucky. Did he figure out what had happened?"

"Well, I'm not sure," I say. "It must have been the brakes. You know – it's an old bicycle. Erling repairs things himself. Sometimes he makes mistakes."

"And were there any other accidents?"

"No."

"Nothing to do with a lamp at work that short-circuited?"

"Not that I can recall. And he would have mentioned something like that."

Gundersen says nothing further. He nods, but slowly. As if he's assessing my premise, and doesn't entirely agree. I think for a moment. Might Erling have mentioned it after all? Something begins to dawn on me.

"Why do you ask?" I say.

Gundersen shrugs. His colleague is coming down the stairs.

"Why did they perform an autopsy on Erling's body?"

He hesitates.

"Just routine."

His hands gather up the sheets of paper and put them back in the folder.

"The cause of death appears to be a heart attack," he says, without looking at me. "And of course there's nothing shocking about that from a medical standpoint. The doctor believes Erling would have had many more years ahead of him had he taken his medications. But – well. He didn't take them. And he was in a high-risk group."

He looks up, fixes his eyes on me. His gaze is steady.

"Still, there's one thing that gives me pause," he says. "Don't read too much into this, Evy, but can you think of anyone who might have wanted to harm Erling?"

Lights flash at the periphery of my vision. Surely this cannot be happening. As my daughters said: Mamma mustn't be left on her own.

"No," I say. "We live a quiet life. There's nobody who would have anything against us."

The year before he reached retirement age, Erling suddenly quit his job with the Norwegian Public Roads Administration to take up a position with Green Agents. He'd been talking about climate change and sustainability and human idiocy – and adopting an ever sharper tone as he did so – for years. He cycled more, took more care over the recycling. Put ever greater constraints on what we purchased, what we threw away, what we ate. He commented on other people's consumption, sometimes in ways that embarrassed me. Still, the change of job came as a surprise. *Pappa's pre-retirement phase*, I called the move when I spoke to Hanne. I thought that must be what it was: for thirty-eight years he had worked for the same employer, turning up for work at eight on the dot, eating lunch at eleven-thirty, performing his daily duties. Perhaps he had grown weary, albeit somewhat late in the day, of the monotony of it all.

Adapting to his new workplace had been challenging. His manager was the young man who came to see me – Kyrre Jonassen, his name is, I remember it now. Not a single one of his colleagues was over forty-five. Erling was hopelessly old-fashioned, but unaware of this himself. Pappa was born a generation too late, Hanne liked to say. Her friends' fathers went on skiing trips with their buddies and were on Facebook.

Erling must have felt awkward at Green Agents, a fish out of water. He complained about his colleagues' laziness and lack of understanding: they wanted to run campaigns on social media, while he wanted to bring legal action against the state.

"Do they think they're going to change the world from their phones?" he asked.

"It's a new world out there, Erling," I said.

He snorted.

"The world is the same as it's always been," he said. "Only hotter, and with less biodiversity."

He must have been disappointed, but he said little about how he felt. Instead, he talked at length about global warming and emission trajectories and changes in the biosphere. And I grew so tired of listening to it. I increasingly caught myself thinking of other things while he droned on.

As we go out to the garage, I tell Gundersen this. It's possible he asked me about it, but I'm not quite sure. As I speak, he nods and makes small sounds of approval. He's a good listener, I think. He makes you want to say more.

The garage door is stiff, it takes a certain strength to lift it. Gundersen helps me, placing his hand beside mine on the handle. His hand is strong, but not especially large. The hairs that cover the back of his hand are pale and fine, and there's something nimble about his fingers. He makes a fist, and together we pull up the door.

"Sorry," I say, smiling at him. "It's a little old."

Along one wall, beside the car, is Erling's workbench. I show Gundersen the spare key, which is in one of the bench's drawers. Then I show him out again, leading him to where Erling keeps his bike, resting against the garage wall. But there's nothing there. Erling's old DBS bike from the nineties, with its taped handlebars, is nowhere to be seen.

"How odd," I say.

Gundersen remains quiet. I walk around to the back of the garage, but there's nothing there either – the bicycle's gone.

That Day, the bike lay beside him in Sondrevegen. At the edge of the road, its back wheel hanging in the air above the tarmac. When I came home that evening, when Bård pulled up at the kerb and let me out, as the car radio played *Wild World*, the bicycle was leaning against the garage wall. Someone must have wheeled it up here, I thought at the time, and since then it hasn't crossed my mind.

"I could have sworn it was here."

But so much is spinning through my head, so many dates and times, and I'm no longer sure of anything. Can I really know, with absolute certainty, that the bike was here after he died?

"When did you last see it?" Gundersen asks.

"I'm not entirely sure," I say. "I don't remember."

FORTY-NINE YEARS BEFORE

"Is this him?" Synne asked, taking the record sleeve from my nightstand. "He looks almost like a woman."

A slim shaft of sunlight entered my bedroom in Røaveien, falling down the centre of the white stone wall and across Synne's body, which was draped over the bedspread. We listened for the music that would soon fill the room. I had raved about it all the way home from school: it's *so* good, just wait until you hear it!

Synne stretched. The window was ajar, and we could hear the traffic outside. The smell of dinner cooking wafted up the stairs to sneak under the door: fried onions, boiled carrots. The first notes of the song sounded, and then the rhythm intensified, the rocking beat filling the air. Then came the voice: high and fine, ethereal.

It was my uncle who had bought me the record. He was taking a trip to London and I had bugged him for a month. Please, I said, *please*. David Bowie. *Hunky Dory*. I can write it down for you – look.

"Listen," I said, holding up my hands and gesturing excitedly with them.

Synne shrugged.

"How do you dance to this?"

Outside, voices could be heard; young men speaking loudly and excitedly.

"Is that Olav?" she asked.

She threw the record sleeve onto the bedspread, got up and ran to the window. I picked up the sleeve and ran my finger over the price sticker in pounds, which featured the name of the record store: *His Master's Voice*.

"It's Olav and his friends," she said. "Come on, Evy."

Downstairs, outside the front door, my brother stood with a group of boys his age. Olav was pointing into the air, as if to show them something, his room perhaps. The others followed his finger with their eyes and caught sight of Synne and me in the window. Something happened to their faces then, to their bodies. They straightened their shoulders, puffed out their chests. I saw it happen. I both knew and didn't know what it meant. Synne waved at them. They waved back. Then they went inside, and we heard the click of the front door.

The tallest of them went in last. He had dark hair and broad, dark brows. Before he stepped inside, he stopped and looked up at me, and his eyes held mine for a second or two.

One afternoon that autumn he stopped in my doorway. I was sitting at my desk and the door was open. He said hello, and I turned around in my chair.

"What are you doing?" he asked.

"Homework."

Silence.

"Norwegian?" he asked.

"Maths."

"Can I come in?"

I shrugged, and he crossed the threshold with the expression of an explorer making his way into uncharted territory. He was so tall that his body swung with every step – it was almost comical. He came over to me, peered over my shoulder. For a while he simply stood there, reading what I had written.

"That's right," he said.

There was surprise in his voice, probably more than he had intended, and this made me laugh.

"Of course, it's right."

"I didn't mean to imply otherwise," he said, blushing.

"Oh, I know."

But I wasn't really sure that I did. I was rather flattered. He was a couple of years older than me, studying law at university with my brother. The other girls he met were probably far more sophisticated than me. And than him, too, presumably.

"Oh, but there," he said, pointing at my exercise book. "That's wrong. You've rounded down the decimal."

I looked. He was right, but I didn't want to give him the satisfaction of seeing me correct it. I turned to face him.

"Did the homework elves send you, or what?"

"My name's Erling," he said.

"I'm Evy."

He held out his hand in a very formal way. It made me want to laugh again, but then I didn't. To save him from blushing again? Or because I was just a sixth-form student, and what did I know about how people greeted one another at university?

Later, he made a habit of it. Every time he walked past, if the door was open he would stop. He leaned his long form against the door frame, and asked me things. How was school? Was I enjoying sixth form? What did I want to do afterwards, did I want to study, what did I want to be? I could hear Olav and the others teasing him for the interest he showed in me. Erling the cradle-snatcher, one of them said once – Olav, maybe, or the one named Edvard. The words twisted in the pit of my stomach – was that how they saw me? I didn't really know what I thought of Erling. He was awkward, a little rambling when he spoke, and so serious.

"He reminds me of my father," Synne sighed. "Would it kill him to smile every once in a while?"

But I liked his seriousness. And I liked that he listened when I spoke, and that he responded genuinely, without showing off. I liked that he didn't speak to Synne in the same way. Sometimes, when I heard Olav and his friends come in, I would open my bedroom door.

One day the following spring, he knocked on my door. It was closed – I was studying for my exams and needed to concentrate.

"Yes?" I shouted – I thought it was Mother – and then he opened the door, swinging his tall body in after it.

"Is this a bad time?"

He was paler than usual.

"No, not at all," I said, putting down my pencil. "Hi, Erling."

He smiled; wet his lips with his tongue.

"Hi. What are you up to?"

We both looked down at my textbooks.

"Homework," I said, entirely unnecessarily.

"When's the exam?"

"In May."

He nodded. His gaze wandered.

"David Bowie," he said, nodding towards the LP cover on my nightstand.

"Yeah. Do you like him?"

"No," he said, as if it pained him to admit it, and then, when he saw my expression: "But maybe I'd like him more if I listened to his music more often."

"It's okay, you know – you don't have to like him."

"Evy," he said. "I wanted to talk to you about something."

His hands were large – they gave the impression that they got in his way. He thrust them into his trouser pockets, as if he just wanted to be rid of them.

"Or, actually, to show you something. Out there."

He nodded towards the window. I got up and went over to it, and then we stood there side by side, looking out through the glass.

"The buds on the birch trees are about to open," he said, pointing.

I started to laugh.

"You wanted to show me the birch buds?"

His cheeks reddened. But he was smiling.

"Not really," he admitted. "It was mostly just to get you to stand up."

I laughed again, the way Synne would have laughed.

"Why?"

I must have seemed much tougher than I really was.

"So I could do this."

He lifted a hand to my face and brushed my hair aside. He looked at me, sort of testing the waters – would I push him away? I felt my stomach flip – it's happening, it's happening, I'd been expecting it for so long, and now the moment was finally here. When did I last brush my teeth? Did I smell good? Would he realise that this was the first time I'd ever kissed anyone, because I didn't know what to do with my lips, with my tongue?

He kissed me. And I thought, so that's what it's like. This is what they're talking about, Synne and the others who know about these things.

"Was that okay?" he asked.

"Yes," I said.

I felt so incredibly proud at finally having done it.

There are so many places it could have started. The smell of the cigarettes my mother and father chain-smoked, one after the other, when we went to the mountains. The small porcelain cups my grandmother gave us to take berry picking, cracked and ancient, with thin, black lines that looked like veins, their fruit basket motifs faded almost to nothing by countless washings. The sound the ripe, red raspberries made as we dropped them into the cups. Why should everything start with Erling?

This is just the beginning, Synne and I told one another as we sat eating ice creams on the fence beside the football pitch that evening. The first boy. Of many, presumably. All those boys out there – the ones at school, Olav's friends, the ones who walked the streets and sat on the bus and browsed the local shops or just hung around in town. Erling was the first, because there would be a long line of them. They were like the raspberries in the cup – all you had to do was pick them.

SIX DAYS AFTER

Silje has brought a lamb stew. She's made it herself, she says, spent God knows how long standing in the kitchen. It's clear I'm supposed to be impressed. She tips the contents of the Tupperware box into a saucepan as she tells me that the most important thing is to leave it to cook for a long time, much longer than you think, so the meat becomes tender. Unfortunately I'm in no fit state to rectify this astonishing situation: my children coming into my kitchen and doing as they please, as if I can't take care of myself. Did I not wipe your noses and bottoms, I want to say. Did I not make packed lunches for you, day after day, year after year? Did I not prepare dinners and breakfasts and pieces of toast for your supper? Do you really think I'm incapable of reheating a simple stew?

But all of this is out of concern for me, I'm sure. It's well intended. There's a time for everything, as they say – a time for giving, a time for receiving. Has the time for receiving arrived? I'm sixty-six. Surely I'm far too young for that?

And anyway – she gets it wrong. She's spent all that time cooking the dish, but now she heats it up on the highest setting, so the meat ends up charred on the outside but remains cold inside. Silje has always been like this. Big projects, extravagant solutions, so much time and energy spent on the execution of tasks that, to the rest of us, don't appear all that necessary. She's hard to pin down, and I don't think I ever really have understood her, or at least, only ever fleetingly. She paints pictures I don't understand, creates installations I'm unable to comprehend. Erling and I have attended all her exhibitions. We've shown up at small galleries, read the labels

43

below the canvases covered in splotches of oil paint that say *Don't come closer*, or *A study of chaos within an orderly society*. We've attempted to connect these titles to what we were looking at, before turning to her and telling her it's nice. We've watched her sigh and roll her eyes: *nice*. I've tried using other adjectives, too, like *powerful* or *expressive* – perhaps even *bleak* or *dark* if I thought that was the kind of thing she wanted to hear – but always with the sense that I don't understand what I'm supposed to think of her work, and that no matter what I say, it will be wrong. The sense that Erling, who left it at *nice*, was at least honest. The feeling that it irritated her when I tried to understand.

"Who's Gundersen?" Silje asks.

A jolt runs through me. I haven't mentioned the visit from the police to any of them, because I haven't quite known what to say. But then she holds up the scrap of paper he handed me, on which he wrote his name and telephone number.

"Oh," I say. "He's a policeman."

"A policeman?"

"Yes. The police were here. Something to do with the post-mortem report."

I say nothing further. I'd prefer not to go into the rest of it.

The bicycle *was* here That Day, when I came home from the hospital. I'm almost certain of it. Someone must have brought it up to the house after Erling and I were taken away in the ambulance. A neighbour, most likely – Maria Berger, perhaps. And now it's gone. But it could have been stolen. I probably haven't had the presence of mind to make sure it was locked up.

But what about Erling's pills in the bathroom cabinet upstairs? No-one other than the two of us has any business being up there. That thin, white strip of eyeball, just visible beneath his lashes; the plastic clip under his chin. And Gundersen: *Can you think of anyone who might have wanted to harm Erling?*

He could be stubborn, of course. And I'm sure his young colleagues at Green Agents have wanted to forcibly remove him at times. I can just imagine it. Kyrre Jonassen, handsome and informal, dressed in worn jeans and a wool sweater.

I received a text from one of them earlier today. Not from Kyrre, but from someone else – a woman. Or perhaps girl is a better word, because the message was full of smiley faces, hearts and thumbs up. *There's still a few of Erling's things here*, she wrote. *Would you like to come and collect them?* She wrote that she was sorry to hear about his death, and punctuated this statement with a crying face and a red heart. Miriam, she called herself. I have no idea what I'm supposed to think of her, but I have a clear picture of Kyrre Jonassen, his strong fingers in their habitual grip on his coffee cup, leaning against a table in the shabby office space as he waxes lyrical about the campaign he's come up with. He uses the kinds of words adored by his generation: followers, likes, algorithms; visibility and momentum. Smiles light up the faces around him. Miriam with the hearts is probably sitting at her desk as she listens, enraptured. The only one who isn't nodding is *him* – the old man all the way over on the right. He crosses his arms over his buttoned-up chest, interrupts Kyrre's impassioned speech, makes a scene.

And then Kyrre's gaze alights on the stapler on the desk he's leaning against. He imagines pressing the sheet of paper he's holding, on which his campaign is outlined in bullet points, against Erling's forehead. Imagines lifting the stapler, thinks of the sound, the feeling in the palm of his hand as he pushes down, hard, so the sharp claws of the staple sink through the skin and into the skull beneath. *You don't like my idea, you fucking out-of-touch arsehole lawyer? Maybe you just didn't read it closely enough?*

"The police came to see you?" Silje asks as she stirs the stew. "Is that, like, routine?"

"Yes," I say, hearing how meek my voice sounds.

45

The day Bård was here, I think. When I went into Erling's study to find the scissors. I stood there thinking that something wasn't right in the room, something I couldn't put my finger on. And earlier that day, Kyrre Jonassen had stopped by. He stood right there, just outside the study, leaning against the door frame. I went into the kitchen to make us some coffee. For how long was I gone? Two minutes? Four? Ten?

I get up and walk out of the kitchen, down the hallway, through the double doors and into the study. The surface of the desk is a shiny, empty expanse. The window is closed, secured with hasps. I stand there and look around and feel my pulse quickening – something is wrong, something is wrong – and now I know what it is.

Taking slow steps, I cross the floor. Stand beside the desk, and run the flat of my hand across its surface. Erling's computer is in the corner. The brand-new keyboard has been pushed all the way up to it, and otherwise the desktop is empty. In other words: Erling's appointment book is gone.

And it's usually always here. Open or closed, right next to the computer's mouse. So all he has to do is reach out to access it.

And there's more: it was here the day after he died. I *saw* it. I'm certain I did. That was the day I stood out in the hallway, listening to my daughters speaking about how I shouldn't be left alone. I had peered into the room and seen them with their backs to me, and there it was, at the centre of the desk. As it always is. It's leather-bound, the year imprinted on the leather in gold. It looks like no other book – you can't mistake it for anything else. It was here then, and that was just four days ago.

When I return to the kitchen, Silje is standing with her back to me. The lamb stew seethes audibly in the saucepan. I stand there,

46

watching her, as my pulse pounds at my temples. Her narrow shoulders, the dishevelled hair she has gathered into a knot on the top of her head. The strong sinews in her neck, which testify to a strength of character her slight build otherwise conceals. She turns to face me.

"Is something wrong?" she asks.

"What do you mean?"

"You disappeared all of a sudden."

"Oh, no," I say. And then: "Silje? The day you and Hanne were sorting through Pappa's things in his study. Was his appointment book there?"

For a couple of seconds we look at each other.

"I think so," she says. "I mean, everything was the same as always."

THAT DAY

Erling walks towards the garage. I'm in the garden with my work gloves on, about to attack the weeds. I didn't really keep up with things last year, and now I'm paying the price – if I'm going to make anything of the garden this summer, I'm going to have to put in some serious effort. I feel dizzy, slightly nauseous. Try to take deep, slow breaths. I glance up and see him. His long, striding legs, his almost swinging gait. His tall, slim body as it disappears behind the building.

When he reappears on the other side of it, pushing his bicycle, he's wearing his helmet, its strap fastened under his chin. With the plastic dome on his head he looks slightly comical, rather like a mushroom.

"I'll be home around three," he calls to me.

"Ride safely," I shout back.

This is the last thing I'll ever say to him. But I don't know this yet.

I watch him as he coasts down the street alongside the fence, until I lose sight of him behind the neighbour's hedge. Then I plant my spade beneath a particularly stubborn patch of goutweed and think: perhaps I ought to write another children's book. Maybe I'll even convince Bilal to illustrate it this time.

Nothing will ever come of this, of course. Time has passed me by, and I know it, but I entertain myself with the idea, it helps combat the nausea. I straighten up, feeling the sun on the back of my neck, and think: maybe we should invite the kids over at the weekend. We had such a nice time at Easter, and it'll be another few weeks before the weather is warm enough for us to take a trip to the cabin on Tjøme. And then I hear her.

Maria Berger is screaming at the top of her lungs – they must be able to hear her all the way up in Makrellbekken. Shading my eyes from the sun, I turn to look in her direction. Am I alarmed? Maria has no qualms about letting everyone know exactly what's on her mind, but this shouting is excessive, even for her. She comes running up Nordheimbakken – I see her storming up the road, the jacket of her yellow tracksuit billowing out behind her like a cape.

"I'm here," I say softly, and she stops beside the fence.

"Evy! You have to come! Quickly!"

Now I see that her features are twisted into a terrible expression.

"It's Erling."

But he left just minutes ago. He literally just tramped across the driveway in his grey suit. I can see him so clearly, every hair sticking out from beneath the helmet, every pore in the smooth-shaven skin of his cheeks. Hear every nuance of his voice: *I'll be home around three.*

I don't know what I'm thinking as we run. I see only Maria's form ahead of me, her yellow jacket like a beacon for me to follow. No thought in my mind but a childish prayer: please let him be okay! Not to God or to Providence or anything like that – just a directionless prayer as we run up Nordheimbakken towards Sondrevegen.

There's a group of people standing around him. A man in

Lycra cycling gear is bending down; next to him a woman in a raincoat is speaking into her phone, and then there's a couple, around our age. The bike lies at the edge of the road, its rear wheel spinning.

Then I see the legs. They're sticking out from the circle of people. The grey suit trousers, the worn trainers. Some of the people look at us, and then they sort of step aside, letting us through.

Erling is lying on his back, his head beside a crack in the kerb. His helmet is still in place, the plastic clip of the strap still fastened under his chin. His eyes are closed, but not fully – I can see a strip of white below his lash line. As if he might open them again if only I could say something to make him listen.

"Oh no," I say, as I sink to the tarmac beside him.

That's all I have to say. *Oh no, oh no, oh no.*

"His wife is here now," the woman speaking on the telephone says. I don't know who she's speaking to, but I get the impression that help is on the way, that someone is coming to fix this. I lift a hand to loosen the strap under his chin, to take the helmet off, and see that I'm still wearing my gardening gloves.

Erling once told me that he would die first. It's pure statistics, he said, I'm a man, you're a woman. We die, and you suffer. I remember thinking, I just can't see it. Not because it filled me with terror, but because it was entirely impossible to picture it. Like trying to imagine how it would be to be blind or deaf, the absence of something that has always been there.

They told me that he died in the ambulance. Which must mean that he was alive as he lay there, flat on his back on the tarmac in Sondrevegen. But it must have been too late, he must have already been dying. There was nothing I could have done to save him, nothing I could have said to bring him back. No way to get his attention, no opportunity to exchange a few final words. To say something more important, more meaningful, than *Ride safely.*

Still, that's how it felt. As if I could have woken him, had I only found the right thing to say. As if I could have dragged him back to this world, but failed.

SEVEN DAYS AFTER

The telephone rings while I'm looking for the appointment book. When I was sitting in the kitchen this morning, listening to the coffee machine gurgling and sputtering, it had occurred to me that it might have been put in a drawer or set on a shelf when the children were sorting through Erling's things. I'm rummaging through the chest in the hallway when I hear a buzzing sound. On the telephone's display, an unknown number.

"Hello?" I say.

"Hi," says a young and enthusiastic voice from the receiver. "This is Peter Bull-Clausen, I'm calling from the law firm Vika Advokatene."

His voice lowers in pitch, as if he's endeavouring to match his tone to the situation.

"My condolences on your husband's passing," he says.

"Thank you," I say dully, thinking, Peter who? And what does he want with me?

"Well, anyway," he says jovially, apparently relieved at not having to dwell on my loss. "As I'm sure you're aware, I managed Erling's assets, and I'd like to invite you and his other heirs to a meeting. Preferably next week, if you're available?"

Outside the hallway window the driveway is like a wasteland. From here I have a direct line of sight straight to the garage wall, where the bicycle is no longer standing.

"I don't understand," I say.

"Well, you see, many people seek legal advice prior to making any investments," Peter begins eagerly.

"No, no," I say. "I just – I don't understand who *you* are. Because our lawyer is Olav Lien."

Peter has no immediate response to this. For a moment there is complete silence, and I say, a little louder:

"I should know, because Olav Lien is my brother."

"Right," Peter says. "Yes, I understand."

His tone is somewhat calmer now, a little more deferential.

"We arranged our wills and property ownership and so on with Olav," I say. "We met with him, the two of us . . . now when might it have been? Around five years ago, maybe?"

"Seven and a half," Peter says helpfully.

"Something like that," I say, a little irritated that he knows this already and only half willing to admit that he's right.

"Yes," Peter says. "But sometimes people change lawyer. Not that this necessarily implies any criticism of your brother. But, you know, it can be good to have an outsider's perspective."

"That's not something we've ever needed."

"Well, this kind of thing is never easy," Peter says. "But at any rate – Erling got in touch a few weeks ago, seeking to invest in some assets and reallocate some property. The final documents were signed the week before he died."

A brief laugh escapes him here. Curbing his gaiety doesn't appear to come naturally to him. I stand by the window, looking out at the empty garage wall against which the bicycle should be leaning.

"So if you and your children could come in for a meeting, that would be great," Peter says. "How does Thursday next week look for you?"

But Erling always informed me of every step he took regarding the family's finances – didn't he? Although it's true I didn't always listen especially closely. I've often indulged him, saying "oh" and

58

"hm-mm" as he spoke – I didn't really think it concerned me. Most of our property is solely owned by Erling, because his father, Professor of Law and Supreme Court Justice Krogh, wanted it that way. But Erling has provided for me. He told me as much often enough. And beyond that – what did it matter? What did I care whether the money was held by this or that bank, whether the cabin was taxed in one way or the other? I'm so slow when it comes to these kinds of things.

Still – he's always included me in his decision-making processes. Insisted on it, even. At the meeting we had with Olav seven and a half years ago, it was mainly the two of them who did the talking. The two lawyers, the two men. What did I have to contribute? I don't know anything about the law; have no particular assets to protect. Erling's thoughts on how we should best manage our finances outweighed mine.

On the chest of drawers in the hallway, my phone begins to vibrate again. This time, Synne's name appears on the screen.

"Hello," I mumble.

"Hey!" she cries, cheerily.

There's a noisy rushing sound around her – she must be in the car. That was where she'd usually call me from, back when we still spoke on the phone once a week.

"How are you doing?" she asks.

"Synne," I say. "I just got the strangest phone call."

I recount the conversation for her. She says *hm* and *oh really* and *but* a few times as I speak, but I just keep going, not giving her the opportunity to interrupt me.

"So, yes," I say, once I've told her everything. "I just don't understand any of this. Why would Erling change lawyers? And why didn't he say anything about it to me?"

"You know . . ." Synne says, the rushing sound building around her. "I think – and don't take this the wrong way, Evy – but you know what Erling was like. He could be a little, well, bristly some-times, couldn't he? A bit tricky to deal with?"

I take a deep breath. A few years ago, Synne and her partner came over for dinner. Synne had just found out she'd been pro-moted, and she was bursting with pride. Manager for a team of fifteen people, she cried as she poured white wine into our glasses. An extra hundred thousand a year on my salary – probably more, if you count overtime. And I'll have real influence when it comes to the company's strategic priorities! Erling looked sullen, his bushy eyebrows drawn down. Synne worked for an airline; she'd been on the ground for the past fifteen years and had worked her way up through the ranks. She'd been instrumental in developing the com-pany's strategy. There was a lot to be gained from offering cheap package holidays – all additional charges stripped away, but with the opportunity to purchase additional extras.

"But surely you understand that's a terrible idea," Erling said.

I hid my mouth behind my wine glass. Synne turned to study him, every muscle of her face screaming *excuse me?* Erling dryly explained what growth in recreational travel would mean for carbon-dioxide emissions. But aren't holidays abroad also about a dream? Synne asked, her mouth pinched. About bringing people together, across borders and cultures? What a load of rub-bish, Erling said – because what use is solidarity if we no longer have a planet to live on? Synne's cheeks turned red. I remained silent. In a cautious voice, Synne's partner suggested that no matter what Erling might think of the company, it was nice that Synne had been awarded a better position. They didn't stay long after that.

"Could it be that Erling and Olav fell out over something or other?" Synne asks now, over the crackling on the line. "Something like . . . I don't know. Something to do with money or rules. And so Erling found someone else to help him?"

"But then why didn't he say anything?" I ask. "I have to call Olav."

But I fail to make the call. I'm about to, I have the number at the ready – all I have to do is press the button. But then a tremor runs through my body, and I just can't bring myself to do it.

Instead, I wander restlessly around the house. Up the stairs, across the landing, through the children's old bedrooms. Then downstairs again. The dining room, the living room, the study. I even stand on the threshold to the cellar. Open the door and peer down the dim staircase as cool air seeps up into the house, that dank whiff of old apples and rot.

It's an unfinished cellar, dug out of the ground, damp and dark. Something about it frightens me, it always has. The heavy smell of decay, the feeling that something dangerous and uncontrollable might ooze its way up from down there to poison everything we have up here. I stand there, peering down at the white stone walls, the darkness below. I change my mind. Slam the door firmly shut and twist the key in the lock.

TWENTY-FIVE DAYS AFTER

The flames devoured the study almost in its entirety. Only charred scraps of the rug remain. The wooden floor has been scorched and subsequently hacked to pieces; the curtains are gone, the walls now bear open wounds. The bookcases with Erling's old books have been reduced to ash.

Some of the damage was the fire brigade's fault. They had to get behind the walls and under the floorboards, the firefighter who talked me through the course of events explained, to prevent the fire from smouldering there undetected. This strikes me as a practical solution: to tear everything down upon the slightest suspicion something is burning. As the firefighter said: It's vital you know what you're dealing with.

Now the room is quiet, abandoned. But the smell still lingers in the air. Bitter and sour at the same time. Acrid, as they say.

According to the police, the window was open, and the bottle was thrown through it. A so-called Molotov cocktail, made from a whiskey bottle half-filled with methylated spirits with a lit rag stuffed into its neck. Fragments of glass were found on the floor.

This was all explained to me when I was interviewed by the police the day after the fire, in a small room with fake plants and harsh lighting. I was wearing clothes I'd borrowed from Synne, and felt curiously ill at ease. The trousers didn't fit – I could feel them pinching in unfamiliar places – and the sweater kept riding up my back. The red-haired woman with the Nordland dialect sat directly opposite me – Gundersen's colleague, the one who searched my house.

She told me about the Molotov cocktail. Beside her sat a firefighter, a tall man wearing a serious expression, his eyelids almost seeming to droop a little. He did most of the talking.

The bottle had smashed against the desk, he said. Its contents fell onto the floor, where the liquid fuel soaked into the rug. The rug was old, bone dry – it must have been extremely flammable. He spoke in a solemn voice, almost sadly, as if regretful of this fact. Then the flames had taken hold of the curtains, devouring them completely before feasting on the bookcases. The books, too, were old and dry. Fodder for the flames, the firefighter said.

Finally, the desk had ignited. By this point the temperature in the room was so high, the air so full of flammable gases, that every-thing was burning. That was likely when I had managed to get out of the house – I was probably standing out on the lawn as the first fire engine rushed down Morgedalsveien. When the fire brigade stormed in, they found the door to the study pulled to – and what a godsend *that* was, said the serious-faced firefighter. Had it been wide open, the air would have been so full of toxic fumes – cyanide, formic acid – that I would have collapsed while attempting to flee. As he said: A single lungful of the smoke in there, and you'd have been done for. We'd have found you sprawled on the hallway floor.

I'm standing in that hallway now. I look down at my feet, trying to take it all in: I'd have inhaled the smoke and immediately col-lapsed. I'd have been unconscious when I died. It was an incredible stroke of luck that I woke when I did, the serious man had said. Especially considering all the smoke alarms were missing their batteries.

EIGHT DAYS AFTER

It would be an exaggeration to say that Ullern church is full. At a stretch you could call it half-full, but even that is probably pushing it. I'm sitting in the front row, between my daughters. Next to Hanne sits her little boy, then her husband, and beyond them sits Bård. Bård's wife and two sons are in the row behind us. On the other side of the aisle sits my mother, along with Olav and his family. Olav has put his arm around Mother's shoulders and is speaking to her in a low voice. He looks up at me, catches my eye and gives me a weak smile. I smile back at him. Then I remember the young lawyer on the telephone and feel the twist in my stomach, the unpleasant, all-consuming feeling that this isn't over. But I've told myself I don't have to mention anything to Olav today. I feel slightly ashamed at just how relieved I feel now that I've let myself off the hook.

The organ plays a powerful chord, then a few lighter ones. I cast a glance behind me. In the middle of the nave sit Synne and her partner. Synne narrows her eyes and inclines her head sadly when she looks at me; her sympathy both comforts and unnerves me in equal measure. All the way at the back, away from our other neighbours, sit Maria Berger and her husband.

Maria moved to the area late. She was different from the other women in the neighbourhood. Her Trøndelag dialect, the big hair, the broad shoulder pads: she was far too modern, far too much of a good thing. She had no appreciation for understated elegance. She laughed too loudly, talked too much, was far too honest – and to top it all off, she was Carl Fredrik Berger's second wife. Many of the neighbouring women knew Carl Fredrik's first wife, and while nobody would claim the original Mrs Berger was any great friend, it seemed there was a certain loyalty there. Or perhaps they felt threatened: if Carl Fredrik could leave his wife and children for someone like Maria, their own husbands might see fit to do the same. It was in everyone's interest that this possibility didn't come to seem too attractive.

So they shut her out. Not in any obvious way that would enable anyone to accuse them of anything, but heartlessly and forcefully all the same. And here I almost have to admire Maria, because whatever else she was, she wasn't stupid. She understood that if she let it show that this ostracism hurt her for so much as a second, then she would lose. She concluded – entirely correctly – that she could expect no mercy from the neighbourhood ladies, that she would gain no favour through fawning and grovelling. And she was smart enough to respond in the way she knew would irritate them the most: by failing to react. She continued to laugh just as loudly, dress just as sensationally. When it came to her dialect, she refused to budge an inch, and as the decades she spent in Oslo naturally sanded it down, she compensated by peppering her speech with words and phrases local to her home town. And not least – she continued to be gushingly warm towards all of them.

Towards me, too – although I've always had the impression that she liked me better than any of the others. I wasn't exactly a fully accepted member of the group either, and she saw that. She's always asked after the family. She asked me about Bård's achievements at business school and Silje's artistic exploits. When Hanne married Ørjan, a boy from Nord-Trøndelag, she went through her network of acquaintances with a fine-toothed comb, then proudly told us about a cousin whose husband came from the farm next to the one owned by Ørjan's parents. She's never done this kind of thing for the other women in the neighbourhood, although nobody can accuse her of failing to be demonstrative: to hear her greeting one of them in the local supermarket, you'd think they were long-lost friends, and it's hugely vexing to them that despite decades of persistent ostracising, Maria Berger remains completely unruffled.

But then came That Day. I've known Maria for over thirty years, but now this one day overshadows all the others. I turn to face the front of the church again. Her yellow tracksuit jacket, the crack in the kerb in Sondrevegen. The plastic clip under Erling's chin, the strip of white between his eyelids. *Oh no, oh no, oh no.*

"Erling Krogh has stepped out of time," says the priest. "Erling Krogh, lawyer, husband, father. Friend, colleague. Dedicated environmental activist. Grandfather. Now Erling has stepped out of time."

There's something about this expression. You take a step to one side, off this endless conveyor belt the rest of us are on, time rushing by without pause, and then you're elsewhere, gone. It's beautiful. Almost as if you're set free.

Beside me, Hanne sniffles. Bård's eyes are wide, his forehead wrinkled above his raised eyebrows, and the expression makes him look pained, panic-stricken. He must not be aware of the show his face is putting on, because if he were, he would have immediately smoothed out his features. I turn my head slightly, to look at Silje. She isn't crying. Her face is frozen like a mask, her jaw tense. She stares straight ahead.

The organ tells us when to stand. In the programme, it says we're about to sing *For the Love of God.* Erling was a staunch atheist, convinced that religion was a curse human beings had brought upon themselves for no apparent reason, other than, perhaps, their weak psychology, their inability to endure random catastrophes. It seems absurd to sing about the love of God before his coffin.

At the undertakers, they had asked me if I'd like to speak at the service – I couldn't think of anything worse. Hanne volunteered, and nobody protested. She's good at that sort of thing. Now she walks slowly to the altar, and I feel such relief: Hanne is doing it, Hanne is wiping away her tears and will get the job done. Up there is the coffin, made of some reddish, highly polished wood. I'm afraid to look directly at it.

"Dear Pappa," Hanne says from the lectern. "I still can't believe that you're gone. It's a little over a week since we last spoke. You gave me some advice about the property market and reminded me to file my tax return before the deadline."

A smattering of laughter from among the congregation. Max points at his mother up at the lectern and says something to his father, a little too loudly. Ørjan shushes him. From the corner of my eye I see Bård pass a hand over his face. Silje's eyes are still dry, but her cold hand is holding mine, and now she gives it a little squeeze.

The conversation with the police seems ever more surreal to me, to the point that I've almost begun to doubt it actually happened. Twice I've had to take out the scrap of paper on which Gundersen wrote down his number, just to see some hard evidence that they were really there. It seems so far-fetched, the most extreme overreaction.

"Pappa was a thoroughly kind man," Hanne says. "Over the past few days, I've spoken to several people who knew him, and everyone agrees that even though he could seem harsh and unreasonable in debates, they never doubted that he was a good person. Everything Pappa did, he did out of a desire to make the world a better place."

Snuffling can now be heard from several places around the church. I, on the other hand, feel strangely disconnected from the whole thing. I put my hands to my eyes, mostly for the sake of appearances.

It's a nice speech that Hanne gives. I like that she doesn't attempt to make Erling seem soft and compliant, that she dares to highlight the more difficult aspects of his personality. She and Ørjan were married in this church, and now she's standing almost exactly where she stood on her wedding day. In my mind's eye I see her, with white flowers in her hair, wearing the tasteful, expensive wedding dress that showed off her shoulders. Ørjan stood beside her, surprisingly handsome in his dinner jacket. His parents are farmers from Trøndelag; they made the long journey to Oslo for the service. His father smiled broadly, his face flushed, clearly moved to be marrying off his only child. His mother was cheerful and gentle and wore a blue silk dress. They seemed so content, the two of them – I remember thinking that. Comfortable in themselves and with each other, and so proud of their son. How must Erling and I have seemed to them? We got married here, too. I walked down this very aisle, in a cheap wedding dress, bearing a bouquet of lilacs.

Silje squeezes my hand. She isn't looking at her older sister, no, she's staring at the coffin. As Hanne takes a brief pause, she turns towards me, and when she looks at me there's something disoriented about her, as if she's just woken up. I turn around to see the effect Hanne's words have had on the congregation, and then I see him.

He's sitting in a pew somewhere in the middle, neither too far forward nor right at the back. Ever since the flowers turned up, I've been wondering if I would recognise him should I happen to see him. I haven't set eyes on him in forty years – and so much time can render a person unrecognisable – but the moment my gaze alights on him, I know that it's Edvard Weimer sitting there.

His hair is combed lightly into a side parting, and of course it's greyer than it was, but still mostly brown. He has attractive, even features; a straight nose, symmetrical eyes. Narrow, nicely shaped lips. He regards Hanne with a questioning expression, as if she's presenting a long train of reasoning with a premise he doesn't quite know if he buys, but which he accepts in order to understand her conclusion.

Just before I turn back around, he catches my eye and nods, almost imperceptibly. For a couple of seconds, we study each other.

Afterwards, I stand on the church steps with my children, shaking people's hands. Everyone walks past us on the way out; people squeeze my hand and mumble *I'm so sorry* or *so good to see you*. Mother is the only one who doesn't do this. She looks at me, astonished, and says: "It's Kari!"

"It's Evy, Mother," Olav says quietly. "Kari has been dead for years."

He puts an arm around her shoulders and leads her away.

Edvard Weimer isn't among the queue of mourners, and I think that perhaps he's already left, but just as we're about to go to the car he comes over to me.

"My dear Evy," he says, taking my hands in his. "It's so good to see you, but so sad that it's under such circumstances."

"Thank you," I say. "And thank you for the flowers."

There's a goodness about him, I think. I remember that I enjoyed being in his company when we were young. We didn't know each other long – he disappeared from our group of friends just after I got together with Erling. He moved to Denmark, and I don't think anyone stayed in touch with him.

"Listen," he says. "There's something I'd like to talk to you about.

I'm sure this must be a busy time for you, but if there's a day that suits, I'd really appreciate it if we could meet."

"Of course, I'd like that," I say.

I mean it, too. Of all the obligations put upon me in recent days, the big and the small, this is the first thing someone has asked of me that I actually want to do.

"Just a moment – I'll give you my card," he says.

He's shorter than Erling, the same height as me. Out of the corner of my eye I see Hanne coming towards us. Edvard digs around in his pocket and hands me a card. It feels luxurious, is made of thick, expensive card stock. EDVARD WEIMER, LAWYER.

"Hello," Hanne says.

"Hello," Edvard says, holding out his hand to her. "Edvard Weimer. I'm a friend of Erling's from university. I very much enjoyed your speech. It was good – personal, but unsentimental."

"Thanks."

We watch him as he walks away.

"He seems nice," Hanne says. "But I can't remember Pappa ever mentioning anyone called Edvard."

I wake in the middle of the night. The light falling through the gap in the curtains tells me that it won't be morning for many hours yet. Erling's side of the bed is cold.

Downstairs, the house is silent. Grey light enters through the windows, and I think about how this time of the day, the hour or two between pitch-dark night and dawn, is marked primarily by the absence of colour. The rooms seem vast and empty in the wan half-light. I look out at the empty terrace. Consider how easy it would be to get into the house from outside. The front door's safety chain is on, but if someone really wanted to get in, they could simply walk around to the back, to this side of the property. The dining-room windows amount to almost the entire wall; the terrace door is practically nothing but glass. One blow with a hard object, and the pane would shatter. You'd have free access.

I go back to the stairs. Walk past the study. Stand there in the doorway for a moment, staring at the desk's empty surface. I remember now – he was sitting there That Day. Busy with something before he set off for the city. He was occupied in here for maybe an hour or so.

What was Erling working on? It was something important, I imagine. But the desktop is empty.

Something draws me to the cellar door under the stairs. Everything we keep down there ends up taking on the same smell: the stench of overripe apples from ages ago, back when we used the cellar to store fruit from the garden. The smell is still in the walls, mixed with the odour of the damp earth just beyond the concrete. There are no windows.

Why I fear the cellar isn't entirely clear to me. It feels as if it's hiding something unpredictable, although I know this is just my imagination. As if something bestial is lurking down there, just waiting for its chance to break free. And at the same time, without me really understanding why, my body tingles at the thought. Unleash the power of destruction! Let it force its way up from the depths and take over our house. Let me see what happens when everything we so meticulously safeguard and cherish goes up in smoke.

But something is wrong here. Even in the gloom I can see it: the door is ajar. The door I find so threatening that it's always kept securely closed. The door I slammed shut and locked, as recently as yesterday. And now it's open.

EIGHTEEN DAYS BEFORE

The daffodils stood in a vase on the dining table; their yellow heads brightened my mood. It was warm enough for us to be able to begin the gathering outside, and there was a bowl of punch, yellow for Easter, waiting on the terrace table alongside a smaller, alcohol-free version for the children. I had set and decorated the table inside for a party, adding the extra leaves so there would be room enough for everyone: ten adults, three children. It was so long since we'd had people over, and it felt wonderful to have a reason to lay the table for a special occasion. To await our guests.

Olav and Bridget were the first to arrive; they had Mother with them.

"Oh, it looks so nice in here," Bridget said when she saw the daffodils.

She was simply dressed, but I could tell from her earrings that she had made an effort. Olav was wearing suit trousers and a shirt. Mother was wearing ski pants topped off with a blouse – they're fairly lackadaisical at the home when it comes to dressing the residents. She looked at me.

"Kari?" she said. "Is that you?"

"No, Mother," I said, and I laughed, because it was such a nice day. "It's me, Evy."

Next came Hanne and Ørjan. Ørjan was busy with Max, who had decided he wanted to wear his sandals and thrown a tantrum when his parents said no; the boy had clearly spent the entire car ride crying hysterically. Hanne wore a stiff expression.

Bård, Lise and the boys arrived ten minutes late. Lise could only stay an hour, they said, then she had to drive Henrik to a football game.

"On Easter Eve?" I asked, surprised, and Lise cast me a desperate look; she'd clearly had the same thought herself.

Silje was the last to arrive. By then everyone was out on the terrace drinking the yellow punch. I handed her a glass.

"What's in it?" she asked, frowning.

"It's all organic," I assured her.

We were all present and correct.

Erling tapped his glass.

"It's so nice that you all could be here today," he said. "Evy has almost worn herself out getting everything just right, and it looks like the Easter lamb will be delicious as usual."

I laughed at this. I certainly hadn't worn myself out. I was just so happy to have people over.

But wasn't Erling's voice a little strained? It sounded choked, as if something were putting pressure on his vocal cords.

The roast lamb was still cooking, so we spent quite a while out on the terrace. Bård's boys played football in the garden; Max found a plastic spade, which he whacked against the terrace railing and the garden furniture. I ran in and out of the kitchen, checking the food in the oven. Outside, I heard Olav speaking in a loud, animated voice – I couldn't catch his words, only his tone. Now and then I also heard Erling's voice, deeper, more monotone.

Then the sound of the doorbell cut through the air. I shouted to those on the terrace that I'd get it. On the front step stood Synne, a bouquet of tulips in her hands.

"For you," she said. "I wanted to get lilacs, but it's too early."

She was well dressed, in a smart suit, and her hair was neatly styled. I stood there in my apron, feeling how my hair curled from the sweat at my brow.

"How lovely," I said. "Would you like to come in?"

"Thanks, but I've got somewhere to be."

Her hand shot out to grab my arm.

"Is everything okay, Evy?"

"Yes," I said. "I'm just busy with the cooking."

"Okay. Well, enjoy your dinner."

I went back into the kitchen. Mother walked past the doorway – I glimpsed her from the corner of my eye and went out to her. The double doors were open, and she was staring into the hallway.

"Where are you going, Mother?" I asked.

"That kind of thing's not on," she said.

Her voice was brusque. It was the tone that had appeared out of the blue when the dementia had really begun to take hold. She had always been of such a gentle disposition.

"No, I'm sure it's not, Mother," I said. I took her by the arm and led her firmly but companionably out to the others.

She tripped on the threshold as we stepped out onto the terrace, almost taking me down with her.

"The food is almost ready," I said.

"I'm not sure we'll have time to eat before we have to go," Lise said to her son. "Maybe I can make you a sandwich."

Eventually, we gathered around the table. When Olav and I were children, Mother used to say a few words about Easter's true message before we ate, and then say grace. Now she was incapable of managing anything of the sort, but I tried in her stead. I couldn't remember the words, I made a few mistakes here and there, but it didn't matter – the most important thing was the atmosphere.

And everyone laughed, raised their glasses in a toast and said cheers.

But Erling was pensive. His forehead was creased in thought, his dark eyebrows sticking out. During dinner, he said very little.

NINE DAYS AFTER

Someone has been in the cellar. I locked the door the day before yesterday, and yesterday it was open. Nobody else has been over to visit since then, and God knows it wasn't me that opened it.

And nobody has any reason to go down there to fetch anything. All they'd find is old furniture and broken household appliances and Erling's emergency stockpile. Other than that, there's nothing but spiders and rot. And that uneasy feeling I don't want brought up here.

This tiny, niggling doubt, too: can I be entirely sure? I've been liable to zone out of conversations lately. I don't remember what people say to me – the doctor, the police, my children. And then there are the items that have gone missing. Surely I can't have opened the door again and simply forgotten?

Because if I didn't, then someone else did. And that means some-one has been in my house, without me noticing. Perhaps even stalked through the rooms, touching my belongings.

Has there been a break-in? Is that why things have been disap-pearing? If so, I should make a report. The scrap of paper with Gundersen's name on it is in the study. It would be the easiest thing in the world to go in there, find the note, make the call. Tell it like it is: I'm afraid that someone has been in my house. While I was out. Or worse – while I was sleeping, while I lay defenceless upstairs. And that would of course explain this other thing, the missing objects.

But then what would happen? What if it really *was* me, if I did it myself? What if I'm in the process of losing my mind, on my way to becoming like Mother? Because there are other things I don't remember. Things Erling said to me, as recently as the day he died. We sat at the kitchen table that morning, we spoke about something, he told me something or other. Something about his job at Green Agents, I think – I wasn't really listening, and I can't quite recall it now.

There are other things, too. I live a quiet life, as did Erling. But if someone were to go searching with a magnifying glass, of course they would find things. I wouldn't like it if people knew everything about me; I like to keep my cards close to my chest. I think of the woman with the Nordland dialect who stomped around upstairs, rummaging through my drawers. If I call the police claiming a break-in, how thoroughly will they investigate me, just how up close and personal will they get? No. There's been nothing but silence from them for a while now. And I can't be a hundred per cent sure that the door was locked. Maybe there's a plausible explanation, something I haven't thought of.

Nor do I call Olav. I know that I ought to ask him about this young Peter Bull-Clausen from the law firm. Bård mentioned it to me after the funeral – apparently Bull-Clausen has called my children, too. Bård was surprised. Isn't uncle Olav your lawyer, he asked me. Yes, of course, I replied. This must be to do with something else. I'll speak to Olav, sort it out. I'll do it soon, well before the meeting on Thursday.

Nevertheless, I've let the days slip by. Tomorrow, I've told myself, for several days in a row now. I'll call him tomorrow. There must be an explanation. Olav will put my mind at ease. I'll do it soon.

The loneliness that pervades the house is unnerving. All day, every day, spent alone in these rooms. The booming of the clock as it strikes the hour; the ticking that chops up the minutes. I think I see things out of the corner of my eye. Darting movements, sudden flashes. They disappear when I try to look straight at them. My hands tremble. My vision wavers. And I look forward to Hanne's arrival, so I won't have to be alone anymore.

"Why on earth were the police here?" Hanne asks.

I'm sitting at the kitchen table while she stands at the counter, chopping cherry tomatoes for the salad.

"I don't know."

She turns back to the chopping board. The way she cuts the vegetables is evident from the slant of her shoulders, I can see just how efficient her movements are. Ørjan runs an organic greengrocers that charges forty kroner for a cucumber; everything they eat comes from there.

"So what did they ask you about?"

"Oh," I say. "I'm not really sure."

I can't immediately recall the conversation with Gundersen. I have some extremely clear snapshots from it, but they're of the wrong things, and therefore irrelevant: the tiny hairs at the bottom of his moustache, a mental image of Fredly turning our bedroom upside down, the nimble fingers beside mine on the garage door. Hanne would never have got into such a muddle. And I can see it in her face, as she scrapes the tomatoes into the salad and turns to me with that wrinkle she gets in her forehead, a perfect V between her eyebrows: here come the questions.

Hanne wants to know what they said, how they said it, what it seemed like their questions were getting at. And then she wants to know about the lawyer. I have few details to offer in that regard, too, and I can't quite explain why I haven't called Olav. I fall short. There's so much I haven't taken in, so much I don't remember. When Hanne asks her follow-up questions, I contradict myself, stammer and stutter. The furrow in her brow deepens, and I know what she's thinking: *Mamma's starting to get confused*. It

87

surges up in me, entirely physical, a loud sob that shakes through my body. I can't do this, I say, I don't know what they said, it's not my fault.

She looks at me in surprise, the wrinkle in her forehead erased.

"No, no, it's okay," she says. "I was just wondering."

"It's the shock," I say. "It's not that I'm starting to get like your grandmother. It's just the situation at the moment."

"Oh, Mamma," she says, putting down the knife. "I wasn't thinking *that*."

She comes over and hugs me. She has strong arms, Hanne; she gives firm, reassuring hugs.

"Hanne," I say as we sit at the table. "Have you seen Pappa's appointment book?"

She looks at me. She was clearly in the middle of telling me something. I wasn't paying attention – I simply can't stop thinking about this. It's been going round and round in my head, and now I've interrupted her. In doing so, I reveal something of myself, I think. I lay bare my current state.

"No," she says, putting down her fork. "I haven't."

Silence falls between us for a moment.

"You see, I can't find it," I say. "And I don't understand where it could have got to."

Hanne says nothing.

"It was here," I say. "In Pappa's study. The day you and Silje were sorting through his things. Wasn't it?"

"I don't know," she says. "I didn't notice it."

"I think it was. You didn't take it?"

"No."

Silence again, and then Hanne shakes her head.

"No – why would I do that?"

I attempt a smile.

"Then it must be lying around here," I say. "Somewhere or other."

"Here," she says, pouring something light and reddish into our glasses. "This is kombucha tea. It isn't carbonated – the bubbles occur naturally during the fermentation process, and apparently it's really healthy. Ørjan's just started stocking it, it's really good."

I nod. I would have preferred a glass of wine with my meal, but Hanne brought along these bottles of whatever it is, and that's just how she is – if she's made plans, then that's how things are going to be.

"By the way, I was wondering if I ought to buy a painting by that Palestinian artist who illustrated your children's books," she says. "You know, Bilal Zou? He's got an exhibition on at a gallery in the city centre. Ørjan and I went to see it. It was incredible. Really moving. And he's so famous now."

Her words screech disharmoniously between us, and I sit up taller, straighten my shoulders. I don't want to talk about Bilal. And I especially don't want to have to see one of his paintings hanging on Hanne's wall, gaping at me every time I go over there to visit her.

"There was one of them I really liked," she said. "Of a burning tree."

She squints, as if she can see it before her now.

"And anyway, you could say Bilal is a part of our family history," she says with a smile. "I thought it might be cool."

She's attempting to communicate something to me with this gesture, I know that. That she appreciates me, perhaps, or more than that, that she recognises what I once was. My throat feels so tight, my face so stiff and strange. She has no way of knowing the impact of her words, because I've said very little about the end of my collaboration with Bilal.

"Wouldn't you rather buy one of Silje's paintings?" I say.

My intention was to steer the conversation in a different direction, but I can hear that my words have come out sounding critical. As if I'm accusing her of not supporting her sister. This is often the way things go between Hanne and me. Something one of us says comes out wrong, and the friendliest of initiatives ends in a misunderstanding. But this time she doesn't appear to interpret my words that way.

"Oh," is all she says, wrinkling her nose. "Well, maybe. I don't know. They're quite expensive, anyway, Bilal's paintings. And we don't actually have the wall space where we live now."

I search for something to say, a new topic to raise, but Hanne beats me to it by asking who the roses are from. The bouquet from Edvard stands on the sideboard: twenty long-stemmed white roses.

"An old friend," I say.

"Who?"

"An old friend of Pappa's from university. He moved to Denmark many years ago, you don't know him."

"The guy who was at the funeral?" she asks. "The one you spoke to outside the church?"

The furrow in her brow has returned.

"Yes."

"What was his name again?"

"Edvard Weimer," I say, lifting my glass to my mouth. Contrary to what was promised the fizzy tea is most definitely *not* good – I find it sour and acrid, and struggle not to show it.

"Ugh," Hanne says, suddenly and violently, and I see that her eyes are filled with tears. "To think that Pappa's gone. I can't believe it. I'm sort of waiting for him to come striding in at any moment, in his worn-out slippers."

She looks towards the hallway as she says this, and I turn in that

90

direction, too. For a moment it's as if we're both waiting for him to enter the room. The grandfather clock ticks, and of course nothing happens, but for a few seconds we wait for him, and it makes me shudder. Then we look at each other and smile uneasily. There's something alarmed in her eyes, I think. In mine, too, probably. As if we are afraid.

"Have a sip of your tea," I say. "You're right – it's actually pretty good."

Once Hanne has gone, I put the safety chain on the door. I tug at it, checking that it's secure. Then I walk the few steps past the study and over to the cellar door. I try the handle.

It's locked now. I locked it again last night, shutting the half-open door and turning the key. I pulled on the handle several times to check, both then and earlier today, but I still feel the need to check it again now. The key is in the keyhole. I pull it out, and put it in my pocket.

I take my box of pills from the bathroom cabinet upstairs. *For the treatment of sleeplessness and anxiety.* I stare at it. Remain standing there like that for a long time, the key burning a hole in my pocket.

That first night, when I returned home from the hospital and stood here, all alone in the house, I thought: I'm not going to take anything, because what if Erling comes back? This was clearly illogical, because I knew damned well that he was dead, that his body lay in the hospital, officially declared empty of life. I understood this, too, rationally. But all the same, I didn't quite trust it, because I had this feeling: Erling always comes home.

But tonight it's different. Now I think: what if *someone* comes back? I have to stay alert, I have to be ready. So I put the pills back. I go into the bedroom. Hide the key to the cellar door at the back of my underwear drawer. Set a chair in front of the bedroom door. It will hardly thwart an intruder, but it will at least wake me if the door is pushed open. Nobody is going to catch me unawares.

I can't sleep. I lie there in bed, tossing and turning. Touch the cold clump that is Erling's side of the duvet and think: that first night, I hoped he would come back. Now I fear it. As if he still exists, a shadow lurking in the corners of the room.

TEN DAYS AFTER

"So how are you doing?" Edvard asks as he turns the car onto Husebybakken.

"Good," I say.

Then I realise that he's really asking about Erling. That when posing this question to a freshly minted widow, there are certain expectations regarding the answer. This is how it is when you keep zoning out of conversations. Erling's death is one of the defining events of my life, it is omnipresent and all-encompassing, and yet I continually have to remind myself of it: Erling *died*, it actually happened. I constantly find myself almost startled at this realisation: is it really, really true?

"I mean, as well as can be expected," I correct myself. "The days keep rolling on by."

"Do they?" Edvard asks. "That's good. In my experience that's what these first few weeks are about. Passing the time. The grieving process itself starts later."

He smiles, sadly but amiably, and I think, this is the care that I want. It's adapted to me, given to me on my own terms.

We weren't especially close back in the day, but when I got in beside him, it felt like getting into the car of an old friend. I consider him as he drives. He has an attractive profile. A straight nose, strong chin. When he smiles, the skin at his temples tightens to reveal the tiny blue veins branching out beneath it.

Once, he knocked on my bedroom door and invited me to join him and his friends. He, Olav and a few others were on their way out – when I opened the door to him, I could hear the rest of them making a racket on the stairs.

"Hi," Edvard said. "I was just wondering . . ."

We stood facing each other. We were exactly the same height, neither of us had to look up or down. I sensed Erling coming over from my desk to stand behind me.

"We're going out dancing," Edvard said. "At Roklubben in Bygdøy. Do you want to come along?"

He had to lift his gaze to look Erling in the eyes, had to tilt his head back slightly. The question hung in the air, an invitation with a hint of something unknown. A student party, the kind Olav and his friends went to. I'd never been asked to join them before, but now I was invited, and all I had to do was say yes.

"We can't," Erling said from behind me. "Evy has to finish her schoolwork, and then we're having dinner with my parents."

I moved my feet, shifting my weight. There would be young people at the club, music to lose myself in, sweating bodies dancing close together. And a hint of something else, too, I suspected, something unmentionable: hands, hips, tongues, sex. This was out there, it was already pulsing through my body, it was within reach. And surely it was possible, if not to throw myself into it, then to at least go there, to be close to it. *Don't be stupid, Erling*, I could have said. *Of course we're going.*

But I didn't. I said nothing. I simply stood there and let Erling speak for me.

"Okay," Edvard said. "No worries. See you later, then."

Olav passed the doorway behind him, nudging him loose with a punch to the shoulder – *come on, then* – and Edvard followed him down the stairs.

The moment was over so quickly. Before I could change my

mind, before I could even consider the consequences of a yes, of a no, he was gone.

The waiter shows us to a table by the window; we have a view of the fjord. I order a sandwich and Edvard does the same.

"You Norwegians and your sandwiches," he says. "When there are oysters on the menu."

"And you're not a Norwegian?" I ask.

"I lived in Denmark for twenty-seven years. Not counting my childhood, I've spent most of my life there."

"But why wouldn't you want to count your childhood?"

He gazes out across the water, gives a little smile.

"Well indeed, why wouldn't I?"

He moved to Denmark to study. Oslo was different back then, he says, the options more limited. He casts a glance at me, apparently checking to see if I agree. In Copenhagen he established a career and then he met someone. He doesn't say much about this, but I get the impression it was a great love affair.

"I thought I'd spend my whole life there," he says. "We were supposed to grow old together. But then cancer came into our lives. I became a widower the year before I turned fifty."

Then his mother fell ill and died. His father was a man of the old school, the kind who might starve to death if left to his own devices. Edvard moved home.

"My father and I had a terrible relationship when I was younger, but suddenly we had a chance to figure things out," Edvard says. "It's impossible to express just how much that meant to me."

Was it also a relief for him to leave Copenhagen following his loss? He doesn't say much about it, but that only means it's all the more present in the little he does reveal. I don't ask, not wanting to pry. But I'm captivated by these glimpses all the same.

I've often thought about that evening in Røaveien in the early seventies: Edvard knocking on the door and asking if I'd like to go out with him and his friends. Erling saying, no thanks, we have other plans.

"And how about you?" Edvard asks. "Did you become a teacher, like you wanted to?"

Now my stomach contracts.

"I trained to be a teacher," I say. "But then the children came, and, well, I was home with them for a while. It wasn't easy to get kindergarten places back then, and there were also certain expectations from the generation above. So I never really made it into the world of work."

He nods. Says something kind about the importance of caregiving, but it stings all the same. I was so smart. I got such good grades.

"I was an author for a while, actually," I say. The statement is inappropriately timed, which in a way is even more embarrassing than my pitiful professional life in itself, but now that I've started I may as well finish. "I wrote a series of children's books. They were illustrated by an artist, Bilal Zou, perhaps you've heard of him?"

I already know that I'll ask myself about this later: was the disappointment I saw on his face primarily my own, something I projected onto Edvard? I thought I'd made peace with it many years ago.

"There was something I wanted to talk to you about," Edvard says.

The coffee is on the table; we've chatted our way through the meal, and I had completely forgotten there was something he wanted to say to me. To tell the truth, I'd thought it was just something he'd said to justify our meeting. I put down my cup.

"The thing is, I met up with Erling a few weeks ago," he says. "At the end of April, pretty much exactly two weeks before he died. He called me, wanting to meet, completely out of the blue."

"You and Erling met up?" I say. "He never mentioned it."

Edvard casts me a searching glance.

"We would meet a couple of times a year."

I straighten the teaspoon on the saucer before me. Erling hasn't mentioned Edvard in many years, maybe not since we were students. And he doesn't have many friends, he doesn't see people very often.

"Yes, over the past few years we made it a kind of habit," Edvard says. "We would go out for a meal before Christmas, and then we'd meet up somewhere for a drink before the summer holiday."

I nod, as if this all sounds perfectly reasonable. Because if I'm honest, if I say that I've never heard a word about this, it will likely seem rather strange, this marriage of ours.

"And for how long did you say you've been doing this?" I say, as if I'm fully aware of their routine and I'm simply trying to pinpoint when it began.

"Oh," Edvard says. "The last five or six years, I would think."

The last five or six years. That's ten or twelve evenings. What did Erling tell me when he was actually going out to meet Edvard? Erling is an honourable man – he doesn't lie.

"I was surprised when he called and wanted to meet in April," Edvard says. "We had a kind of pattern, you see, and we'd already agreed on a date in May. But I accepted his invitation, of course, and we met at a bar. We had a nice time, and just when I was thinking that was all it was about, a catch-up over a drink, Erling said . . ."

He clears his throat.

"I've thought about this a lot, Evy, and I've concluded that I simply have to say it as it is. Erling was afraid that someone was trying to harm him."

For a moment it's as if the restaurant is unusually quiet. As if everything going on around us has hushed for our sake. I think of the two police investigators in my house; the empty space in the bathroom cabinet where the bottle and boxes of heart medications should have been. The appointment book. The open cellar door.

"I just can't see how that could be right," I say, more to myself than to Edvard. "It sounds so far-fetched."

Yet at the same time: the bicycle accident – the one in March, which Gundersen mentioned. And is it really routine to do a full autopsy when someone with a heart condition keels over?

"I know," Edvard says. "That's exactly what I said. I asked Erling why on earth he would think that. Erling replied that he'd fallen prey to a couple of accidents – he genuinely believed they might have been attempts to take his life."

Someone had cut the brake cables on his bike, he told Edvard, but there were other incidents, too. His lamp at work had short-circuited, and would have given him a major shock had it not been for the circuit breaker. He checked the connection afterwards, and he believed that someone had tampered with it.

"Erling was aware how all this sounded," Edvard says. "He said: 'As you well know, I'm not exactly inclined to paranoia, Edvard, because I have fairly sober thoughts about my own significance.' Well, I couldn't argue with that – but at the same time there was no denying that he *sounded* a little paranoid."

He casts a glance out of the window, then looks back at me. The seriousness changes his face, and all at once he looks old.

"I asked if he had any idea why someone might want to hurt him – and he said he did. And then I asked if he had any thoughts about *who* it might be. And Erling said that, yes, he had his suspicions."

For a second or two it feels as if I'm hanging in mid-air, nothing beneath my feet, nothing to hold me.

"Who?" I ask quickly, my voice hard.

He takes a deep breath and holds it for a moment, then lets it out in a long exhalation.

"He didn't say. He wasn't a hundred per cent sure, he said, and so he didn't want to name names. He said: 'This isn't an accusation you can just throw around willy-nilly. If you're going to accuse someone of something like this, you have to *know*.' But he was certain he was going to get to the bottom of it. By the time we met up again in May, he said, he would be sure."

Edvard sighs.

"So I tried to get him to go to the police – I said he had to, if he really believed that someone was trying to kill him. And I said that he ought at least to tell me who he suspected. I think I even said it might be dangerous for him to keep his suspicions to himself. But he believed he had found a way to neutralise the threat posed by this individual. Well – what could I do? I told him he could always come to me, and I promised him I would look after you, in the unlikely event something should happen to him. And now something has happened. And, Evy, when I found out that he died just two weeks after telling me all this, I realised I never should have let the subject drop until he told me who he was afraid of."

There's something pained in his expression now, and his shoulders slump a little, as if this sense of guilt is an actual, physical burden he carries.

"The police came to see me," I say, and my voice sounds distant, as if I'm recounting something that happened in a dream. "They called me a few days before the funeral and said there was no trace of his heart medications in his body. Nor could we find the boxes or bottle of pills – we looked everywhere. And other things have disappeared from the house. His bicycle. His appointment book."

And the cellar door was ajar. But I choose not to mention this. I blink, and push the image of it away.

He was supposed to cycle into the city to Green Agents that day, too – it was maybe a couple of months before he died. After just ten minutes he returned to the house, and I called out to him – are you home already? I heard him on the stairs, and when I came out of the bedroom he was standing in the bathroom, in the process of pulling off his dark-brown gabardine trousers. Down the length of his calf ran a wide channel of dark-red blood, sticky against the hairs of his leg. His face was bleeding, too – a trail ran down his cheek and onto the strap of his bicycle helmet. Red stains seeped through one of his shirtsleeves.

"My God," I said. "What happened?"

"I fell."

He mumbled the words as he studied the wound on his knee.

"The brakes on my bike weren't working. Luckily I noticed before I'd made it all the way down to Husebybakken, so I hadn't yet picked up too much speed. I just crashed into the Bergers' fence. Still, I hit it pretty hard."

He took a ball of cotton wool from a drawer and carefully wiped the blood from his face, studying the gash in the bathroom mirror. It didn't seem to be very wide. And presumably it wasn't very deep, either. But he was pale. The hand in which he held the cotton wool was trembling.

I looked at him, standing there in his white underpants and bloody shirt. The fear made him seem small, vulnerable. I thought, this is how it starts. First he'll no longer be able to manage on his bike. Later, it will get harder to find the right train, to step aboard and disembark in time. Then he'll struggle to drive the car. I didn't want to think about any of that, so I went back into the bedroom, and left him standing there alone.

In the car on the way home I tell Edvard about the bicycle accident. I tell him about the missing bottle and boxes of pills. All of them had labels with Erling's details and dosage instructions. They had been in the bathroom cabinet for more than two years. I'd read the labels so many times.

On one of the first evenings after That Day, I opened the bathroom cabinet and looked at the bottle and the boxes. All those brand names: Metoprolol, Digoxin, things like that. *Erling Krogh, to be taken once a day, as directed by your doctor.*

My mind was still struggling to function at the time, the accusation wasn't yet fully formulated in my head, but it was getting there. This first-rate doctor in her thirties, the one Erling believed to be so competent, so undramatic and straightforward, so *sensible*. She had failed. It wasn't enough. She had prescribed a solution, and yet he'd still had a heart attack and collapsed while out riding his bicycle. I didn't think, *This is all her fault.* But I wasn't that far off. I stood there and looked at the boxes of pills. That was just a few days ago, and they *were* there.

By the time we're back in the car, driving towards Montebello, the sky has clouded over. It was so lovely just now, shades of gold strewn across the beach and the fjord, but it's being worn away, the city is turning grey and colourless.

Before I get out of the car, Edvard says: "How would you feel about meeting up again?"

*

Erling's study is oriented so the sun never really enters it, and now, in the afternoon, with the hall's double doors closed, it is dim. I stand in the doorway and look inside. Remember the feeling I had on Friday, that something was missing. At the time I had thought it was just his absence. But now I know better.

Did Erling fear for his life? Did he think someone wanted to kill him, and did he suspect a specific person? He was supposed to meet Edvard again a week from now, and by then he believed he would know for certain. So what was supposed to happen before that? Had he arranged to meet the person he suspected?

Erling made a note of all kinds of appointments. He meticulously wrote them down, in the book that is now missing.

TWENTY-FIVE DAYS AFTER

The dining table is set for dinner. I stand before the place setting that must be mine; lift the tablecloth and carefully run my fingers over the object I've attached to the underside of the tabletop. Beside the plate lies my phone. The text is already written; all I'll have to do is tap send. But I have to do it at the perfect moment. Everything depends on me getting this exactly right.

When I close the double doors, the burnt smell is less insistent. There's a hint of it here in the dining room, too, but with the doors closed it doesn't invade the senses the way it does just outside the study.

Once I had been granted permission to enter my house again, the fire brigade advised against me staying here. It's an old house, and old houses generally tend to be safe following such incidents, but at the same time they were obliged to inform me that toxic gases can linger. The firefighter who let me back in asked if I wouldn't rather stay at a hotel. Insurance companies tend to cover that sort of thing, he said. But I didn't want to. I had a plan.

All through the conversation with the police, I had the sensation of being outside my own body. I sat there, pulling at the fabric of the borrowed sweater, picking at the thighs of the uncomfortable trousers. Listened calmly, as if I were being presented with a distressing story that concerned someone else. I tried to appear appropriately affected, but simultaneously failed to see the relevance to my own life. As the terrible particulars of the events leading up to the fire were outlined for me, I found that my mind spun instead around small, curious details. Like how the window had been open, when I was sure I hadn't opened it. Or how there were no batteries in the smoke alarms – not in the study or the hallway, or on the upstairs landing. Despite the fact that Erling never removed the batteries without replacing them.

I listened to the firefighter, and was far calmer than you might think. But what I needed to do had already begun to dawn on me.

FORTY-FIVE YEARS BEFORE

It was four in the morning. I should have been tucked up in bed, fast asleep. Instead, I sat on the windowsill, counting the cars on Røaveien. There weren't many, not yet, but every now and then the hum of a motor would rush past, and I would ask myself who was in the car, where they were going. On the wardrobe door hung the wedding dress. Every time I caught sight of it, I thought of the hard buds on the lilac bushes outside the teacher training college, and of the double doors in the house in Montebello.

The first time I visited the house, I stood in the driveway looking up the steep hill to the front door. The house was large, but not flamboyant. The walls were stained black, the building surrounded by pine trees that offered shade from the sun. It was attractive – that's what Mother would have said. But the hill that led up to it was long and steep. Erling was already halfway up it; he turned and called out to me.

Just inside the front door there was a small vestibule where the family hung up their coats. The hallway further in was referred to as *the hall*. I had only ever seen such a grand term used about people's homes in books – it made me fidgety and nervous. Leading off *the hall* were three doors. One led into the kitchen, which was the domain of Mrs Krogh, and where I was occasionally granted an audience so I could assist her. The second was the pair of heavy double doors, which led to the family's inner sanctum. At my house, Erling and I sat in my room listening to records and snogging, but here I wasn't even permitted to *see* his childhood bedroom, and throughout all my visits the double doors remained closed.

The third door led into the living room. As we walked in, the grandfather clock struck the hour, booming through the house.

"Well would you look at that," Mr Krogh said. "You're early."

Erling's proposal was fairly standard, the kind one would expect from a man like him. We were sitting on the tiny veranda of his bedsit; I was playing Joan Baez on the portable record player, and he said he wished I could spend the night. Mother wouldn't like that, I said, and I imitated her voice, her drawling southern dialect: *That is not the way you were raised.*

"If we got married you could stay," Erling said. "Then you could stay forever, Evy."

I laughed at this. But by the time I got home that evening, I already relished the idea. A ring on my finger, a new name. The key to a nice apartment, with a sign on the door that read *Krogh*. A great deal would accompany that name. Money and standing – but not primarily that. More a kind of *adultness*. People would have to admit that I had done well for myself. And we were going to spend our lives together regardless, so why not now?

The date was set for early in May, so we would be back from our honeymoon well before my exams. I had few opinions about the party or the dress, but I was determined to carry a bouquet of lilacs from the bush outside the teacher training college. When it had blossomed the year before it had been magnificent – an explosion of purple. The scent of it had seeped into the lecture halls, so strong and perfume-like that it was almost impossible to believe it wasn't manufactured, that the plant simply grew out there all by itself. Just look at how nature surpasses us human beings, I had thought, and there was something beautiful about it. Something a little frightening, too.

And lilacs bloom in May. Sometimes early in the month, some-times a little later. It depends on the kinds of things that can't be controlled, but I didn't think of that until it was too late. That was probably the mistake. The dress was bought, one with a simple and clean silhouette. Father counted his pennies – how much would the wedding cost? It was customary for the bride's parents to pay, and Erling was the son of an important man. Mr and Mrs Krogh invited my parents to Sunday dinner, and said that they wanted to keep things simple.

"These days you hear about young people arranging weddings as if they were royalty," my future father-in-law said. "I find that kind of thing both extravagant and unsavoury."

"Absolutely," agreed his wife. "It's so vulgar. We're so happy that Evy is a sensible girl from a decent family."

From the corner of my eye I saw Mother swell with pride. Father smiled a relieved smile: despite their money and status, the Krogh family were frugal. Their home was sensibly furnished, there was no sign of excessive luxury. At first I thought this made the house in Montebello relatable, but later I wasn't so sure. All their belong-ings had history and significance, and I mean *all* their belongings, including objects like soup tureens and vases. At my house, things like that were just there to be used. And I hadn't yet been let through the double doors.

April was cold. The lilac buds were currently no more than hard little lumps. I began to think of it as a sign: if the lilacs bloomed before the wedding, it would mean that my decision to get mar-ried had been the right one. And if they didn't, well – that was a bad omen.

*

The wedding dress hung there on the wardrobe door, mocking me as I sat on the windowsill, my heartbeat thumping, *one, two, three, four*, everything's going to be fine, *one, two, three, four*, I'm going to be married, it's a good match, *one, two, three, four*, but, but, but *but*. Quiet as a mouse, I crossed the bedroom floor and went out onto the landing, tiptoeing oh-so softly down the carpeted stairs. I caught sight of my face in the mirror above the telephone seat – my wide eyes, my bright-red cheeks, like a child with a fever. My fingers were pale and sweaty as I dialled the number. It rang, and I tried to calm my breathing, which raced and raced, as if I'd been running. It was the middle of the night; nobody answered. I let it ring, and when the telephone disconnected, I called the number again.

"Hello?" a sleepy voice finally answered.

"Synne," I whispered. "The lilacs!"

"Evy?"

"The lilacs haven't bloomed yet."

There was a hissing on the line. Synne yawned loudly.

"No," she said. "But it's also too early in the year for them. As I've told you, many times."

I nodded. Listened to the hissing, the sound of the world out there.

"I'm scared I'm about to do something stupid."

"Don't you want to get married?"

My reflection was hollow, my face like a mask.

"I don't know," I said.

It felt as if everything I had been, all my acquired knowledge and the things I held to be true, were playing cards in my hand. The kind that can be collected up again, reshuffled and dealt out anew.

"We can run away," Synne said. "If you want, I'll come and get you right now, tonight, and then we'll take my car and drive to

Stockholm and stay there for a few days. I have a little money, we could hole up in a guest house until everything blows over."

My chest began to heave again, and only then did I realise that I must have been holding my breath. Synne had quit secretarial school and got herself a job as an air hostess – she earned her own money and owned a small car. What she said was actually possible.

And my heart pounded: *one, two, three, four.* This feeling that had pulsed through my blood all night, the sense that it was now or never. The engagement ring that I had exclaimed over in the autumn, the new name that would be mine – the grown-up, orderly life I had so desired when we planned all this – it was as if the lilac buds were warning me: What are you giving up, in exchange for it all?

And I imagined myself taking off the thin, sensible engagement ring and putting it in an envelope, along with a letter to Erling. Then creeping back down the stairs, floating like a spirit through my childhood home and out the front door, closing it silently behind me and running to the gate, where Synne would be waiting for me in her little VW Beetle. And then we would drive, Synne shifting gear after the turn, and we would just keep on driving.

And afterwards? Who knows – anything could happen. I could run away for good, travel the world, visit England, Spain, the USA. Meet a powerful man, tall and dark-haired, with a big car and a house by the sea. Or meet with misfortune, poverty, death. Maybe end up dumped in a ditch somewhere, or throwing myself off a cliff in despair. I had no idea, everything beyond the confines of life as a Krogh seemed unknowable and boundless, as if Synne's little Beetle was a boat facing roaring rapids, so much bigger, so much wilder, than the tiny stream that ran through the suburb in which I lived and in which I would marry.

And I already knew I would never leave. Morning would come, and with it my wedding day. I would put on the dress.

"It's a bit too late to pull out now," I said into the telephone.

My voice sounded surprisingly normal. So it was possible, in the midst of this breathlessness, this wild and free-flowing state.

"What would they do with all the gifts?" I said. "No – I've come this far, I have to see it through. And of course I don't want to lose Erling, either."

For a moment there was silence, only the hissing in the receiver, and then Synne said: "Probably just as well. And thinking about it, I have to go to work tomorrow."

A few hours later, she called back.

"I managed to get hold of some lilacs," she gushed. "My cousin from Tønsberg is coming to town, and they're flowering in her garden. They're white – I hope that doesn't matter?"

"Oh Synne – thank you so much!" I cried back.

And I thought: *this* is the sign.

But as I was getting dressed, I felt unsure. The lilacs outside the school were purple. Wasn't it precisely *those* lilacs I wanted, from precisely *that* bush?

But I was too sensible to believe in signs. And if I needed one, I'd been given it: I would walk down the aisle bearing lilacs. So I pulled the wedding dress over my head, Mother did up the zip, and I was driven to Ullern church, where I married Erling Krogh.

ELEVEN DAYS AFTER

Olav came over a day or two after Erling died. He had Bridget with him, and Bård was here when they arrived. Some neighbours had also stopped by; the house was far too crowded. I'm sure there was an expectation that I should play the hostess, or maybe that's just how it felt. I made coffee, unpacked all the baked goods everyone had brought and put them on a serving plate. My hands shook the entire time, I remember that clearly. Again – it's mostly these kinds of memories that have stuck: my hands trembling and me putting them into my pockets, clasping them in my lap, trying to hide it. Erling's slippers, which I don't know what to do with. Olav and Bård standing out on the terrace; Olav looking up from their conversation to stare straight at me. Bård was the one doing the talking, is the impression I got. But I was inside and they were outside, and I heard nothing of what was said.

Later, we stood in the hallway. The neighbours had gone; it was just family. Olav set his heavy paw on the dresser, his fingers thick as sausages. The double doors were open, for some reason or other – we could see through them towards the study and the stairs, and I remember that this embarrassed me. But thinking it might seem brusque, I didn't close them. I went into the kitchen to put the cinnamon rolls into boxes they could take home with them. They stood there in the hallway, beside the open doors: Bridget, Olav, Bård.

But this doesn't necessarily mean anything. There are many other people who could have taken the appointment book. The day before, Hanne and her family came to visit; earlier in the day, Silje stopped by. A day later, Kyrre Jonassen came – and yes, Synne was here, too. Even Edvard could have been in the house – he might have delivered the bouquet of flowers himself. The front door might have been unlocked.

Before Olav left, he told Bård that he would check his files and give him a call. Bård thanked him. He didn't say anything to me about what it was Olav was going to check. It could have been anything, of course – it didn't necessarily have anything to do with Erling, and nor did I ask.

I've loaded bags of groceries into the car, and as I turn out of the supermarket car park and onto Sørkedalsveien, I drive in the opposite direction of the house. I'm reluctant to go home. I have no plans for the day. As far as I can remember, none of the children have said they're coming by. And I don't want to go back to that lonely house on the hill.

In spite of everything, it never truly became mine, the house. It's still filled with the Krogh family's possessions, their customs, their ticking grandfather clock. And I would really prefer not to see the study and the terrible yet alluring dank cellar.

So I drive. Up one road and down the next. Through Røa, an area from my childhood that is no longer recognisable, with its tall apartment buildings with huge windows and terraces, its estate agencies and cafés selling coffee in cardboard cups. I drive past the house we grew up in, Olav and me. Where Erling leaned against the door frame to my room. But it's a different house now, with a huge extension.

Olav and Erling were friends back then. Weren't they? But with the exception of the dinner party at Easter, it's a long time since Olav and his wife have been to visit us. It's a long time since we last visited them, too. This kind of thing happens, of course, without anything necessarily being wrong. But Erling's stubbornness and

pietism may have rubbed them the wrong way, especially considering Olav's penchant for overconsumption: all the new cars, the
sports equipment, the trips abroad. People change as the years go
by, you can end up pulling in different directions. Perhaps end up
with less in common, less to talk about. But we're family. We've
been close for so many years. That binds people together, in spite of
everything. Doesn't it?

I cross the city limits and drive into Bærum, along roads that
become increasingly unfamiliar. I don't know where I'm going –
or maybe on some level I do. When I reach Asker, I realise, at least
in part, why I've chosen to head in precisely this direction, because
I'm becoming uneasy now, I have this sickening feeling in my
stomach, but still I tell myself that it's good to drive, good to see
something new. It's only when I'm no more than five minutes
from his house that I say to myself: is this really about to happen?
Am I really about to see if Olav is home, and actually have that
talk with him?

The house was newly built when they bought it. It's huge, bordering
on gaudy, with actual columns before the front door. In the porch,
stuck into a flowerpot, is a sign that says BALANCE WELLNESS. An
arrow points to the entrance to the basement, from which Bridget
runs her practice. I squint in that direction; it looks dark, she must
be out. But Olav's car is in the driveway. I press the doorbell and
hear its friendly notes.

His face is almost a blank when he sees me, and for a moment he
just stands there, his mouth half open, his broad jowls hanging,
expression empty. Then it's as if he comes to – the muscles in his
face begin to work, his cheeks pulling his mouth into a wide smile.
Something ignites in his eyes.

"Well hello, Little Sis," he says. "What a nice surprise."

Then he pulls me into a bear hug. He walks ahead of me into the kitchen, chattering away as he goes, telling me how nice it is that I've come, he only wishes I'd called first, so he could have set aside more time.

The kitchen features a bar counter with two stools placed in front of it. One of them is pulled out; before it is a plate with a half-eaten sandwich on it. Olav takes a seat on his stool, and it creaks under his weight. I take the other.

"Where's Bridget?" I ask.

"Oh," Olav says. "She must be out somewhere. I mean, I think she's having lunch with some ladies in Asker. Today is Thursday, isn't it?"

His shoulders are bulging in his shirt; he's put on weight in recent years, though he's always been burly. He filled out a little after he got married, but it's only in the past five or ten years that he's become veritably fat. I count backwards: it started when his daughters moved out, when he and Bridget were left alone. Bridget, on the other hand, only seems to get thinner and thinner. Whenever I see them together, I often catch myself wondering what their dinners are like.

"So how are you doing, Sis?" he asks.

"I'm not entirely sure," I say. "I miss him. I feel sort of . . . empty."

But I'm unable to really feel the weight of this. I know that the grief is there, but I tiptoe around it. If I don't disturb it, perhaps it might leave me alone.

"God," Olav says. "I just can't imagine it. If Bridget were to collapse like that."

My brother. The guy who knew everyone, whom everyone liked. How many of his friends are left? The people who accompany him on skiing trips and summer holidays on the Riviera are often business contacts.

"Thank you for bringing Mother to the funeral," I say.

"Of course," he says. "But she's getting worse. She gets confused a lot – like when we were leaving the church. I hope that didn't upset you too much."

His phone lies on the counter beside his plate, and he casts a glance at it before he looks up at me again.

"Olav," I say. "Is it true that Erling changed lawyers?"

The genial smile is ripped from his face in an instant, and again he looks at me with that empty gaze. There's a trembling in my stomach. I don't recognise him when he's like this, he seems almost a stranger.

"How did you find out about that?" he asks.

"He called me," I say. "The new lawyer. He sounded like a young man."

Olav scratches his head, thinking. As if recovering himself.

"I did wonder if I ought to tell you, Sis. It wouldn't have been right, from a legal perspective, but since you were present when he signed his last will, I could have got away with it. But then I thought . . . Well. I don't know. You don't just storm blindly into people's private affairs, you know?"

"Olav, what does the new will say?"

My voice is small and afraid. I am in no way certain that I want to know.

"I don't know," he says, spreading his huge paws wide. "I know nothing about it. It was, let's see, about a month ago. No, less than that – a couple of weeks. Just after Easter. Erling called one day and said he'd consulted a new lawyer."

"And what did you say?"

"What could I say? I asked him why, of course, but he only said he'd decided it would be more appropriate to consult someone outside the family."

His fingers pick at the crusts on the plate, and he looks at them, wrinkling his brow. How well do I really know my own brother, I think. Now, as a sixty-year-old? What were he and Bård discussing out on the terrace, a couple of days after Erling died? What was it Olav was supposed to check for Bård in his files?

"He sounded so distant," Olav says. "And that wasn't exactly a pleasant thing to hear. He rejected me, in a way. He could have at least given me a reason – he is my brother-in-law, after all."

He looks up at me and smiles. There's something uncomfortable in it.

"But it may have been difficult for him, too, of course. Erling isn't exactly one to express himself with tact. *Wasn't*, I mean."

He sighs.

"This must all be so hard for you, Evy."

His hand moves to take mine, and the feeling shoots through me – I don't want him to touch me. Olav doesn't seem to notice. Or at least, he grabs my hand regardless, and holds it tightly.

"I should have said something. When he died, at any rate. You shouldn't have found out about it this way."

"Do you remember Edvard Weimer?" I ask.

Olav lets go of my hand.

"Yes."

"Have you spoken to him?"

"I saw him briefly at the funeral."

He's being somewhat cautious here, I think. A little hesitant.

"Edvard says Erling thought someone was out to get him," I say.

Olav studies me. There's something judgemental in his eyes. Perhaps in mine, too. As if we're measuring each other up. All that can be heard is the buzzing of the refrigerated wine cabinet.

"You know," Olav says, his voice steady. "I've always thought there was something a little strange about Edvard Weimer. Something a little underhand, or . . . I'm not quite sure how to put it. As if he can't be trusted."

I shift in my seat. I shouldn't have mentioned Edvard.

"It's so strange that Erling never mentioned the new lawyer to me," I say instead, steering us back to business.

Something shifts in Olav's eyes.

"Are you sure that he didn't?"

"Not that I can remember," I say. "Why? What do you mean?"

He shrugs.

"Oh, I don't know. Just that maybe you weren't really listening."

What did Olav speak to Erling about at the Easter dinner party? I see them in my mind's eye, standing together on the terrace. Olav speaking, Erling listening with a furrowed brow. I was running in and out, seeing to the food, so I didn't catch everything that was said. Olav's voice is loud and boastful, it could be heard everywhere, I must have heard him. Erling appeared to listen sceptically, saying little. Not long after this, he called Olav and dismissed him.

But if he believed that someone was trying to harm him, I think as I manoeuvre the car down the narrow roads of Olav's neighbourhood – yes, more than that, if he believed that someone wanted to *kill* him, that they had even made attempts on his life – then *surely* he would have mentioned it to me. I press my lips together, squinting at the slip road that will lead me onto the motorway. Erling wasn't a mysterious man. He was straightforward, he said what he meant. Was he really filled with doubt and living in fear, right there beside me, without ever saying anything about it?

I think back to the day I found him cleaning his study – it must have been a week after the Easter gathering, two at most, because I remember that the daffodils were still on the table. I was topping up the water in their vase when I heard a banging and clattering in the hallway. In the study, Erling stood bent over the desk, with rubber gloves on his hands and a scarf pulled over his nose and mouth. Beside him was a bucket of water and an arsenal of spray bottles containing various cleaning products. In one hand he held a cloth, dripping with water and suds, which he swiped across the desktop in long, thorough strokes. Behind him was the long-handled broom, which presumably was what I had heard him hauling around.

I stood in the doorway and watched him. His khaki trousers were worn thin at the knees and along the pockets, and he had pulled the bright yellow washing-up gloves over the cuffs of his shirt. The scarf made him look like a bank robber from a Donald Duck cartoon. I asked him what he was doing. He looked up and said he was cleaning. It wasn't easy to read his expression under the bank-robber scarf. Beside him was the wastepaper bin, and I could see the keyboard from his computer sticking out of it.

"I cleaned in here on Tuesday," I said, but he only shrugged and said he felt like giving the room a good going-over.

I felt this like a punch to the gut. I was the one who cleaned the house. Of course, one could argue that I'd taken less care with it in recent years than I did when I was younger, but still, there are better ways to let someone know you're dissatisfied. I took a step into the room.

"Don't come in!" he shouted.

Urgently. As if he were afraid.

"I'm sure it isn't *that* dirty," I said.

On That Day, we drank our usual morning coffee at the kitchen table. We had a conversation. I'm sure we did – we must have done. Let's see. He read the newspaper. Or at least I think he did, that was his usual habit. And then he said something. Told me something or other. But what? I frown. Why am I unable to remember?

Erling never mentioned Edvard. And since the appointment book is gone, I can't check whether they actually met up in April, as Edvard claims. Nor can I check when Erling met with the new lawyer. I'm unable to determine if it was before or after the Easter dinner party, before or after he told Edvard he was afraid.

Was Erling murdered? Did someone steal his pills, trick him into taking placebos instead, or replace them with something harmful? I see him outside the house with his bicycle, adjusting his helmet. *I'll be home around three.* Or that same morning, at the breakfast table. What did we talk about? When I try to remember our conversation, why is there nothing but a blank?

THAT MORNING

I wake up late. By the time I make my way down into the kitchen, the coffee has already been taken from the machine and poured into the cracked thermos jug. My head is heavy. Searching among the cups in the cabinet, I find one I like. I take a seat at the kitchen table, look out through the window at the drive. The gravel is almost gone, we ought to top it up. God knows what the neighbours think – they can all see it, and probably have a few choice words to say about it.

Outside, there's a rustling from the stones, and along comes Erling, walking with his head slightly bowed. He's always moved this way, as if he's constantly in the process of passing through a doorway that is just a little too low. In his hands he holds the newspaper. He gives me a nod then disappears from my line of sight. Shortly afterwards, the lock on the front door clicks.

He goes straight to the kitchen cabinet and takes out a coffee cup edged with a pattern of flowers. He examines it closely. This irritates me – does he not think it's clean enough? It's like when he was cleaning his study, and I take it as a criticism.

Then he sits down opposite me. Pours coffee into the carefully inspected cup. Unfolds the newspaper. He frowns as he reads the headlines. Mumbles about something he's dissatisfied with, something at Green Agents. I think: maybe I'll spend a bit of time working in the garden today. Erling sighs deeply. There's some sort of irregularity it has fallen to him to sort out.

"It's really quite concerning," he says, his dark eyebrows pulled low. "But only for me, luckily enough. And now I think I've found a solution. By the time I get home, it'll all be done with."

"Right," I say.

I'm not really listening. I'm mostly thinking about the garden. If I make a start on the weeding today, I'll have it finished before the flower beds bloom.

TWELVE DAYS AFTER

Miriam is short, with wide hips she swings confidently as she approaches me. Her hair is black and curls in perfect corkscrews, and she gives me a big, friendly smile that seems to spread through her entire being.

"Evy, isn't it?" she says.

For a moment I think she's about to hug me, but instead she takes my hand and shakes it heartily. She manoeuvres us past desks at which her colleagues sit with headphones in their ears, their laptops open before them. As we walk, she cheerfully tells me about how she's been thinking about Erling's possessions, apparently unconcerned that her prattling might disturb anyone. I look about me. Around ten desks are scattered about the room, and along one wall there's a small kitchen nook, where two young men are deep in conversation. I can only imagine what Erling must have thought of his young colleagues, talking loudly about their plans for the weekend while he was trying to work.

"Here," Miriam says, as we reach a desk towards the far end of the room.

"Was this his desk?"

"No, this one's mine. He sat over there."

She points to a desk over by the wall. A girl wearing large headphones and thick-framed glasses is sitting at it, staring intently at her screen.

"Here are his things," Miriam says, picking up a cardboard box. "I've gathered them all up."

In the box there's a small pot plant, which is apparently called a "peace in the home". There's also a stack of papers, printouts of judicial information and legislation, as well as strategic documents featuring boxes and arrows and phases like *offensive campaign* and *forward-leaning*. On one of them Erling has made a note, apparently disagreeing with some statement: *But the basis for existence!!* Two exclamation points. That seems somewhat excessive, I think.

Erling had been retired for almost six months when he died, but he still came into Green Agents weekly – often a couple of times a week – and kept his desk space. He would cycle to the office and spend a few hours here, then cycle home again. Panting up the hills to Montebello.

"Can this really be good for your health?" I once asked when he arrived home out of breath.

"It's keeping me alive," he panted in reply. "And anyway, it provides a signal effect."

"Signal effect" was a term they used at Green Agents, not something Erling would usually say. So perhaps they had rubbed off on him after all. Maybe he rubbed off on them, too, it isn't beyond the realms of possibility.

"Is that where the accident happened?" I ask, nodding towards the workstation where the girl with the glasses is sitting.

"The accident?"

"Something to do with the lamp," I say. "Apparently it short-circuited?"

"Oh, that. Yes, that was there."

"May I take a look?"

"Of course."

Miriam walks ahead of me. She apologises to the girl with the glasses, who nods vacantly and returns her attention to the all-consuming screen. I cast a glance at it, and see that it is covered by a huge spreadsheet. I look at the girl again. It appears that she not only understands the significance of the table's figures, but also reads something utterly shocking in them. Beside her stands a completely ordinary desk lamp.

"He used to have a different one," Miriam says. "An older one, made of metal. The police took it away."

"The police?"

"Yes. They were here a few days ago."

"What did they say?"

She shrugs.

"Not much. They asked about Erling and looked at his desk."

I take a deep breath. Erling told Edvard that he wasn't one to get paranoid. That he generally had fairly sober thoughts about his own significance.

"What happened, with the lamp?" I ask.

"He was changing the bulb," she says. "And it just went *poof*. The entire floor lost power, the caretaker had to go fix something in the fuse box. Something to do with the earth in the lamp. The fuses trip automatically, apparently, to prevent accidents from happening. It was easy to fix – I mean, everything was back on again within the space of a few minutes. But Erling seemed fairly stressed out. He was white as a sheet. If the fuse hadn't blown, he could have suffered a major shock, he said. He was changing the bulb, holding the lamp with both hands."

Miriam raises her eyebrows.

"Afterwards, he looked the lamp over again and again. Unscrewing the bottom, stuff like that. Later that day he came to me and asked whether anyone had been at his desk, or been in the office outside working hours. I'm a kind of gatekeeper here, you see – I'm the one who keeps track of who's in the office and when."

She laughs. She has a generous laugh, friendly and inviting. I would have liked to laugh along with her, in a way, but I'm unable to. My throat is dry, my face stiff.

"And what was your reply?" I ask.

"I mean, people come and go. But nobody had asked after him that week and nobody had gone through his things. All I found was that he'd let himself in during the evening, two days earlier."

"Erling?"

"Yes. The pass registers when you let yourself in outside of working hours. I'm not really supposed to share that information, but I thought it was okay that I tell Erling. It was about him, after all."

She smiles at me. I look at the new desk lamp. The girl with the table of figures casts a quick glance my way, but says nothing.

As I'm about to lift the cardboard box of his things, I catch sight of the note on the document. *But the basis for existence!!* Erling has written in the same style since I first got to know him, his letters elegant and slanting. I would recognise his handwriting anywhere, and suddenly a shiver runs through me: he'll never write anything ever again. This script was his alone, and all that is left of it is loose notes, arbitrary words. For an instant I'm overwhelmed by this realisation; I find myself gasping for breath. I quickly regain my composure, but Miriam has presumably noticed. She gives me one of those looks, full of pity.

But it awakens something else, too, this document strewn with Erling's scribbled comments. My husband might have been a man of pen and paper, but these young people – they must do all kinds of bookkeeping digitally.

"There's something I was wondering about," I say. "Do you have any kind of, I don't know . . . appointments system?"

She looks at me, and I explain: a web-based system, perhaps, where you register plans and meetings, things of that nature.

"Oh, yes, we have a shared calendar," Miriam says. "But Erling wasn't its most enthusiastic adopter, so to speak."

"Would you mind checking it for me anyway? I'd like to know if he'd agreed to meet someone. On the day he died."

Miriam consents and sits down in front of her computer. I can feel my pulse vibrating at the base of my throat. Why am I asking? I don't actually want to know. It was just a sudden impulse, I'm acting without thinking.

As she types away on the keyboard I close my eyes – it feels as if I'm floating away. It isn't my job to go poking around asking questions. The police are doing their job and that should be enough.

"It looks like he used it, at least," Miriam says. "But, hmm. That's strange."

"What?" I say, my eyes still closed.

"Look at this," she says, and I open my eyes again.

The screen is filled with a calendar covered in pink and green boxes, all neatly organised. At the top is Erling's name. Below this the week is drawn out, day by day. On That Day there are two boxes: *11 am: Strategy meeting. 1 pm: Private appointment.*

"That's a function that allows people to connect their work calendar with their private calendar," Miriam explains. "But Erling didn't use it."

Miriam clicks something, expanding the small, pink box.

"I don't think I've ever seen him mark anything as private before," she says.

We stare at the screen. He's set aside an hour and a half. As he had said to me, that morning: *I'll be home around three.*

THIRTEEN DAYS AFTER

Mother sits with her eyes glued to the TV, watching the tennis. Her chair is a deep shade of red, and even from where I'm standing, over in the doorway, I can see that there's an absorbent pad beneath her. The white, clinical material sticks up behind her stooped shoulders. She's wearing a blouse over a T-shirt, and the grey jogging bottoms I bought for her last autumn. She's wearing an adult nappy, I know that. Sometimes the edge of it peeks above the waistband of her trousers – it makes me feel queasy to see it. Her hair is cut fairly short, but it's matted all the same. It's greasy, her fringe is stuck to her forehead. The air in the room smells extremely sour, of greasy hair follicles and perhaps urine.

"Hello," I say.

She slowly turns her head, pulling her eyes from the tennis match. She doesn't say anything when she sees me, just gives a brief wave, then returns her attention to the TV. I enter the room, take the plastic chair from where it stands beside the door to the bathroom, and pull it over to sit beside her.

"How are you?" I ask.

She mumbles something without taking her eyes off the screen.

"That's good," I say.

They expect me to visit her often, the nurses, the assistants, the staff. They're always telling me it means so much to her that I come. I have no idea what I'm expected to do when I'm here. It's not as if we can have a conversation, and it seems strange that me sitting in the chair beside her as she watches TV should make such a great difference. That would surely hinge on a kind of interaction, an exchange of some kind – if not meaningful sentences, then at least words, sounds? One of her first nurses explained that even though the dementia had robbed many of her routines of their substance, there was still meaning in them: they were reassuring and predictable, understandable because they could be recognised. And so I chatter away to her regardless.

"So you're watching the tennis?" I ask her.

I can hear that my voice is high-pitched, irritatingly jovial.

"Load of rubbish," she mumbles.

She doesn't move her eyes from the screen.

"I went to see Olav the day before yesterday," I say.

She remains silent, so I add:

"He still lives out in Asker, with Bridget, you know."

"Tart," she mumbles.

Personality changes are part of the disease. That's what the first doctor who asked to speak with me alone said. Alongside the loss of dignity, this is what's most difficult: my mother was so proper. She never would have called someone a tart.

"They have a lovely place out there."

On the TV, the ball is hit from one side of the court to the other. I have no interest in this sport, know nothing about its rules or challenges. But I've always enjoyed seeing clips of the audience, a large group of people turning their heads in unison, back and forth, back and forth. The synchronised yet spontaneous nature of it.

"Well, my house is rather empty now," I say. "You know, after Erling died."

She turns her head. For a moment she fixes her gaze on me, properly, and somewhere far behind her grey eyes, something stirs.

"Nothing but fish," she says then.

"Yes," I say. "Nothing but fish indeed. That's actually a fairly accurate description."

The hair on her head is so thin. I can see how each strand is attached to her skull, can almost see how she would look if it all fell

146

out. She has hundreds of wrinkles around her eyes, but the skin of her cheeks is still smooth, and despite the dirty greyness that hovers about the rest of her – even her lips, even her tongue – her cheeks are slightly flushed.

Sometimes I think that everything Mother was, all the youth and lightness she possessed, even as a grandmother, has been cast from her. But she still has this hint of pink in her cheeks. I've never had such a rosy complexion, and I admit that it's always irritated me.

"It is," Mother says. "It is, it is."

She's searching for the right words. That was the first sign, I remember, she'd want to say completely ordinary words, *porridge*, *apple*, *tree*, and couldn't find them. We stood around her, nodding and smiling. Helped her, encouraged her. Eventually, all our efforts only made her irritable. That was the second sign.

"The children visit often, though. Silje and Hanne, and Bård, too. Sometimes they bring your great-grandchildren with them – do you remember them, Mother?"

A low mumbling sound escapes her, I can't tell if she's trying to say something.

"You saw them at the funeral," I say. "And at the dinner party at our house at Easter. Do you remember? All my grandchildren were there. Olav and Bridget, too. And Erling, of course – it was before he died. Do you remember? At our house in Montebello?"

"Somebody went," she says.

It's there again, that gleam deep in her eyes. She fixes me with her gaze for a moment, and with a sudden flash of clarity she seems to see me and know who I am. She wants to tell me something.

"Through the doors," she says. "Into Erling's study."

"What do you mean, Mother?"

She frowns, staring off into space, not quite able to grasp it.

"There was someone . . ." she begins.

My breath quickens.

"Who was it, Mother?"

She looks back at me and says, her voice crystal clear: "I've always believed no-one else had any business being in there."

This sudden jolt, back to when she was a functioning person, to when she had opinions it was possible to relate to and understand, stings, because in a flash I see what we've lost. But in what she's saying there's also something else: a ringing bell. I grasp her thin, bony hand.

"Who was in Erling's study, Mother?"

She looks at me, and then it's as if she loses her grip on what she had managed to grab on to, somewhere among those ever more tangled neural pathways. She looks at me with uncomprehending eyes.

"No," she says, quietly, almost to herself. "It isn't possible."

"Mother," I say urgently. "Who was in Erling's study?"

"It'll be fish again for dinner. What stuff and nonsense."

I sit in the car, breathing. In and hold, out and hold. This is something Bridget taught me after she took one of those courses in Sandefjord. *Focus on each breath.* It seems too simple, but it helps all the same.

Someone went, I think. Through the double doors, and on into Erling's study. Of course, I remember this from the day of the dinner party, that she was in the hallway, that I accompanied her out to the others on the terrace. Had someone else stepped away at that moment? Bridget was there, I remember, and I think Lise said something. Erling was there, too. But other than that? Can I be certain that everyone else was in the garden? Or might one of them have been inside, behind the double doors, in the study?

I miss Erling. It bubbles up in me, pushing against my throat so I can't breathe, against my eyes so I have to squeeze them shut. I miss his reassurance, his calmness. His tall, slightly stooped frame, still slim as a young man's. I miss him as he was, with his silver-grey hair and dark eyebrows. I miss his physical form, the body that has been by my side for almost fifty years, sheltering me from life's storms.

My phone buzzes, making me jump. My hands shake as I pull it out, inhale and hold, it's there in my handbag, I grab it but I don't have full control of my hands. It slithers free twice before I finally hold it up and see Edvard's name on the screen. Exhale and hold.

"Hello," I say.

My voice is almost nothing but air.

"Hi, Evy," Edvard says. "Is everything okay?"

"I don't know," I whisper.

"Where are you?"

Half an hour later I'm sitting opposite him in the library bar of the Hotel Bristol. He's wearing a suit – he's come straight from the office – and even in my sorry state I notice how appealing he looks. There's something soft but professional about him. Were I having legal problems, it would calm me to sit across from him.

He orders first, and when he asks for sparkling water to accompany the meal, I do the same. The waiter withdraws.

"So," Edvard says.

"So," I repeat.

He smiles, and I have the urge to talk about something else. I just want to sit here with him in this room, among the many tables and hushed human voices, all the food. I want to swaddle myself in the idea that we are beyond time and space, on our very own satellite.

"I was just at Green Agents," I say instead. "I was picking up some of Erling's belongings and was able to take a look at his desk."

"Oh?"

"The desk with the lamp," I say. "The one that short-circuited. Apparently the police have been there, they took it away."

I tell Edvard how Erling's pass was used to enter the building a few days before the lamp blew, and how Erling had a private appointment entered in the calendar on the day of his death. Edvard nods pensively, but he doesn't interrupt me until I mention the new lawyer.

"That's strange," he says. "Did Olav know anything about the content of the will?"

"No, nothing. What do you think?" I ask, suddenly anxious. "Is there something going on here that I ought to be afraid of?"

I feel the knot in my stomach, the one that pulled tighter every time I thought about calling in on Olav: who is this young lawyer with the excitable voice, and what kind of message does he have for us?

"I'm not privy to the details, of course, but it isn't necessarily anything to worry about," he says. "The will was signed a few weeks ago?"

"Yes. Olav said that Erling called him about it just after Easter."

"So just after he told me he thought someone was out to get him. When he said he'd found a way to neutralise the threat posed by the individual he suspected."

At this moment, it's as if a realisation settles over us. We look at each other and share it, each knowing what the other is thinking. And despite the seriousness of the situation, there's a faint tingling in my body, as if there is also a kind of thrill in it: we're in this together, Edvard and I – this is something we share. I feel a heat bloom in my cheeks, a decisiveness in my chest.

"We're going to see the new lawyer tomorrow," I say. "So I presume we'll find out what's in the will then."

"If you like, we could meet for coffee afterwards," Edvard says. "I might be able to shed some light on what comes up," he adds – he's a lawyer himself, after all. But there's no need for him to justify the invitation; I'm already nodding, of course I'd like to see him.

The waiter returns with our food and drinks; we sit in silence as he sets everything on the table before us.

"And there's something else," I say, as soon as the waiter has departed.

"Oh?"

Almost breathless, I tell him what Mother said. Edvard listens, his expression thoughtful.

"I see," he says. "So just before the Easter dinner party, Erling is frightened by the electrical fault, which he interprets as an attempt on his life. And shortly after this he changes his will. It's enough to make you wonder."

"Exactly."

"Who did you say was at the dinner?"

"Erling and me," I say. "Bård and Lise, Hanne and Ørjan, Silje. My three grandchildren. Olav and Bridget, and Mother."

"So only immediate family."

"Yes. Synne stopped by, too, but I only spoke to her at the front door."

"Hm."

"Of course, what Mother said doesn't necessarily mean anything," I say.

"That's true."

"She gets fairly muddled these days."

For a while neither of us says anything. But the silence isn't an awkward one.

"The shrimp is good," he remarks finally.

"Another sandwich," I say, and he laughs.

"Indeed. When in Norway, do as the Norwegians do."

"Was she Danish, too, your wife?" I ask.

Something flickers across his face. Not pain, exactly. More a kind of wonder. I'm not sure why I'm asking, but I'd like to know more about her. The fact that he never mentions her only serves to make me more curious.

"As Danish as rye bread," he says.

"Do you miss her?"

Another pause.

"Yes."

We each take a bite of our respective sandwiches. Chew for a few seconds.

"Do you miss Erling?"

"Yes," I say, swallowing. "I miss the sounds he made, his footsteps throughout the house, his habits. I miss having him there. But in a way . . . uff, no, that would sound terrible."

"What?"

"I moved straight out of my parents' house and in with Erling. I've never lived alone."

He gives me a searching look.

"So there's also a kind of freedom in it?" he guesses.

I hesitate.

"I'm not sure freedom is the right word. Or, yes, perhaps it is. A kind of ease, at any rate. If I want to replace the sofa – well, I can just do it. Does that make sense?"

"Yes," Edvard says. "It does."

"Don't think that I'm not grieving. I miss him terribly. My entire body still aches when I think about That Day."

I close my eyes at the thought of it. When I open them, Edvard says, slowly and thoughtfully: "I've never told anyone this before, but I also felt that way. It wasn't contrary to the pain. Truly, it wasn't – I was utterly crushed. But at the same time . . . to be master of my own house . . ."

He raises his eyebrows.

"For a long time I was afraid there might be something seriously wrong with me, for thinking that way."

"And are you still afraid that's the case?"

"No," he says. "I'm no longer afraid of that."

TWENTY-FIVE DAYS AFTER

Everything is ready. The envelope is affixed to the underside of the tabletop, hidden beneath the tablecloth. Beside it I have taped my sharpest kitchen knife.

I've disposed of all the other things. The bicycle, the boxes and bottle of pills. The length of gas pipe, and what remained of the appointment book. The decision to do all this wasn't an easy one to make, but it was necessary. Once it was done, I felt a great sense of relief.

Taking slow steps, I return to the hallway and open the double doors. Walk past the ruins of the study and over to the window. A grey mist has settled over the neighbouring gardens, but through the fog I see a pair of parallel headlamps moving up Nordheimbakken. I already know that it's them. I can tell from the speed at which they are travelling, see how they slow down before turning into my driveway. This is it. They're here.

FOURTEEN DAYS AFTER

Peter Bull-Clausen's office is located on the fourth floor of a tall commercial building that is all glass and metal. Bård hurries in as I'm waiting for the lift. He appraises me with a vacant gaze, as if he's just woken up and doesn't quite know what he's doing here. Then he smiles.

"Hi, Mamma."

He gives me a hug, smelling of coffee. As he releases me, the lift doors ding open.

"To think that we've ended up here," I say.

"I know," he says, and I'm not sure whether he really understands what I mean.

But it doesn't matter. I cast him a sideways glance. I can feel it in my heart, that he's still my little boy. His shirt is smart and freshly ironed, he's wearing dark jeans and casual shoes. Over his shoulder he carries a bag, presumably with his laptop in it.

Bård works in property development. From what I've gathered, the idea is to acquire empty plots cheaply and then sell them on to developers, without having to do much more than acquire the land and produce a few illustrative charts and drawings of trees and bushes and modern buildings; people carrying cups of coffee and pushing prams. These creations are then furnished with marketable names, like *Hoff Marina* or *Lunden Gardens*.

Bård seems to spend his every waking hour working. He spends dinners at our house engrossed in his phone; the same is true whether he's sitting on the lawn at the cabin on Tjøme or if we visit him and Lise at their house. It's as if he's constantly writing and sending messages, reading replies and forwarding them, weaving his way between the thousands of contacts that comprise his network. He often wears this weary, somewhat overwhelmed expression: what demands does the world wish to impose on me now?

"Are you doing okay, honey?" I ask.

I stroke his arm. For a moment I want to hold him, as I did when he was a child.

"Yes," he says, surprised. "I'm doing okay."

The girls have already arrived – we find them in reception. Hanne gets up the moment she sees us; Silje is standing behind her, reading something on the wall. She also looks exhausted – worried, almost. There's a look about her eyes that I'm not used to seeing: the skin is a little puffy, a little swollen.

"Where did you park the car, Mamma?" Hanne asks once she has hugged me.

"I came by train," I say.

"You did?" Hanne says, casting a critical glance in Bård's direction. "One of us could have picked you up."

"It's fine, really," I say.

Bård steps to one side and goes over to Silje, gives her a hug. He's avoiding Hanne, I think. Hanne, who has taken charge of the situation, who has so many tasks she'd like to delegate. To him – who already has so much on his plate.

"I can drive you home afterwards, anyway," Hanne says.

"That won't be necessary," I say. "I'm meeting up with someone."

"Oh? Who?"

Now they're looking at me, all three of them, and I feel a heat in my cheeks. I'm probably blushing. Which is stupid, because there's no reason for it, and I understand how it must look, what they must think.

"Edvard Weimer," I say. "He was a friend of Pappa's from university. You met him at the funeral."

"Him?" Hanne says, frowning. "I thought you said you and Pappa hadn't seen him in ages?"

"We hadn't," I say. "But I've met up with him a few times since Pappa died."

I look at them, at their surprised faces.

"He and Pappa had kept in touch," I add, for the sake of appearances. "And it's nice to spend time with someone who was a friend to your father."

Bård nods. Hanne still looks sceptical – I can see it from the corner of my eye.

Peter Bull-Clausen is short in stature and has longish blonde hair he wears swept back from his forehead. He's smartly dressed, with such pointy-toed shoes they're reminiscent of those of an old-fashioned court jester. He comes out to reception to greet us, shaking each of our hands, introducing himself and registering our names while he somehow keeps a loose conversation going: did we have any trouble finding the office, it was good we managed to find a day that suited everyone, May is such a busy time.

The meeting room is too large for us. There must be space for fifteen people around the table, and we cluster together at one end: Peter sitting at the head, with Hanne and me on one side and Silje and Bård on the other. Peter conjures up a folder of documents, which he begins to leaf through.

"I've prepared an overview for you," he says. "To make it a little easier for you to follow. There's a lot of legalese here."

He smiles widely and apologetically as he hands out the documents. I glance at what is passed to me but I'm unable to focus on it; the letters are tiny black insects on the white page. On the other side of the table I see Bård with his head bent, reading intently; beside me Hanne does the same. Silje just sits there and stares into space as she absently fingers the sheet of paper.

"In summary," Peter says, "a few weeks before he died, Erling transferred ownership of his property, that is, the house in Nordheimbakken, to Evy. In addition, he had recently invested rather heavily in it. Let's see here . . ."

Peter's fingers riffle through some documents.

"Ah yes, here it is! Yes – he has advanced half a million kroner to a contractor who is going to tear down the garage and build a new one, with an apartment above it. I'm sure you'll already be aware of this, Evy."

I only stare at him. Tear down the garage? Build an apartment? Peter sees my confusion.

"An application for planning permission was made to the authorities, let's see, in early March?" he says, as if to jog my memory. "And permission was granted at the end of April. The sum for the contractor was transferred just a few days before Erling died, actually."

My children are looking at me, all three of them. I stare at the sheet of paper in front of me. There are words such as *heirs* and *abode* and *probate* and *bankruptcy court.* This is Erling's language, not mine. It's as if I'm watching us from a distance, as if I'm standing at the other end of this enormous table and observing this pitiful gathering: a mother, her three grown-up children and the ever smiling Peter Bull-Clausen.

"We never spoke about it," I say.

"Maybe you just didn't quite take it in, Mamma," Hanne says, quickly placing her hand over mine.

"But Mamma and Pappa had separate estates," Bård says, straightening the sheets of paper on the table before him, then flicking through and straightening them again. "Pappa told us that.

Right, Hanne? And didn't you have one of those sorts of chats with him before you got married? About how the cabin belonged to Mamma, while the house belonged to him?"

Hanne doesn't answer. Peter Bull-Clausen nods obligingly, as if this is simply about clearing up a minor misunderstanding.

"Yes," he says. "It appears to have been that way previously, but after these latest changes, whereby he transferred everything to Evy, things now stand a little differently."

Bård appears to find this complete and utter madness. Hanne turns to the lawyer and says: "But surely Mamma can reverse the planned extension?"

"The agreement has already been entered into," Peter says, with an apologetic if slightly too broad smile. "It was Erling's express wish that this be done. He wanted to invest in the property."

"But Pappa also had quite a few other assets," Bård says as he leafs through the pages Peter handed out. "Didn't he?"

"Indeed – and now we come to that," Peter says. "As I already mentioned, the cabin on Tjøme belongs to Evy. You also jointly invested in a small apartment in the city centre, let's see, around ten years ago?"

I nod.

"In April, Erling transferred his ownership stake in that property to Evy, so she's now the sole proprietor."

The three of them look at me again, and I think I detect something reproachful in Hanne's gaze.

"But with the exception of the house and the cabin, Erling and I owned everything jointly," I say in my defence.

"Not the apartment," he says. "That is now owned by you alone. You signed the documentation on . . . here we are, the twenty-first of April."

He hands me a document. I glance at it – the letters seem to wobble and dance, but I can see it, my name is there, and yes, it appears to be my signature. Dated a week and a half before That Day, I think. That's not so long ago.

"I don't understand," I say, and then I look up, look at Hanne. "I don't remember this."

Hanne turns to Peter. "Is it still valid, if Mamma doesn't remember signing it?"

Peter turns to face me.

"Do you contest that this is your signature, Evy?" he says, his voice friendly.

I try to think back to April, but find nothing specific to grab on to. Only the dinner party at Easter. The daffodils, the yellow punch. Olav prattling away out on the terrace. Erling listening, a sceptical expression on his face.

"Erling brought me some paperwork," I mumble.

"If you don't contest that you are the one who signed it, then the document is valid," Peter says.

His apologetic smile is even wider now. He seems to be the kind of person whose smile increases in proportion to how uncomfortable the situation is.

I frown. Examine the sheet of paper in front of me. Erling has made these decisions, and I haven't paid attention. Whenever he's asked me to sign something, I've simply done it. Why would he want me to own the house? My father-in-law insisted that it be Erling's alone, and we've respected his wishes for all these years. Erling always assured me that I'd be taken care of through the cabin.

"Further investments were also made on Tjøme," Peter continues. "Erling purchased two plots adjacent to the cabin, which are currently undeveloped."

"But . . ." Bård says, "did Pappa take out a loan, or something?"

"He had quite significant funds in his accounts," Peter says.

"So then what do we inherit?"

The lawyer's smile widens yet again.

"Ah yes, about that," he says. "Evy is, as I mentioned, the sole owner of the house, the cabin, the plots of land, the forthcoming garage apartment and the apartment in the city centre. And what remains of Erling's assets, beyond these properties, is to be divided between the three of you. As far as I can see, this primarily constitutes the money in his accounts, and, ah yes, in addition to his current account he had a savings account, the balance of which is around 58,000 kroner."

The amount smacks onto the table. It's as if I can see it lying there, on its shiny surface, trembling. For a while no-one speaks, and then Bård clears his throat.

"So you're saying that Pappa had, oh, I don't know, we must be talking about several million kroner in his bank accounts, but just weeks before he died he spent all of it, apart from 58,000 kroner?"

Peter is silent for a moment. Then he says: "Erling wanted to invest in property."

"Which is now all solely owned by Mamma?"

"Yes."

Hanne and Bård exchange glances. Silje is still gazing into space, wearing her vacant stare.

"Well," Bård says. "I think I speak for all three of us when I say that of course we want Mamma to have enough to live well. But I have to say, I can't help wondering why Pappa would do all this. I mean, could it be that he wasn't in his right mind? The thing with the garage seems preposterous. And the fact that he bought two plots on Tjøme? And that Mamma now owns everything, without even being aware of it? It seems to me that he was becoming a little unhinged at the end, so surely it must be possible to reverse it?"

"I'm afraid not," Peter says. "These are binding agreements. The acquisitions have already been made. Evy could choose to sell, but that's up to her."

"But . . ." Bård starts, and then Hanne sends him a look and he silences himself.

"Maybe we can talk further at a later date," Hanne says in a businesslike voice, addressing Peter. "I think we all need a little time to digest this."

As she speaks, she nods at the sheets of paper Peter has photocopied for us, as if they are what needs to be digested. I imagine us stuffing them into our mouths, devouring them.

"Of course," Peter says generously.

"This is utter madness," Bård mumbles.

He's wearing that expression again, the one he had at the funeral: eyes wide open, forehead wrinkled so the folds of skin appear stacked one on top of the other. Hanne puts the papers in her bag, her movements brisk. Her hands are neatly manicured. For a moment the image of the painting she wanted to buy flickers before me: Bilal's flaming tree.

"I think we should just respect Pappa's wishes," Silje says suddenly, her voice loud and clear. "He's obviously done this for a reason. It's his money, we have to accept that this was what he wanted."

For a brief moment there is total silence, and then Peter says: "That's an excellent way to approach this."

It sounds false, like when an adult praises the scribbles of a child who is old enough to do better. We get up from our chairs.

"Do feel free to reach out if you have any further questions," Peter says.

If I really concentrate, I can remember Erling asking me to sign something. When could that have been – perhaps a couple of weeks before he died? He padded into the living room, where I was lounging on the sofa with a glass of wine in my hand, watching a silly Western that was about to reach its climax. He handed me some documents, offering an explanation I didn't hear: he was going to make a few amendments to our property portfolio, make our investments work a little harder.

Did I sign them? I must have done. All I remember is feeling a little irritated that Erling was disturbing me in the middle of the film, that he came barging in, bringing me details about things that belonged in his domain. And then I remember what happened in the film, the great duel at the end. I'm unable to recall anything else.

A silence falls between us as we walk back towards the reception area, and to break it I turn to Peter, who is still standing in the meeting room doorway.

"Um, where is the bathroom?" I ask.

The young man lights up, apparently happy to be of assistance.

"At the end of the corridor, on the right," he says. "You can't miss it."

"This is all extremely interesting," Edvard says.

He leans across the table towards me. His brow is wrinkled in concentration.

"But Erling was so frugal," I say. "Why in the world would he want to build an apartment above the garage? And what are we going to do with two extra plots on Tjøme?"

I take a breath, hold it in my chest. Recall Erling's crazed fit of cleaning in the study; the rubber gloves and bank-robber scarf.

"Might he have been losing his mind?" I ask.

I think of Mother. The early, insidious signs: little misunderstandings, logic that seemed obvious to her, but the rest of us could make no sense of.

"Did the lawyer offer any explanation?" Edvard asks.

"Investments."

The restaurant in which we are sitting is small and secluded, on a backstreet behind Youngstorget. The food is French-inspired, and – as Edvard promised – it is delicious. I eat chicken, *poulet à la provençale*. The waiter is clearly French, but I have no wish to test out my language skills. So many years have passed since I took the course in Paris, and besides, I never completed it.

"One way of looking at this," Edvard says thoughtfully, "is that he wanted to give you room to manoeuvre. Had you maintained separate estates, you wouldn't have been able to remain in the house. And had he requested joint ownership, certain limits would have been placed on what you were able to do with the assets. But now you have full right of disposal over everything."

"That's true."

I'm not sure what I'm supposed to think about this. It feels like a responsibility I'm not entirely ready to take on. But there is also something intoxicating about it: *I'm* the one with all the money now.

The children were upset after the meeting. When I returned from the toilets, I heard them talking among themselves. My footsteps were inaudible on the carpeted floor, and the folding screen in muted colours hid me from view.

"I agree that it seems crazy," Hanne's voice said. "But right now, the main thing is to find out what we can do about it. And preferably without worrying Mamma."

"I just don't understand how it can be *allowed*," Bård said. "I'm tempted to ask Uncle Olav about it."

Neither of the girls responded to this.

"What worries *me* is that Edvard guy," Hanne said. "He turns up out of the blue just after Pappa dies, supposedly a close friend. And now he's taking Mamma out to eat. Like on a kind of *date*, or something."

One of the others laughed a little at this – Bård, I thought, from the sound of it – and this wounded me a little: is the thought really so ridiculous? But at the same time, I felt a fluttering in my stomach when Hanne said the word *date*. Is that what this is?

"I mean it," she said. "Pappa has transferred all his assets to Mamma, and then he dies, and suddenly this guy keeps popping up wherever you turn. We've heard nothing about him before now, but he and Pappa were apparently *oh-so* close. And Mamma is rich now, of course. Those plots on Tjøme – how much might they be worth? In addition to the cabin and our plot? Not to mention the house, with an extra apartment above the garage. I spoke to Edvard at the funeral, too, and to be honest he seemed like a bit of a sleazebag. He had *gold digger* written all over him. And Mamma says that the police have been over, snooping around the house."

This knocked me sideways. Is that how things appear from the outside? I stood there behind the folding screen, thinking of Edvard's gentle, kind eyes.

"So what are you suggesting?" Bård said. "That Mamma is about to fall victim to a criminal super-seducer?"

There was laughter in his voice again, which twisted the knife once more

"Why not?" Hanne said. "I think that if you consider all these things together – first the stuff Pappa has done, and then Edvard suddenly taking Mamma out to dinner – there's reason to be concerned."

"Sure," Bård said. "But what can we do about it?"

Nobody responded to this. Then Silje said: "I can't see Mamma wanting to go out on a *date* right now. It's only two weeks since Pappa died."

"Don't be so naive, Silje," Hanne said. "Mamma has a history of being quite selfish – and pretty often."

A shiver ran through me – what did she mean?

Bård cleared his throat.

"The thing is – and here I'm assuming that all three of us are on the same page – that inheritance would have come in really useful right now. I figured Pappa probably had a fair bit in his savings account, and I thought . . ."

His voice trailed off; some of them shifted position.

"Well, let me put it this way," he said. "Does anyone have any-thing against me contacting Uncle Olav?"

Silence for a few beats. Then Silje said: "I have no problem with that."

Again they fell quiet. Perhaps glances and gestures were exchanged.

"Sure, go for it," Hanne said. "Yes – go ahead, Bård. Just keep us updated."

"Of course."

"Just, you know, Uncle Olav can be a little . . ."

She let the half-sentence hang there in mid-air.

"Oh, I know," Bård said.

"Now I think we'd better stop talking," Hanne said. "Mamma will be back any minute."

On my way to the restaurant to meet Edvard, I thought about what they had said. The thing about the money, of course, and Bård's frustrations – how he clearly needs his inheritance – but mostly what Hanne said about Edvard. Disturbingly enough, it doesn't frighten me. On the contrary, I can't help thinking, might she be right? Is Edvard interested in something more? Is he interested in *me*?

When I was nineteen, Edvard stood in the doorway to my room and asked whether I'd like to join him and his friends on a night out. And this time, *I'm* the one who gets to decide, I think – this time neither Erling nor Hanne nor anyone else can decline on my behalf.

To begin with, this isn't what we talk about. Edvard tells me about a criminal case he's following through the courts – not one of his, but a colleague's. I listen intently, making suggestions that Edvard takes seriously – yes, he says, one could certainly argue that, that's a rational point to make, but shall I tell you how the defence would have responded? For a while it feels as if I could be his colleague. A less experienced and knowledgeable colleague, of course, but still a voice worth listening to. I'm not so stupid that I'm unable to see this whole situation from the outside, too, and I ask myself whether Hanne might be right, whether Edvard is flattering me in order to soften me up. But that isn't exactly what's happening, because he offers me resistance, doesn't agree with everything I say. No, what touches me is simply that he listens. That he takes my opinions seriously, takes the trouble to properly respond. Did Erling not do this? I don't know, I can't remember the last time we spent an evening deep in conversation.

Have we ever spoken that way, Erling and I? Over the past few years we've mostly lived in near silence. Of course we've told each other about recent events, the headlines in the newspaper, how the cupboard door is hanging loose on its hinges, or what we did that day. We've exchanged information, apparently listened to one another. But how much do I really know about what was on his mind? All the troubling things that have happened lately, the kind of things I haven't wanted to hear about: the fall from his bicycle, the day he scrubbed down the entire study, his mouth covered by the scarf. He had accumulated a stockpile of canned goods in the cellar, and his career change had been so sudden – one day he came home and announced he was resigning from his position at the Public Roads Administration and would be starting work at Green Agents.

"Why on earth would you want to do that?" I had asked.

I offered up possible reasons. Was he bored at work? Was there too little to do, or was it his new manager? Erling shook his head.

"I can't think of a single issue that's more important than climate change," he said, in his dry, matter-of-fact voice. "*Everyone* should stop doing what they're doing and start working on behalf of the environment. Right now."

Privately, I had thought it was about Erling being afraid of reaching retirement age, a fear of old age itself. Of the many long days at home with me. But to what extent did I ask him? I think I simply accepted it – okay then, this is just the way things are now.

Only when the food is on the table do I tell Edvard about the meeting at the lawyer's office. He listens attentively as I speak, and says nothing until I'm finished.

"If I were to try to piece together what a person might be thinking when doing something like that," he says now, carefully setting down his fork, "my first question would be to ask if he was trying to ensure his assets wouldn't fall into the hands of his heirs."

"I don't know," I say. "Why would he want to do that?"

Edvard is quiet for a while.

"I don't have children," he says then. "So I can't imagine what this must be like for you, Evy. But with things as they are . . . is it possible the person Erling was afraid of is one of them?"

"One of the children?"

"Yes. Or possibly your son- or daughter-in-law?"

I think of six-year-old Hanne, clinging to me when I came home from Paris, holding on tighter and tighter and refusing to let go. Eight-year-old Bård, who had simply stood there and stared at me, somewhat stand-offishly, with his big, serious eyes. Silje, a newborn, angry and red. And Lise, the go-getting GP who got together with Bård when they were just nineteen. Ørjan, the son of farmers from Nord-Trøndelag, with his blonde curls and passion for sustainability and fair trade.

No, Edvard doesn't know what he's saying. He's right – he can't imagine what any of this is like.

For a while we eat in silence. Edvard is considering something, I can tell – his brows are drawn down, and there's a far-off look in his eyes.

"What's on your mind?" I finally ask him.

His eyebrows lift again, and he smiles.

"Let's talk about something more pleasant," he says. "But before we leave the subject: how would you feel about the two of us taking a trip together to the cabin on Tjøme? We could take a look at your new plots, see whether anything there makes us any the wiser. Perhaps even later this week?"

I feel the suggestion as a fluttering in my stomach.

"That sounds like an excellent idea," I say. "I can do any time."

THIRTY-NINE YEARS BEFORE

The headmaster presumably once had a thick head of hair, but now it was thinning from the top down. He was wearing a casual tweed jacket with a crumpled shirt underneath, and something about him – the slow way he poured our coffee, perhaps – told me he was one of those people who just cannot be rushed, who quite simply refuse to get stressed, who allow things to take the time they take. His office was messy, the plants on the windowsill suffering from neglect.

"A very warm welcome to you, Eva," he said.

"Evy," I corrected him, and for a moment he looked confused, scanning his desk for the right sheet of paper.

"Evy, of course," he said when he was unable to find it. "Welcome."

This was my first job. I had fallen pregnant before I'd finished my teacher training course, and Bård was just over a year old when I became pregnant with Hanne.

I had enjoyed the time I spent with the children. That's what I said, if anyone asked: is there any job more important than providing your children with the best possible start in life? But I'd been looking forward to this – to getting started. To dressing smartly, to taking on responsibilities. To putting into practice all I had learned.

"I'm sure everything will run like clockwork," the headmaster said. "You'll be the form teacher for 4B. They're a good group, I think. Energetic and eager to learn."

I smiled. 4B. Twenty-five ten-year-olds. With open minds and books covered in brown paper. The headmaster got up. A strict-looking receptionist handed me a bunch of keys, and then we walked out into the corridor. Children all around us, with their baseball caps and trainers and pigtails, their laughter and their shrill, cutting voices. Their intensity astonished me. All the physical agitation, all the nudging and the shoving. But this was break time. In the classroom, it would be different.

"Ellen," the headmaster shouted, waving over a young teacher with a blonde ponytail. "This is Evy, she's new today. Could you show her to 4B's form room?"

Ellen led me into a long corridor where it was a little quieter. She was a head shorter than me, and younger, too. Not by much – three or four years perhaps – but we must have looked as if we were from different generations. Me, smartly dressed in my pleated skirt and patent shoes; she in her dungarees and trainers, like the teenagers at the shopping centre. The shirt she was wearing beneath her dungarees wasn't even ironed. But she said nothing about the differences between us, only how good it was that I was there and could take the class – the school year was already underway, after all. I'd have to jump onto a speeding train, but I'd be just fine. She smiled cheerfully, showing me her dimples. Was I a recent graduate?

"No," I said. "I completed my training in seventy-six, but I had a baby straight afterwards."

A couple of boys rushed past us, and Ellen called after them: Markus, we *walk* in the corridors, remember? One of them looked at her and smiled, then slowed his tempo to something that could just about pass for a walk. Ellen rolled her eyes, but she smiled, and as the boys went by, she ruffled Markus's fringe.

"He's one of yours," she said when they were gone. "I'd keep an eye on him, if I were you. He's a lovely boy, but he can be quite the rabble-rouser. You need to be firm with him."

She opened the door to the classroom, and there it was: an open space, twenty-five chairs at twenty-five desks. The teacher's desk, with an office chair. The blackboard was a large blank slate, as yet unmarked.

Form 4B tumbled into the classroom like a wild river of meltwater – they splashed and spluttered everywhere, the rush of voices like the roar of a waterfall. I had to hiss *shhh!* several times before they settled down.

"My name is Evy," I said. "I'm your new teacher."

Some of the girls closest to the window turned to face each other. I wrote my name on the blackboard, and when I turned back to the class, two of the pupils were out of their seats wandering about. I called them back to their desks, and the pair of them looked at me. Only one of them sat down, and the other took a good deal of persuading to get back into his seat.

I told them that I was married, and that I had two children. Some of them nodded. A girl in the front row asked what my children were called, and while I was speaking, the nervousness began to bubble up in me again. To prevent the dam from bursting I asked them to take out their Norwegian textbooks. I found the sound of twenty-five hands digging around in twenty-five school bags far more overwhelming than it should have been.

The next period was maths. I attempted to explain multiplication by two-digit numbers. Every time I turned to face the blackboard, chaos erupted behind my back. Markus snapped a girl's pencil in half; the girl screeched and flailed her arms around, and while I was attempting to break up the argument, half the middle row ran over to the window.

As I was doing my best to get them back into their places, the door opened. There stood Ellen, in her dungarees. I tried to roll my eyes ironically at her, but I could feel the desperation pulsing along my jaw, in my lips, at my throat.

"Hello!" bellowed Ellen with all her might. "Now sit down, all of you!"

Her cry cut through the racket. Silence fell. The middle row shuffled back to their seats.

"Jon Ivar, take off that cap," Ellen said. "Marianne, go sit in your place, *no*, I don't want to hear why, just go and sit down, right now. And Markus, you *know* you're not allowed to draw on the desk. One more time and it will be straight to the headmaster's office."

A kind of stillness fell over the room. Ellen stood there without speaking, looking them over. They looked up at her, each and every one of them.

"Now behave yourselves for Evy," Ellen said.

I cringed – she was instructing my class to be nice to me. I felt like such an idiot, standing there in my skirt and prissy woollen sweater.

Towards the end of October I asked Erling how he would feel about me stopping working.

"I'm thinking of the children," I said. "Hanne is still so young, after all. And Bård seems a little down in the dumps. I think it might be good for them to spend less time with the childminder."

Erling went along with my rationale. The kids are only young for such a short time, I argued. It seems such a shame for them to be away from us practically all day every day. And besides, I have my misgivings about that childminder, I said. I arranged my features into serious folds and expressed myself with caution – nothing was *really* wrong, the children were safe with her, I was certain of that – but from a developmental standpoint, was it enough? Hanne suffered from such moods, and they shifted so quickly. And Bård was so sensitive, he needed to be around adults who really *understood* him.

Erling agreed. This had actually been his position from the start, he said – not that there was anything necessarily wrong with the childminder, but it's best for children to be with their parents. He earned good money, we had a small mortgage and extremely moderate expenses. We had arranged our finances wisely, and now it was paying off. We had the freedom to choose. And should we now believe it best for the children to be home every day, we actually had the means to make that happen.

Relief swelled within me. The rowdy class, the constant struggle to contain the chaos. Some mornings, I cried in the shower, although I said nothing of this to Erling. I simply leaned my forehead against the tiles and felt the weight of all those battles – I fought them daily, and often, I lost.

Of course, I would return to work later. Make use of my education and my skills. But when the timing was better. Yes – all in good time.

"Ah, yes, it's such a shame you have to leave us," the headmaster said.

It was my last day, and there I was, back in his office. He was wearing the same shapeless tweed jacket.

"I know, I wish I could have stayed," I said. "I've grown very fond of my class. But I have my own children, and unfortunately things didn't work out so well with the childminder."

"I understand," he said. "Well, Ingeborg will take 4B until Christmas, and there are other applicants for the position, so it will all work out, I'm sure."

He seemed to look straight through me. He was done with me, already in the process of planning the next semester. I had disappointed him. He doesn't know, I thought hotly, he doesn't understand what it's like. It's easy for him to imagine everyone can be like Ellen.

"Perhaps I'll come back," I said. "In a few years' time, when my children are older."

"Yes, yes," he said, without looking up. "Of course, do feel free to apply."

I felt the receptionist's eyes boring into my back as I walked out of his office. She said nothing, and nor did I.

FOURTEEN DAYS AFTER

"Hello, Evy." Miriam's voice is warm as she answers the telephone. She's saved my number, I think, surprised – she knows it's me calling.

"I'm so sorry to bother you," I say breathlessly.

I speak to her as I walk. I'm actually on my way to the T-bane station, but the lunch with Edvard is still buzzing through my head, and my feet seem to be acting of their own accord, taking a slightly more circuitous route. I can't be sure that this isn't by design.

"No problem at all," she says.

"I was just wondering about something."

I come to a standstill outside the grocery store. No, it isn't due to simple chance that I've ended up here. On the other end of the line, Miriam is quiet. She's waiting for me to speak, so I blurt it out:

"Do you think Erling was going crazy?"

"Crazy?" she asks.

"Yes. Did you ever think he appeared to be losing his mind?"

She takes a breath.

"No," she says. "No, I never thought that."

"You saw him at work," I say, because I feel the need to explain myself. "Maybe you saw a different side to him. Because I think . . . I don't know. Some of the things he did towards the end were a little odd."

Silence. I peer through the shop window at the crates of vege-tables as Miriam thinks for a few moments. The young woman standing behind the counter inside is engrossed in her phone.

"He seemed completely normal at work," Miriam says. "Maybe a little, how to put it – preoccupied? But only for the past few weeks. As if he was worried about something. But that's all. His mind was crystal clear, as far as I could tell."

"Thank you," I say, releasing my breath in a sigh and allowing the relief to fill my voice.

"Evy," Miriam says. "Now *I'm* starting to feel a little worried. Is everything okay?"

"Oh, yes," I say, studying the rustic crates of vegetables and the pale counter of untreated wood. "Everything's fine. Thank you very much."

As I hang up, I take hold of the door handle and enter the store.

The girl behind the counter looks up. She has long, brown hair that hangs in a messy braid over her shoulder, and a gold ring in her nose.

"Is there anything I can help you with?" she asks me.

"Yes," I say, from my position beside a row of baskets offering broccolini from Hadeland. "Is Ørjan here?"

"He's in the back. Just a moment."

While the girl looks for Ørjan, I look around. The shop is neat and tidy. The vegetables are arranged in crates, all labelled in looping handwritten script on tiny blackboards. The prices are steep. A white countertop with chairs set in front of it runs the length of the window, where people can sit to enjoy a coffee and a pastry. There are no other customers.

"Hello, Evy," Ørjan says as he walks out onto the shop floor. "How nice to see you."

He puts his arms around me and gives me a squeeze. He's a generous hugger, and he holds me tightly for a long time. Then he offers me a coffee and asks me to take a seat.

I consider him as he pours the coffee. He's tall and slim, with attractive blue eyes and blonde curls, which his son has inherited. The first time I met him, I thought he was too soft for Hanne. All her previous boyfriends had been strong, ambitious men. She'd had her heart broken by several of them, and just after she split up with the last one, she had come home with Ørjan. To heal her crushed heart, I had thought. Not to get married and have children.

I've occasionally wondered how their marriage suits her – and how it suits him, they're so different. But maybe that's precisely why it works. Assuming it does work, of course. Hanne rarely confides in me. Despite the fact that we speak on the phone fairly often, there is no deep confidence between us. I've likely muttered about Erling changing his job, or sighed when he wouldn't let me replace a broken piece of furniture: *you know how Pappa is*. But while Hanne often complains about work, or about the kindergarten staff or the odd broken appliance in their apartment, I never hear her complain about Ørjan.

But maybe this isn't down to a lack of closeness, I think. Perhaps they're genuinely happy together.

"Here you go," he says, setting the cup on the white countertop and taking a seat beside me. "Coffee from Guatemala. From a farmer there who we're in contact with. We'd prefer to sell only Norwegian produce, but you can't exactly farm coffee beans in Vestfold."

We sit in silence for a little while, looking out at the street through the window. It occurs to me that we've rarely had a proper conversation, Ørjan and I. When Hanne is there, she's the one who speaks for the family – Ørjan is content to simply agree or supply the odd detail. Perhaps this is my fault. Maybe I always address her, treat him as a hanger-on.

"How are you, Ørjan?" I ask.

"Oh you know, pretty good," he says. "Getting by. Things are busy, both at work and at home."

He laughs. He laughs often, I think – he's a bright and happy sort of person. Hanne, on the other hand, is more demanding. I wonder whether he makes her happier, or whether she puts a damper on his good mood.

"Max is getting so big," I say. "And he must be sleeping better by now, I suppose?"

"Yeah, but you know how it is, there's always something. Friends coming over to visit and after-school activities and everything he has to learn."

"And what about Hanne? Is she doing okay, do you think?"

"Yes, fine."

"Sad at losing her father?"

"Of course," Ørjan says, his eyes serious. "Yes, of course she is. And she's incredibly stressed about this whole thing with the house."

I take a deep breath. This whole thing with the house? I search for a hook to hang these words on, but find none. Ørjan explains: surely I must have heard about the planned development of new semi-detached properties in Kjelsås – didn't Hanne show me the prospectus? She heard about them from a friend who had bought one. You put down a deposit, and the house will be ready in around a year's time. There are now only two units left, Ørjan says, and Hanne's getting more and more stressed with each one that's sold.

I nod and nod, as if I'm already well aware of all this, as I attempt to locate what he's telling me among the telephone conversations I've had with Hanne over the past few weeks. I can't remember her ever mentioning this.

"The bank says we need more equity in order to be approved for a mortgage," Ørjan says. "And Hanne got worked up when Erling said you weren't able to help us out. I mean, I understand, of course I do. I told Hanne we couldn't just expect you to lend us the money, but you know what she's like when she's made up her mind about something."

He laughs a little. I try to laugh, too. Did Hanne ask us for money? Did she go to Erling and not me? Why has neither of them said anything?

Ørjan frowns, his expression turning serious.

"It can't be easy for her, that that was the last conversation they had," he says. "She was incredibly close to him. His opinion really mattered to her."

He's probably right about this. It's ten years since she got her current job, working for a chain of kiosks. She threw her entire heart and soul into it. Have you seen all the people sitting bent over their phones on the tram, she asked as we sat around the table eating Sunday dinner. Research shows that our ability to concentrate is in decline, we have to log off Facebook and read physical books! Hanne wanted to make illustrated weeklies and colour magazines trendy again. Do you like architecture and art? Stylish glossies from overseas! Are you an intellectual? Weekly journals carrying essays about society! Interested in fashion? *Vogue, Elle, Cosmopolitan* – we have it all! Erling just shrugged. He found it pretentious.

"When did you say it was again, the last time they spoke?" I ask.

"She called him a couple of days before he died," Ørjan says. He wrinkles his brow, thinking. "Or maybe she met up with him, actually, I'm not sure. I think things were a little tense between them. You know how stressed Hanne gets when things don't turn out the way she planned."

"You know," I say, "this is the first I've heard about the semi-detached properties in Kjelsås. Erling never mentioned it to me, and neither did Hanne."

"Hm," Ørjan says. He looks out of the window.

"I can't think why they wouldn't have mentioned it," I say.

"No, I've no idea," he says.

*

There was something Ørjan wasn't saying, I think, as I sit on the train home. He looked away, like he was holding something back.

I have the same feeling as when I stood behind the folding screen at the lawyer's office and heard my children talking about me – and yes, the same as on the day that Hanne and Silje stood in Erling's study discussing how they were going to take care of me, without bothering to ask me what I wanted. Why don't they ever involve me in these conversations? I think of Erling, the way he padded into the living room in his ancient slippers when I was watching the film: Evy, could you sign this?

But he's had strange ideas before. The deeper he dug into books and research on climate change, the more certain he was that the world as we know it is on the brink of collapse. A few years ago, he gathered together various necessities including a camping stove, canned foods and cash, and hid it all in a safe in the cellar. He had shown it, almost ceremoniously, to the children and me: in the event of a crisis, we'd have all we needed to survive for a while. Because climate change would lead to the breakdown of society.

It's only a question of time, he said. The price of food will increase, and the planet will become ever more uninhabitable. It's vital to be prepared.

This treasure trove, which would save us in the event of the coming apocalypse, was meticulously locked away. The procedure to open the safe was an intricate one: the first key was hidden behind the stack of apple crates in the main storage room, in a small tin can with a flowery pattern. It unlocked a drawer in the linen cupboard, which was hidden at the back of another of the cellar's storerooms, so we would have to scale stacks of old garden chairs and broken lamps to get to it. In the drawer was a jewellery box containing another key. This one finally admitted you to the safe, so if you knew the code – and also knew that it was located in precisely *that* storeroom, hidden behind a broken travel cot and a huge radio cabinet from the 1950s – you could open it and get your hands on the stash: the canned foods Erling believed would be so valuable, bottles of clean water, methylated spirits for the camping stove, packets of pasta, powdered foods and beef jerky – purchased from an army surplus sale – and an old lunchbox containing seventy thousand kroner in cash. This was how we would survive the apocalypse.

Erling impressed the details of the system upon all four of us, making us repeat them: the stack of apple crates, the linen cupboard, the jewellery box with its padlock, the safe. Behind his back we exchanged despairing eye-rolls; perhaps indulgent smiles, too. This was around six months before he quit his job with the Public Roads Administration, and I would come to look back on these doomsday preparations with ever increasing concern and ever decreasing humour: what on earth was going on with Erling?

Was this the point of the apartment he wanted to build above the garage, or the plots he had acquired on Tjøme? Rage surges up in me: he's treated me like a child. Never respected me enough to ask for my opinion. Maybe that's why it feels so good to spend time with Edvard. Because I've been so starved of being heard.

I take out my phone and write him a message: *Would you be free to go to Tjøme tomorrow?*

THIRTY-FOUR YEARS BEFORE

I had rented a room in an apartment hotel on the rue de Paris. There was a bar-tabac on the way to the Metro station, and every day when I returned home from the language school in the afternoon, a group of men would be sitting there drinking and chatting. Glances were cast in my direction as I walked past, along with laughter and comments in a certain tone. It frightened me – I felt there was malicious intent behind their words, but I didn't understand enough of the language to know exactly what they were saying.

My room had a kitchenette tucked away in a nook, and a toilet in a tiny closet. In the mornings I ate hunks of baguette and drank coffee which I heated on the hotplate; there was no fridge, so I had the bread either with jam or on its own. Then I would gather up my things and walk down the rue de Paris to the Metro station, past the bar-tabac, where in the mornings it was just people drinking coffee. Plunging down into the station's long, intricate underground corridors, I followed the signs for one line, then another. I squeezed myself among the impatient Parisians in their smart overcoats and fought my way back up to the pale February light at Saint-Placide, a little less than an hour after I had descended below ground.

When I had planned the trip from home, from our bedroom, while Erling sat downstairs in front of the TV, it had seemed ideal that the language course offered only four hours of teaching a day. I imagined myself striding out of the school at lunchtime, ready to use what I had learned. I imagined spending the afternoons in

museums and galleries, in enthusiastic discussions with connois-
seurs and bohemians: *mais comme elle est belle, cette peinture!* I
wasn't prepared for how exhausted I would feel after four hours of
studying the rules for *subjunctif* and *passé simple*. The class finished
at one o'clock – by which time my brain would be mush, and I
would find a cheap café close by and order bread and soup, which I
greedily devoured. Then I'd walk back to the Metro and allow it to
rattle me back to the rue de Paris as I stood shoulder to shoulder
with people with empty faces.

The agreement was that I called home on Saturdays. In the
reception there was a coin-operated telephone, and I dropped a few
francs into the slot. Bård was awkward, inarticulate – he would
usually respond with either a yes or a no. The more I asked, the
more silent he became. Sometimes I'd hear Erling coaching him in
the background.

"Why don't you tell her about school, Bård?"

Hanne fluctuated between speaking and whining, asking over
and over again when I was coming home, and how long it was
until then.

Erling and I exchanged a few words at the end of each call. There
was something unfamiliar in his voice then, an impure, trembling
sound. He asked how I was doing and if I was having fun. Of course,
I chirped, I had been to the Louvre, seen incredible works of art – did
he know just how small the *Mona Lisa* is in real life? He was scared
out of his wits, I knew that, but I didn't want to think about it. This
was the first time I had been alone. The first time I didn't have to
answer to anyone, the first time I didn't have to take responsibility for
others. Surely that had to count for something? Surely it must be an
important experience, something to cherish, to hold on to?

In a household with two working parents, there are presumably
many different ways in which those parents might choose to
organise their lives. For us, however, the traditional marital division

of labour was upheld: Erling earned money for the family's upkeep, while I was responsible for the daily running of the household. This felt natural, but sometimes slightly unfair: Erling worked from nine to five-thirty, with paid holidays and the right to time off in lieu. My work was never-ending.

The house on the hill in Montebello was his, signed over to him as an advance on his inheritance. The stipulation that we maintain separate estates seemed reasonable enough when it was proposed in the Krogh family's usual, unsentimental way, but it also gave me a queasy feeling. It wasn't mine, this house I took care of. I had no rights to it, I was little more than a maidservant. Every other week I took water and floor soap into Erling's study and got down on my knees in front of the desk, a monstrosity Erling had inherited from his father: tropical hardwood, with carvings along its edges, intricate flowers, leaves and spirals. Dust would settle deep within these embossed patterns – and a huge amount of rubbing was required to get it out. Sometimes, as I was doing this, I would imagine my mother-in-law, the formidable Inga Krogh, on her knees on the dark-green wall-to-wall carpeting as she attempted to force tiny particles of dust out of their niches, as if it were an honourable tradition for the women of the Krogh family, one we proudly passed down the generations.

Erling felt no responsibility for ensuring that his house was kept clean, or that there was food in the fridge. Or that his children had full bellies and clean clothes to wear and were well rested. When he got home from work, he settled down in his favourite chair. If he set the table or did the washing-up, he acted as if he was doing me a favour.

But so what? In the biggest houses in Montebello, the wives invariably stayed home, and we agreed that this was preferable to going to work. What a privilege, to get to spend so much time with our children! Could you imagine having to change places with your husband, we sometimes asked each other. I recalled my miserable months as a form teacher. Children benefit from their mothers staying at home – it's good for them. It's good for mothers, too. It's a privilege to be able to afford it.

The only domestic domain Erling took it upon himself to manage was the family's finances. And, admittedly, he took this very seriously. He set a monthly household budget, gave me the allocated funds and kept accounts. This all seemed very old-fashioned to me. The neighbourhood women had generous bank accounts that they dipped into as they wished, but in our house, frugality was regarded as the ultimate virtue. Erling despised wastefulness. Anything beyond the most basic everyday expenses had to be discussed with him. The payslips were in his name; it was up to him to approve or deny any outgoings.

"Two hundred kroner each for the tickets," he might say if I suggested taking the children to the theatre. "Plus sweets in the interval, cloakroom charges, parking in the city, and yes, you'll need a ticket, too. That soon adds up to a thousand kroner for an afternoon. I don't know, Evy – is it really worth it?"

So I could state my case, if I had the energy for it: their friends are going, it's culture, it's part of giving them a rounded education. And he would counter with the new skiing equipment we had just purchased, which had taken a huge chunk out of the monthly budget, and why couldn't we just read the book instead of going to the show?

"It costs to live," he would say, and then he'd rattle off a list of all the expenses I knew nothing about: electricity, down payments on the cabin and the car, insurance. "And, as you're well aware, we have only one income."

If I really believed an expense was important, I could usually force it through, but the discussions were draining. More often than not, I found I couldn't be bothered to battle it out. When he began to summarise our outgoings, wearing that expression that would slip across his face – the pinched mouth, the furrowed forehead, the narrowed eyes – I tended to cave. And at the same time, humiliation burned in my gut: I was a grown woman who had to ask for permission to take her children to the theatre.

I was not unhappy. It was just how it was, and many had it far worse. But I was tired. No matter how hard I worked, my work was never done.

My father died on an ordinary Tuesday. He was fit and healthy, not yet seventy, and one afternoon when he and Mother were at the supermarket, he collapsed in the frozen foods aisle. The loss was so meaningless, so sudden. It had never occurred to me that it might happen so soon. I should have told him everything I wanted him to know while I had the chance; asked him for some pointers on how best to live my life. But I didn't, and now it was too late. I was thirty years old and I felt lost, orphaned.

Synne said: come with me to the mountain hotel! She could get us a good price through work. We could drive up on the Friday, stay until Sunday. Eat well, dance, forget all the sad stuff. Erling said: we can't just go throwing money around. He held forth about interest rates and the state of the markets; described the challenges facing the Norwegian economy. Who was I to come here rhapsodising about dance floors and breakfast buffets? Didn't I understand the pressures of being the family's sole provider, the weight of the responsibility he carried?

Yes, I understood. I had intimate knowledge of his arguments. I called Synne and politely declined.

*

Immediately after this came the first of three bouts of a stomach bug. I wiped up the vomit and comforted each child in turn: first Bård, then Hanne. I plucked remnants of half-digested spaghetti from the landing rug until I had to empty my stomach myself. I got up in the night with sick children while ill; tried to offer comfort as I stood bent double over the toilet. Erling slept on a mattress in his study so he wouldn't catch the virus.

I don't think he believed anything about this arrangement was insensitive or cruel. I don't think any of the people we knew did either, or that I even did myself. I think that we, Erling and I, simply believed that that was how things were. The purpose of our marriage was to enable Erling to go to work every day, so that the money came in and the family endured. The division of labour was sensible. I think he would have been genuinely astonished had anyone suggested otherwise.

When my father died, I inherited a little money. As was only right, I paid down the car loan and contributed to the family's expenses, but I also kept a little back for myself. At a trade fair some years earlier, I had picked up a brochure about French language courses in Paris, and now I dug it out of a drawer. *Apprendre le français à Paris!* the cover declaimed in colourful letters, above an image of young people sitting on a lawn. They looked so happy, so carefree. They were probably speaking French, effortlessly and fluently, telling one another about what they would do that day, where they would eat, *soup à l'ognion*, perhaps a little *apéritif* first. And I wanted to sit there with them.

Flights, accommodation and the French language course, as well as some spending money. The inheritance from my father would cover it. I had the funds and I could make the decision myself.

*

"I've always wanted to learn French," I said to Erling.

I had agonised over how I would broach it. Eventually, I landed on bringing it up casually, at a time when we were relaxed, enjoying ourselves. I chose a Friday evening, three weeks prior to the start of the course. We were sitting in front of the TV, each with our glass of wine. The sitcom being broadcast on NRK was fairly amusing, and Erling was in a good mood.

"Really?" he said, without taking his eyes off the TV.

"Yes," I said. "I think I'd be good at it, too. I have an ear for languages – you know, my high school English teacher always said so."

"Well then why don't you just get stuck in?"

He took a sip from his glass. I studied him – from the corner of my eye, so he wouldn't notice.

"There's a school in Paris," I said. "A kind of conversation class, where you learn the basics. I picked up a brochure a while back, and it says that if you have enough prior knowledge, you'll achieve an *acceptable conversational level* after just three weeks."

He glanced at me, confused, as if trying to determine if there was a point to these apparently irrelevant pieces of information with which I was presenting him.

"Not to mention that you get to live in Paris," I continued, quickly, cheerily. "And I've always wanted to live in Paris. You know, the city of light and all that."

My smile was too wide, I could feel it, but I was unable to do anything about it. I so desperately wanted his approval.

"You mean you want to go to France?" he said, astonished.

"Yes," I said, before hurrying to add: "Just for a few weeks. Three – or preferably four."

"Alone?"

"Yes."

For a moment he stared at me with that expression of his, as though he thought I was crazy, and then he began to laugh. But it wasn't a mocking laugh. It was more that he seemed genuinely entertained, as if my suggestion were a joke I had come up with to amuse him.

"You, alone in Paris?" he said, still laughing. "You've never been anywhere on your own. You can hardly read a map – we only just about manage to figure out where we're going when we drive to Denmark in the school holidays."

He was laughing openly at me, inviting me to laugh along with him: yes, you're right, what a comical thought that I might manage something like this. That was what pushed me over the edge, I thought later, the fact that his laughter was so inviting. Had he mocked me or met me with active resistance, I might have backed down. But he found the whole thing so hilarious it didn't even occur to him that I might be serious.

And I thought: I'm a grown woman. I have an education. True, I haven't really used it for much, but I *do* have it, and I got good grades, so I managed *that*. I have money in the bank and a good head on my shoulders, I can take care of myself. After all, I administer this entire household and keep us all alive, with no assistance but the money I manage to squeeze out of him. Does he think I can't do it? Does he think I'll come crawling home, with my tail between my legs?

"It's a three-week course," I said, my voice a little flintier now. "You can rent an apartment through the school."

The laughter died on Erling's face and he stared at me. He was wearing the smile of a man being presented with the utterly absurd. And then slowly – so slowly I could see it happening – an element of scorn crept into it.

"I see," he said. "And how do you think we're going to afford that? A three-week course, return flights and an apartment in Paris? We're a single-income family, in case you'd forgotten."

As if he owned me. Those thousands of discussions about money remained imprinted in my body, and now I felt a tingling, malicious pleasure rippling beneath my skin. He thought I was living at his mercy. But he had no idea.

"There's nothing for you to worry about," I said, and I felt so light, almost weightless. "I have the money – I'll pay for all of it. I think I'll book flights for a couple of weeks' time."

I don't think he thought I'd go through with it. I don't think he ever imagined I'd be able to do it all myself. Over the next few days we said no more about it, and he seemed to think I'd been crying wolf, that I'd proposed the trip only to scare him.

I didn't tell the children until the day before. I don't know, I must have thought that was the best way to handle it. They both began to cry.

"Everything will be absolutely fine," I said, comforting them. "Pappa is going to take good care of you."

The French teacher was named Laurent. He had messy, dark-brown hair and rimless glasses, and he spoke informally, addressing us using the familiar pronouns and our first names. He was the same age as me. From what he told us about himself, in informative sentences, designed for maximum learning outcomes – *je m'appelle Laurent, j'habite dans un appartement vers Porte de Lilas* – I understood that he didn't have children. Presumably he was single, although I'm sure he was presented with many opportunities to change his status. Something about his slightly dishevelled appearance probably made women want to take care of him. I could see it in the faces of certain female members of the class, and nor was I completely unaffected myself.

Sometimes I saw him on the Metro, on the early morning stretch from Châtelet to Saint-Placide. The first couple of times, I just stood there, watching him. He sat bent over a book, engrossed in what he was reading, oblivious to what was happening around him. The third time, I was afraid he was going to miss the stop, because when the Metro pulled into the platform at Saint-Placide he sat as if in a trance, and gave no sign he was getting up.

"*Bonjour*," I said, walking over to him.

He looked up, confused, and then he smiled at me from behind his rimless glasses.

"*Bonjour*, Evy."

My name sounded different in his mouth. As if this was the way it was always supposed to be pronounced, with the emphasis on the Y. As if everyone else had been saying it wrong.

*

One afternoon, I bumped into him on the street, just outside the school. He said hello, kissed me on both cheeks, and I thought, does he see me as a friend?

"Do you have plans?" he asked.

"I'm going home to make dinner," I said.

"Would you like to join me for a drink?"

We found a table at a café not far from the school. He complained about something to do with his apartment, there was a leak, *mais bon*, he would just have to get it fixed, although it would be expensive. I nodded. I was so elated to be sitting there, at a café in Paris, in conversation with an attractive young Frenchman. Little more than a month ago I'd been on my knees picking up half-digested strands of spaghetti from the floor, and just look at me now. I imagined a former version of myself standing outside by the window: she peered in and saw us and couldn't believe her eyes.

When our drinks were brought over, a few of the other students from my course walked past. They caught sight of Laurent and waved and smiled, and a moment later they came tumbling into the café. Only when they had made it over to our table did they see me. One of them, a young American by the name of Tim, gave us a slightly questioning smile, as if he was wondering if we were on some sort of date.

"Have a seat," Laurent said. "*Venez.*"

Rob and Tim were childhood friends, and they had been on the course for several weeks. Rob was the louder of the two. I liked Tim better – he could be arrogant, but at the same time there was something kind about him. With them was a friend named Eric, who was visiting them from Wisconsin. He told us he was travelling around Europe – he would be moving on to Spain next, he wanted to see the bullfighting and live like Hemingway. Laurent nodded in a proper and exceedingly French way. Then after twenty minutes he apologised and said he had to get going. He kissed me on both cheeks, shook the boys' hands and was out of the bar before I'd even realised he was leaving.

The Americans had planned to stay out for a while, and asked whether I'd like to join them. They looked at me, all three of them, with their young, open faces. Tim was fairly attractive, as was Eric, but it was getting late. The version of myself standing out on the street, the one who was watching me hop from one group of friends to the next here in Paris, was impressed, but she too checked her watch. Surely I wasn't going to stay out much longer? Who could say what it would be like to walk past the men in the bar-tabac in the middle of the night? And anyway, I was supposed to call the children early in the morning.

But then I thought of Edvard knocking on the door of my bedroom in Røaveien and inviting me out. Wasn't the entire purpose of all this – this city, the language school, the rue de Paris – precisely to not have other plans when someone comes knocking?

The first bar was fairly quiet. I started to find Eric more entertaining. The boys were a few years younger than me. They tried to seem worldly-wise, but it was clear that they were starry-eyed, impressed by almost everything they saw. There was something appealing about them – the fact that they were young and strong, that they leaned forward when I spoke, that they held my gaze. Eric's eyes seemed glued to me, which I found troubling and thrilling at the same time.

The second bar was a discotheque. I danced with Eric. He put his arms around me. He was young and clumsy, but led well all the same. It was a long time since I'd danced that way, with a man's steady arm around my waist.

I have an image in my head of us dancing – I'm smiling, euphoric, as a disco ball turns above my head. I can't be one hundred per cent certain that it was like this, but that's how I think I remember it: an ecstatic dance – and then nothing.

When I woke, I was lying in a bed, a blanket pulled halfway over me. Beside me, Eric was sleeping. There was a gap between the curtains, and the light coming through cut a line across the blanket and up the wall behind us. I sat up.

My head was heavy, my mouth dry and woolly, and above all else I felt the need to drink something. I looked around. I saw the sleeping boy beside me. His mouth was open, a thin strand of saliva had dried at the corner of his lips, and I thought: did we . . .? Surely we can't have . . .?

I was, at least, fully clothed. Or half-clothed – my tights were off, and I couldn't see them on the floor, but I was still in my underwear. My skirt was bunched up around my waist, but I was wearing it all the same. He was wearing a sweater and his underpants. At least we weren't naked. Still, I felt a churning pain in my stomach. How could I have let this happen – what was I thinking?

I got up, staggered across the room. Something about my body felt strange, as if I didn't quite recognise it. Were these my hands? Were these my legs? I searched for my tights, getting down on all fours and digging through the mess on the floor – crumpled trousers, dirty socks one by one, a bag, a football, French language textbooks – but I couldn't find them. I went into the living room. At least the door to the bedroom wasn't closed. Surely that must mean that everything was above board? If something had happened, surely we wouldn't have left it open?

In the living room, I found Tim asleep on the sofa. Rob, I couldn't see. I glanced around their untidy, dirty apartment. Thought: I have no memory of this. How did I get here? Did we take the Metro, did we take a taxi? Did I walk through the door over there? The last thing I remembered was the disco ball.

In the hallway I found my boots, my coat, my handbag. My hands were freezing cold as I opened the bag, but everything was there: the Metro pass, along with a hundred francs I had withdrawn from the bank the day before. On the sofa, Tim stirred – I heard him groan – and a column of panic rose from my stomach. I had no desire to see him now, like this. I shoved my bare feet into my boots, pulled my coat around me, slung my bag over my arm and silently closed the door behind me. I ran down the stairs and out into the February cold, slamming the front door and walking as quickly as I could down the street. I didn't stop to get my bearings until I was several blocks away.

I've never quite managed to put this non-incident into words. I still don't know what it was, how I could describe it for someone else. I'm unable even to define it for myself. As a result, I never mentioned it to Erling. Nor to Synne, either.

Because you don't end up in that kind of situation through no fault of your own – I must have done something wrong. But what, exactly, I'm unsure. Where, specifically, did I go wrong? Was it when I accepted the drink with Laurent? Was the problem that I didn't get up and leave when he did? Should I have left with him, or should I have waited until he had gone, and then left? Was the mistake that I didn't say goodbye to the American boys outside the bar, but instead got into the taxi with them, went with them? Maybe everything was fine right up until I agreed to go to the club. Was my misstep that I drank, or that I danced?

Hadn't I wanted to flirt? Didn't I hold Eric's gaze for just a little too long, hadn't I hinted at the possibility of something happening? But did I want to be taken back to the apartment? Can I know that

I said yes, or that I was asked? On the other hand: can I be certain that the suggestion wasn't mine?

What should I think of the American boys, what was their role in what happened? Did they take advantage of a woman who'd had too much to drink, or did they take me with them because I was too drunk to go home alone? If something did happen, it can be interpreted in many ways. A one-night stand. A drunk woman, and a man who responds to the situation. Did he (or they? Is that a possibility? I can hardly bear to think it) have a plan, right from the start, when he entered the café? Might somebody have put something in my drink, and if so, who? The American boys, or someone else? Were they my assailants, or did they rescue me?

And as to whether anything really happened, I don't know. There are signs that it did: a feeling in my lower abdomen that day, a kind of soreness. A sense of unfamiliarity in my body. And, of course, I was lying there, half-naked, beside him in the bed. Other signs point to something else: I was still in my underwear, at least, and the door to the living room was open. As to which side of the scales outweighs the other, I don't know.

People talk about things they have experienced, about the worst or the best things to happen to them, but common to all these incidents is that they *actually happened*. The worst thing about that night in Paris is that I don't know.

But there's another thing, too. When I returned home again, a short time later, I discovered that I was pregnant. The day I did the home test I could hear the ticking of the grandfather clock all the way from the upstairs bathroom. I heard its rhythm as I sat there and said to myself: No. No, no, *no*.

Having another child would not be a disaster in and of itself. Erling and I had talked about it, although admittedly that had been some time ago. And besides, if something had happened in that apartment in Paris, it was extremely unlikely that it would have resulted in anything like this. Erling couldn't keep his hands off me in the weeks after my return – it was far more likely the child was his. Purely mathematically, too: if you counted the days, Silje was probably conceived towards the end of my first week back home.

But I couldn't rule it out. Technically, it was a possibility. I began to dread the birth, imagining that the child would be a copy of Eric, a tiny version of the boy who wanted to live like Hemingway. Those first days, alone with Silje in the hospital, I ceaselessly leaned over the Moses basket, examining her face for signs of someone else. But Silje was strong and hot-tempered – her little face was entirely her own. I thought: I'll just wait and see. The truth will out, sooner or later.

As she grew older, I sometimes found myself looking at her and thinking: where did she get *that* from? A distinctive frown line as she concentrated, a tendency to become so immersed in things that she lost all sense of time and place. A fiery rage that could appear suddenly, as if thrust upon her, which I recognised in neither Erling nor myself. But then she might speak with Erling's uncompromising voice, take on an expression that was the spitting image of her father's, and I would chide myself for ever having doubted it.

For long periods – that grew longer and longer as the years passed – I set aside that night in Paris. I folded it up and put it in a drawer that I have never since opened. But there is no getting away from the fact that Silje, so different to her siblings in her approach to life, is the one Erling held in the very highest regard.

"I haven't appreciated you enough," Erling said the night I came home.

I had expedited my return journey, leaving Paris a week earlier than planned. Hanne clung to my body from the moment I stepped through the door until she fell asleep, refusing to let go. Bård was more reserved. He kept his distance, only warming to me when I took out the gifts I had brought them.

When the children were in bed, Erling and I sat on the living-room sofa, each with a glass of wine, so we could talk. Erling turned his wedding ring on his finger, looked down at his hands as he spoke. Perhaps he hadn't always been the best husband, but he would be better, everything would be better now.

"You do so much for us, Evy," he said. "You mean more to the children than anything else in the world, and I . . ."

He cast a quick glance at me, and said, his voice cracking:

"Well, you mean the world to me, too."

He looked down at his hands again. Turned and turned the thin gold band that had encircled his finger since the day we were married.

"But Evy . . . You can never leave us like that again. Do you understand? It's something you can never, ever do."

His tone of voice, the way he pressed his palms together, should have shown me what admitting this was costing him. But I was too far gone. I had left part of myself behind in that dirty apartment in Paris, and I felt as if I was observing the world through a windowpane.

I was just so endlessly exhausted. Outside it was dark, but the light on the terrace was on, and the house was warm. And I had got away with it. That's what I thought: I was home again and everything would be okay.

FIFTEEN DAYS AFTER

Edvard parks in front of the wooden sign that announces KROGH, painted in white letters with Erling's careful brushstrokes. On the drive down, I told him about my conversation with Ørjan. We discussed what it might mean, and briefly touched on why Erling didn't tell me about Hanne asking him for money. Now we walk together in silence. A certain gravity has replaced the excitement I felt at lunch yesterday. To reach our cabin, you have to follow a little path from the parking area, over a hill and between a couple of larger cabins that have a view of the fjord. It's overcast today, and the air is heavy and humid.

"Here we are," I say as we emerge from the trees into the clearing where the cabin lies.

It's small and unassuming, without electricity or running water. Around it there's a lawn that isn't much bigger, beyond which the forest closes in again. It's five hundred metres down to the jetty, but you can't see the fjord from here – at most you might catch a glimpse of it between the pines when the sun is bright and glitters on the water. We come to a stop, standing side by side, and consider the small, red-painted hut.

"It's nice," Edvard says.

"It could do with modernising," I say.

As I look at the cabin, this is what I see above all else. We bought it in eighty-one – it was old even then – and Erling has done almost all the work on it himself. It has no terrace, no annex. It has oil lamps and a gas stove, and water has to be collected from a well a good ten minutes' walk away or bought from the petrol station en route and hauled along the path from the parking area in heavy drums. Even the simple act of preparing dinner is a slog.

We cross the lawn, walking over to the front door. The lock is fairly new, because Erling believes in keeping the place secure, and he hasn't allowed the cabin to fall into complete disrepair. You have to look after what you have – that was his motto. But there is little luxury here. For someone who appreciates the finer things in life, as Edvard does, it must look dismal.

"It's fairly basic inside," I say as I turn the key in the lock, hearing how this sounds like a warning.

I set my shoulder against the door, and shove it open.

"It's cosy," Edvard says diplomatically as we stand in the living room. And then: "Very Erling."

This latter statement is undeniably true. There's something peculiar about coming here like this, on a spring day just before the season starts. I look around. The ancient sofa we inherited from my parents, the lace curtains handed down by my grandmother, the tiny, low windows. The uneven wooden floor. The tiny kitchen nook, with its gas stove and butane tank, a bowl for the washing-up, an oil lamp hanging above it to light our bedtime routines, and the doors that lead to the two bedrooms, both with home-made bunks. When we bought the place, I had thought it was idyllic. Now I find it run-down and bleak. I wonder what has changed most, the cabin or me.

"What's that smell?" Edvard asks.

I sniff the air – there's a strong, unpleasant odour. As if someone has defecated in a corner somewhere.

"I don't know," I say. "Maybe a rat died in one of the walls."

"Does it usually smell like this?"

I look at him. His eyebrows are raised, his brow creased.

"We've had problems with rodents before," I say.

The beds in the bedrooms are neatly made, as we left them when Erling and I shut up the cabin last summer. Now the cabin is mine alone. Along with the plots beyond it, which extend all the way down to the water. What am I going to do with all this land? The cabin never became what I hoped it would be when we bought it, I've never really enjoyed spending time here. The summers always dragged. Exhausting and excruciatingly boring at the same time.

In the living room, Edvard is leafing through the cabin's visitor book, which lies on the living-room table.

"Nobody has been here since last year?"

"It's a summer cabin," I say. "It's uninsulated. The season begins at the end of May and lasts until the end of August."

He slowly turns the pages. My head feels heavy, drowsy. I didn't sleep very well last night, but I managed to avoid taking my sleeping pill. I was thinking about this trip with Edvard – I didn't want to have to lie about using medication, should he happen to ask. The others have stopped informing me about important matters, treating me as if I'm somehow unreliable. I don't want him to see me that way, too. So I'll just have to put up with feeling a little tired. I take a deep breath, feel my eyelids drooping. I can have a nap in the car on the way home.

"It smells pretty strong for a dead rat," Edvard says.

"Yes," I say lethargically, slowly turning towards him. His face is like a mask, his skin pale, his eyes wide open.

And he's right – the smell is strong. I sniff the air again. It's hard to make it out, my mind is working so slowly. I can't quite seem to pull myself together. Edvard puts an arm over his nose and mouth – it looks as if this movement happens in slow motion, and yet he starts to look afraid, a sense of urgency dawning.

"We have to get out, Evy," he says, his voice low and intense. "Now!"

I try to answer, but I feel weak at the knees, and just then there's the sharp jangling of smashed glass, because Edvard has lifted one of the brass candlesticks from the living-room table and flung it through the window. He staggers towards the front door, opens it wide, and then takes a few steps back, grabs me by the arm and pulls me out. As everything begins to turn black, the spring air slaps me in the face, and I stagger down the steps, crumpling onto the lawn as my knees give way, gasping for air, as Edvard stands bent over, taking deep, panicked breaths.

The firefighter stands with his legs planted far apart. He addresses us in a tough, macho voice, as if we're boisterous recruits upon whom he needs to impress the seriousness of the situation. Yes, he says, there has been a gas leak: butane gas from the container below the counter had been seeping out over time and filled the entire cabin. Generally it takes a fair amount of gas for the situation to become hazardous, so it's rare to see incidents as serious as this, but the cabin was filled with a huge volume of gas – it could have been disastrous.

"The cabin is surprisingly well sealed," he says, setting his clear grey eyes on Edvard and me in turn, as if we are in some way to blame for this.

Emergency personnel fill the lawn around us. There are several inside the cabin, too, wearing breathing apparatus. Earlier, a serious young woman in her thirties asked me to take her through what happened, from the moment we arrived until we called to make the report, while Edvard stood with a man on the other side of the clearing – presumably the same questions were being put to him. I'm still tired, and my head aches. A young man in red overalls and a reflective vest examined me, he was from the ambulance service, I think, but I don't know where he is now. The authorities have taken over the cabin, made it their own.

In addition, gas containers are strictly controlled, the firefighter with the wide stance tells me. Especially ones like ours, which is pretty old.

"My husband did most of the repairs himself," I say. "Maybe he made a mistake. You know, he was rather good at those kinds of practical things, but still . . ."

"You have to be extremely careful when maintaining gas equipment yourself," the firefighter says reproachfully. "This could have been much worse. You were lucky."

Edvard and I nod gravely. The firefighter explains that the leak occurred where the hose is connected to the container, but had that been the sole issue, the situation wouldn't have been so serious.

"What surprises me here, is that the hose is cracked and broken," the firefighter says. "Ancient, it seems."

"Erling liked to reuse and recycle," I say mechanically.

"So I gather," the firefighter says. "But there are fairly strict controls carried out on this stuff. As I said, these situations can end in disaster. But accidents are rare because we check the equipment. And I see that this system was inspected only a year ago. Is that correct?"

"I don't know," I say. "My husband took care of that kind of thing."

"And your husband has passed away, is that right?"

He clears his throat.

"It's worth your while making yourself familiar with this stuff. We recommend that everyone in the household understands the system and knows how it should be inspected."

For a moment I wonder whether he's this way at home, too. I imagine him standing before a flock of blue-eyed children, instructing them in how to operate a fuse box or a heat pump.

"Well, it says here that the hose was replaced at the inspection a year ago – a brand-new one was installed. And this hose – it's far older than that. So I'm not sure what to think. Surely there's no reason to replace a brand-new hose with an old, cracked one?"

"I don't know," I whisper. "I can't think of one."

"I'm sure Evy is exhausted," Edvard says from beside me. "She's been through a lot lately – and the police in Oslo have been involved in connection with her husband's death, isn't that right, Evy? I think it would be wise to send them this information, too. I can give you the name of the relevant contact, if you like."

He turns to face me, takes hold of my shoulders.

"Evy," he says kindly. "If you're tired, you're more than welcome to go and sit in my car. I'll be there in a few minutes. We should probably stop by the out-of-hours doctors' surgery in Tønsberg, and then I'll drive you home. Does that sound okay?"

"Yes."

It feels so good to let him sort everything out. My head is heavy and weary. I walk slowly, so slowly, up the path between the two large cabins, over the hill and over to the parking area. I let myself into Edvard's car. By the time he follows me, I've almost fallen asleep.

The journey home from Tønsberg is quiet. I hardly speak, just lean my head against the window and doze all the way back. Every now and then I cast a glance at Edvard. He sits there calmly, looking thoughtful. His brow is furrowed, his expression focused. I remember the way he looked during Hanne's speech at the funeral, as if he were listening to a number of claims about which he felt sceptical, but which he accepted in order to make an assessment and reach a conclusion.

"Someone might have replaced the hose to the gas tank," I say when we reach the city limits.

He allows a few seconds to pass before he answers.

"Yes. Perhaps someone did."

"We're the only ones who have keys to the cabin. The children and me."

He reaches out, puts his hand on my arm.

"I'm so sorry you're having to go through all this, Evy. So very sorry."

We drive in silence for a little while longer, and then he says:

"How do you feel about going home? Will you feel safe alone, do you think?"

"Well," I say. "Where else would I go?"

For a couple of seconds he's quiet – it's as if he's hesitating – but then he says: "It just so happens that I have a guest room. Now, I really don't want to overstep any boundaries here, but if you'd feel safer, you're always welcome to stay with me."

It's as if I can hear the heavy ticking of the grandfather clock in my living room all the way from here; the grinding of the seconds, the slow rhythm that draws me in. I think of the heavy, dark furniture that once belonged to my in-laws, all the old, hostile objects waiting for me in the house in Montebello. But what would people think?

And there's something else. A tiny irregularity I don't understand, buzzing around at the back of my mind.

"I should probably go home," I say. "I can't be afraid to be alone in my own house."

The toothbrush is rough against my gums. The box in the cabinet calls to me – just one little pill, something to help me sleep, something to knock me out and stop the adrenaline rush, ease this sense of imminent danger. I open the cabinet door, examine the box. *Evy Krogh. For the treatment of sleeplessness and anxiety.* But what if someone comes? I've put the chain on the front door, but the terrace door could be smashed using a garden chair – it would be easy. I don't want to be half-tranquilised if someone breaks in, so I leave the box of pills well alone.

The space where Erling's pills once stood is empty. This medicine, that was supposed to protect his heart. Why didn't he take it?

That Day, when he lay on the tarmac with the white strip of eyeball visible below his lash line, prone but still alive – I imagine myself taking off his helmet. See him blink, then open his eyes and focus his dying gaze on me. And I speak to him, manage to wake him with my questions, haul him back to life. Have you taken your medicine? When did you last see Edvard Weimer? Who owns the house, who owns the cabin? And – and this I hardly even dare think – who do you think is out to get you?

But I didn't manage to do this, and a few minutes later, he died.

I brush my hair with slow strokes. Study my face in the mirror. I was attractive once. Wasn't I? Not in the way Synne was, and not like Bridget, either. But sweet. What have the years done to my face? The skin hangs more loosely; the eyes are now slightly sunken, and I have indeed put on a little weight. But isn't it also true that I don't look all that bad? It's a long time since I've thought this way. Since I've turned towards a mirror and thought: what would a man see, were he to look at me?

As I put my toothbrush in its place, beside the box of pills, I think about the feeling that stirred in me when Edvard asked if I would like to stay in his guest room, the thing that has been buzzing around at the back of my mind since we stood on the grass outside the cabin. He told the firefighter he would give him the name of the relevant person in the Oslo police.

But how would he know it? I've said no more than that the police came over to see me. I've never mentioned Gundersen by name. And the little scrap of paper with the telephone number on it, the one Gundersen gave me when he was here – I haven't had that with me the times I've seen Edvard. No – it's on Erling's desk. And as far as I know, Edvard has never once set foot in Erling's study.

FOUR DAYS BEFORE

I woke because he was getting out of bed. At first I thought he was just going to the toilet, but there was something about his movements that told me something wasn't right – they were jerky, unsteady. Still half-drunk with sleep, I sat up.

"Erling?"

I heard his footsteps out on the landing. Considered collapsing back into bed and simply going back to sleep, but then pulled myself together. Was I thinking of the yellow washing-up gloves, the scarf that had covered his mouth? All the odd things he had been doing lately, or his accidents? I got up and followed him.

No sign of him on the stairs, but I could hear him downstairs, so I went after him. I caught a glimpse of his figure in the hallway, but it was dark, I couldn't see him properly. Just his silhouette, a tall man in the darkness. One of the treads creaked beneath my foot, and the dark shadow suddenly turned and shot towards me. A sob escaped me as something brushed my arm, sending me backwards.

Was I caught off balance, and therefore liable to tumble over from a mere nudge? Or was I pushed hard?

Before me I saw Erling's face, contorted into something I didn't understand: the eyes wide open and the jaw bulging, the skin around them pulled tight as a drum. In his hands he was holding the long-handled broom – that was what he had pushed me with. He was holding it like a weapon.

Then his expression changed. The intense, terrifying scowl vanished, and his features became his own once more.

"Evy?" he asked.

"What on earth are you doing?" I whispered.

"I thought I heard someone."

He turned his back to me again. I got to my feet. Taking hesitant steps, I followed him. He seemed to have forgotten me, his attention was focused on what might lie ahead.

The door to his study was ajar. He tiptoed in that direction. The darkness engulfed him again, and I saw only his outline, the broom he brandished as a weapon. He approached the door. Carefully pushed it open.

Then he went in. I followed. There was no-one there. Erling stopped in the middle of the room. Stood there in his pyjamas, leaning on the shaft of the broom. Turned his face towards me. The grey, soon-to-be-white hair. The dark brows. He was both familiar and unknown, at once vulnerable and sinister. Moonlight lanced through the window, leaving a pale stripe across the desk's surface. The brand-new keyboard, the closed appointment book.

"Nobody in here, at least," he said.

His voice was thick, trembling. I was trembling, too. I glanced at him, unable to think of anything to say. He looked around the room. Didn't turn on any of the lights. It was gloomy, but my eyes quickly adjusted to the darkness.

"Evy," Erling said.

Haltingly.

"Yes?"

"Did you open the window in here?"

"No."

I looked over at the window. It was ajar. Erling went across to it and pushed the pane. It swung out – it wasn't locked in the open position. He looked at me, I looked at him, and we stood that way for a few long seconds, staring at one another.

TWENTY-SEVEN YEARS BEFORE

Vernissage, it said at the top of the letter. It was printed on fine, thick paper, and my name and address had been handwritten on the envelope. A distinguished typeface invited me to a private party for Bilal's new exhibition, *Imagine*, which would open in a few weeks' time at a gallery in Frogner. *And guest*, it said. I stood in the living-room doorway and looked at Erling sitting there on the baby-blue sofa, wearing his worn slippers. I thought, there's no point even asking him. But maybe Synne would like to come.

He had been working as an on-call substitute at Silje's kindergarten. The mothers gossiped about him: have you seen his clothes, he looks like a gangster, and who knows what he's hiding in that bag he always carries with him? Have you heard how he talks? He sounds like the people who hang around under the Vaterlandsbrua bridge when they're interviewed on the evening news. And have you heard – apparently he's a refugee. Who knows what he's experienced. Not to mention what he's done. Of course it's awful that he's had to live under occupation and oppression. A terrible business, all of it. But still! That sort of thing changes people. Numbs them, increases their tolerance for the suffering of others. Not that Bilal is to blame for his trauma. But you have to ask yourself: is this the kind of person we want looking after our children?

He must have been in his early twenties back then, and it was true that he had a guarded look about him, something hard and uninviting written across his face. As far as I could see, he was never harsh with the children, but nor was he particularly friendly, either.

In fact, it seemed he wasn't especially interested in them. The temp job was simple enough – he needed no special qualifications. This was true for all the on-call staff, but he was the only one people objected to.

As a general rule, Bilal could be found at the art table. Which was where Silje also usually sat. She was good at drawing, and she idolised him; any day he was called in to work was a good day for her. Once, when I arrived to pick her up earlier than usual, I stood watching them in secret, half-hidden behind a bookcase. The big man with the hard face, holding a crayon so gently between his fingers. He was sitting on a tiny child-sized chair, his knees splayed out on either side of his body as he leaned forward, focused on nothing but the sheet of paper in front of him.

The little girl with blonde pigtails who sat beside him was also drawing, but she kept glancing at him, studying what he was doing. Attempting to reproduce his work on her own sheet of paper.

I was in no rush that day. I walked over to the table and sat down with them. Silje showed me what she had drawn. She glanced at Bilal, over and over – did he see her, did he hear what she said? His drawing depicted a girl with pigtails. It was Silje, without a doubt. She was holding out her hand, and a butterfly had landed on her palm. He had given her big, surprised eyes, and he had captured her round little chin perfectly.

"You draw so well," I said.

He didn't answer; simply finished the drawing, signed it and handed it to Silje.

"Here."

He's sullen, I thought. But not hostile. He's just not especially talkative. I wasn't going to be influenced by the other mothers in the neighbourhood. I knew better than that.

"Do you illustrate stories, too?" I asked him.

My tone was playful. He looked at me blankly, and shrugged.

But there was something in his eyes, too. Such deep, dark eyes – they hinted at a sea of emotions moving within him.

"There's a story I tell Silje," I said. "It's about a little girl called Martine, and one day she makes friends with a mouse."

I did my best to be present for Silje. Bård and Hanne were growing up fast. Hanne was in the last year of primary school, Bård would soon be finished with secondary school, and although I tried to put Paris behind me – what the trip had cost the family, what it had cost me – it remained a wedge driven between us: I left them once, and when I returned, something had changed. None of us could forget this. But the uncertainty around what had happened in that apartment in Paris was mine to bear alone. I had to live with it, unable to share it with anyone.

I did what I could to alleviate the guilt. To some extent, I did penance through Silje. I might have abandoned her siblings, suddenly and without a good enough explanation, but for her I would stay close, be available, offer myself up. I tried to do penance with the older children, too, but they were so big, they didn't really let me in. With Silje, I had access. So I sat on the floor and played with her, I bought coloured crayons and fancy paper from the hobby store, I drew and cut and glued, and every night I either read her a story, or made one up. Silje was my baby girl – with her, I still had a chance.

Bilal drew as I told him the story, and when we were done, he gave me the drawings. That evening, while Erling sat in the living room watching TV, I spread the illustrations on the bed. There were four of them, tiny artworks conjured from nothing more than wax crayon and lead pencil. Martine had soft curls, big chubby cheeks and huge, marvelling eyes. The mouse had a wet nose, delicate whiskers, and fur so lifelike you could see how soft it would be to stroke it with a finger. Over the next few days, I jotted down my story, and one Friday evening, when Erling and I had shared a bottle of wine, and I was slightly tipsy and bubbly in the head, I took an envelope from the study, slipped my text and Bilal's drawings inside, and marked it with the address one of the biggest publishing houses in the country, copied from the telephone book.

The next day it seemed ridiculous, a foolish dream. I didn't bother to put a stamp on the envelope and post it. I hid it in my underwear drawer instead. And, of course, I said not a word about it to Erling. But all the same, I felt a lightness in my heart when I thought about it: I had a secret. Should everyday life become too suffocating, there was a way out.

And in the end, I sent it off.

To my surprise, Bilal was the hardest person to convince. The publisher liked the idea – they thought the story was delightful and they loved the drawings. I could hardly wait to get started, but Bilal took it remarkably hard that I had sent in the drawings without asking him first.

"But they like them," I said to him.

"Still," he said.

His face was empty, and he turned away.

I didn't know very much about him. Only the rumours that still circulated: he'd had dealings with criminals, he used drugs, he once killed a man. Gossip should never be taken seriously, and there most likely wasn't any substance to it, but part of me understood that he'd experienced things I couldn't comprehend. My problems must seem petty and self-absorbed compared with his.

And still I wasn't quite able to let it go, because I wanted this so much, I *needed* it. An actual publisher was interested in my story – I'd be able to call myself an author. It was within reach, it could be added to my not especially impressive CV and brought out at parties when people asked me what I did. It could justify the long hours at home during the day in which nothing happened. I could become someone – but it all depended on Bilal. The publisher was ready, they wanted us both. So I begged him to come with me to the meeting – surely you can at least do *that*, I said. I offered to pick him up, to drive him home again, to speak to his manager to ensure he got time off with pay. I pestered him for weeks, and in the end he reluctantly agreed.

At the meeting he said little. Anna, who would be the book's editor, did most of the talking, and I also talked a lot, babbling away, feeling the need to fill the silence. I was the one who had failed Bilal, I was the one who had sent in his drawings without asking. I tried to make it up to him by praising him unreservedly. At one point Anna said something I didn't quite catch that appeared to get through to him, and for a few minutes they spoke enthusiastically about the choice of materials for the illustrations. Something came to life in Bilal's face. As we left the offices, I still wasn't entirely sure what it was she had said, but he had signed the contract.

The first book sold well; the second was also a minor success. Bilal surpassed himself – his illustrations were scarily lifelike. My story was also praised, and I was invited to schools and libraries to read aloud. Sometimes the children brought copies of the books to these sessions. Parents asked me to sign them, while the children pointed out which of the drawings they liked best.

And I was good at it. I liked reading aloud, enjoyed speaking to the children. I was able to use my educational training, and there was no pressure this time, I had no problem ensuring that the kids were well behaved. I earned a little money, too, and was able to contribute to the family's finances. This was when we bought the baby-blue sofa; I also invested in a stereo system. I took the children to the theatre and amusement parks and paid for it all myself.

When it came to the third book, Bilal took his time. Publication was delayed by six months because he failed to deliver. He was no longer working at the kindergarten – he'd taken on other illustration jobs. Anna mentioned in passing that he was illustrating another children's book for her. At the kindergarten, someone said they had seen a calendar featuring his drawings. But the plan was that he would still complete the illustrations for the third book, *Martine and the Deer Family* – it just might take a while. I waited. I was impatient to get the book out there – and not just for the money. Silje said she could draw the pictures for me, and I ruffled her dishevelled mop of hair and said, thank you, sweetie. When she showed me her efforts, I failed to muster the enthusiasm I should have shown her.

Luckily, Bilal delivered in the end. Several weeks past the new deadline, but at least the book did get published. It made it into bookshops six months before the invitation to the private viewing arrived in the post.

Synne came with me. She drove, while I sat in the passenger seat. I didn't say much, I was thinking about the idea I'd had for a fourth book, about a bird with a broken wing who needs Martine's help. I imagined the drawing of the little bird with a splint and plaster cast; how Bilal would create something truly captivating. How the children would sit on the edge of their tiny seats and hope against hope that the poor thing would pull through.

"Bilal," Synne said with a sniff. "It's a bit of an odd name, don't you think?"

The gallery was in an old villa in Frogner. We approached through a small front garden, down a path lined with square stones and small torches. Inside, it seemed bigger than it appeared from the outside, comprising several spacious white rooms. Bilal's drawings and paintings covered the walls. I took a glass of bubbly from a tray, and Synne and I began our tour of the exhibition.

Along one wall there were drawings of a small family, a mother with warm eyes and long, wavy hair, and her two children, a boy and a girl, both with soft curls. Bilal had drawn them in several situations: in a boat, in a bed, sitting under a tree. The mother's gaze was tender as she looked at her children, but there was also pain in it, a kind of portent of what was to come, which elicited a prickling beneath the viewer's skin.

On the next wall, the children were alone. The boy was looking after the younger girl. The eyes of both children were afraid; the boy's were angry, too. This duality in his gaze, fear mingled with anger, was expressed with heartbreaking precision. We moved on to paintings of birds in flight. They were beautiful, graceful. The last one depicted a dead bird on a beach.

In the next room, the boy with the curly hair had become a teenager. We saw him walking past soldiers, the hood of his hoodie pulled up over his curls, the look in his eyes ever more furious. He was bigger, harder, more threatening. We saw him fleeing a city alone on a dark night – his sister had disappeared from one image to the next, and this sudden absence seemed somehow more intense than if there had been a drawing to explain what had happened, as if all this young boy loved could vanish at any moment, without a trace. The boy hid in a lorry. He was beaten, he sat alone on a bed in an institution, listening to music. He held up a knife, threatening some unseen person, who could just as easily have been any of us in the gallery.

The final wall featured paintings of birds again. The very last image presented the boy's sister as a child, with a bird in her arms. She pressed her nose into the creature's soft feathers. It was the largest image in the exhibition, probably two metres tall, painted with beautifully precise brushstrokes.

"Jesus," Synne said as we stood before it, her voice thick with emotion.

I thought of the bird I wanted Bilal to draw for the Martine book. After seeing this painting, it seemed an impossible thing to suggest.

The buzz of voices was low and reverent at first, but soon the wine had its usual effect, and the guests became accustomed to the images' tragic narrative, or at least enough to dare to speak more loudly. People were throwing labels around, I heard them in the fragments of conversation around me. The word *genius* was used a couple of times; *talent* was on everyone's lips. Synne was unusually quiet, and then all at once she was telling a story about how a few years back she had worked on a flight on which a young refugee had been forcibly returned to his unsafe homeland; he had sobbed in desperation the entire journey. Her eyes shone as she spoke. I looked away, not wanting to hear.

Anna stood before the painting of the sister and the bird.

"Aren't they just incredible?" she said to me. "I'm trying to get Bilal to agree to publish them in book form, too – it would be so moving, and a huge success, I'm sure. He's sceptical, but he was last time, too, as I'm sure you remember."

She smiled knowingly. And I think it was there and then that I understood there would never be a fourth Martine book. Bilal had outgrown me. Everyone could see it – Bilal himself, Anna, and each and every one of the gallery's guests. I was the only one who hadn't understood.

In the car on the way home, as the last few glasses of bubbly swished through my cerebral cortex, I thought of the painting of the boy with his knife turned on the viewer. With a certain skill, I thought. As if he knew what he was doing.

SIXTEEN DAYS AFTER

How does a person end up getting injured? What kinds of accidents take people's lives? I'm used to thinking about these questions from the opposite perspective: *Don't go out in the dark without your reflective vest,* I used to say to the children. *Don't swim too far out, look both ways before you cross the road.* But what if it's the other way around? Say you wanted to facilitate someone harming themselves. Or more precisely: you wanted to harm someone.

Someone who believes in reusing and recycling, who has old equipment, who undertakes repairs himself. An old desk lamp, an old bicycle, an old gas stove. Say you tamper with these things, lay the groundwork for an accident.

It's five o'clock in the morning and I'm in the kitchen. I've hardly slept, but no matter, I'm awake now. My throat burns, my head swims. Lights flash in my peripheral vision. Let's just say someone wanted to lay the groundwork.

Erling wasn't careless. Despite his dogmatism when it came to make do and mend, he had respect for health and safety. He followed protocol, called in professionals when necessary. Causing either of us to have an accident wouldn't have been easy, because Erling took great pains to block any route that might lead to one. You'd have to be patient. And maybe that patience ran out. Perhaps someone decided more drastic measures were needed.

And so where would that someone turn? The gas stove is an obvious target, because gas accidents do happen. Rarely, but every now and then. And that someone might ask themselves: what other accidents do people fall victim to? Errors in medication dosage? Cycling accidents? Fire? Drowning? Electric shock? Poisoning?

We inherited our toaster from my parents – it's ancient. Erling has repaired it a couple of times, got it working again. For a moment I stand with it in my hands and remember my father leaning over it when I was a child, fishing out the slices of toast. But then I remember the feeling from the cabin: the nausea, the drowsy indifference. Edvard's hand grabbing my arm and pulling me out. My heart is beating fast. I take out a rubbish bag and toss the toaster into it.

But that's not all. What about the dried goods? How easy would it be to slip something into the coffee tin or into the flour, and then simply wait? One by one, I take these staples from the kitchen cupboards. Sugar, pasta, rice – all of it has to go.

My pulse slows as I work, because now I'm taking control, attempting to save myself. What if someone put rat poison in the jam? Every jar goes straight in the bin. What if someone brushed a toxin onto the cutlery? I fill the sink with boiling water and squeeze half a bottle of washing-up liquid into it. As I stand there scrubbing, I catch sight of my reflection in the kitchen window, and I meet my own crazed eyes. Here I stand, at five in the morning, in my nightgown, in the process of sterilising the knives and forks.

And I think of Erling frantically scrubbing down his office, as if he were hunting for signs of something dangerous, or poisonous perhaps. I think of the perfectly usable keyboard he threw away. The night he went downstairs brandishing the long-handled broom as a weapon. At the time, I thought he was losing his mind, but now I know better.

But the woman reflected in the window looks insane. If I were to say anything about this, nobody would believe me. Not the police, not my children or my brother. Only Edvard. Yes, I think – Edvard will believe me. But then there's the thing with Gundersen, the scrap of paper with his name and number on it. Edvard couldn't possibly know about him, yet he seemed to all the same.

The receptionist looks at me sceptically when I introduce myself – have I really come to the doctor's surgery without an appointment? I only just manage to convince her to call Lise and let her know I'm here, and I can hear in her voice that she expects Lise to ask her to send me away. She seems almost a little disappointed when she's told to let me wait. I nod and find myself a chair in the waiting room.

I'm not entirely sure what I think I'm going to get out of this, it was a spur of the moment thing. Ørjan told me something about Hanne, I thought – what might Bård's wife tell me about my son? This morning Edvard sent me a message asking how I was doing. *If you're free, I'd love to meet up for dinner some time soon,* he wrote. I haven't replied yet. I'm sure there must be a simple explanation, but how did he know the names of the police officers who visited me?

"Hello, Evy," my daughter-in-law says as she emerges from her office, rubbing her hands with sanitiser.

"Hello," I say. "I hope I'm not disturbing you?"

"No, of course not," she says wearily, in a tone that tells me that's precisely what I'm doing. "Would you like to come into my office?"

The other patients glance up from their phones. What privileges must I have, they seem to be wondering, to be asked in before them, to be greeted by my first name?

Lise's office is small and cramped, with a window that looks onto a car park. There's a bench with a paper cover for patients to lie on, next to a low bookcase with a model of a pelvis on top of it. On the wall above the pelvis there's a drawing of a human being without skin, showing all the muscles, tendons and internal organs. Lise takes a seat at the desk and offers me the chair beside it.

"How are you?" she asks.

"As well as can be expected," I say.

This is a half-truth, at best. I hardly slept prior to my episode of paranoia-fuelled mania, and nor could I sleep after it, either, I only dozed. This morning, I didn't want to risk drinking coffee from any of my cups. I drove to the supermarket and bought bread and sandwich fillings, not daring to eat anything that had survived last night's purge, because what if there was something I hadn't thought of?

But I can't say anything about this. So I turn the question back on Lise: how are things with her?

"Oh, you know. Good. Busy."

She looks exhausted, I think. When she met Bård, they were both in high school. They got together just before their final exams, when she was nineteen, sweet, good-natured and head over heels for my son. There was nothing exhausted about her then. Erling and I agreed that she was the perfect girl for Bård. Dependable, sensible. Not afraid of hard work.

Now she wears her hair gathered into a ponytail. She's strikingly free of vanity – she finds Hanne's proclivity for expensive shoes and beautiful leather handbags entirely incomprehensible. In many ways, she seems the type to have married young. Someone who wanted to build a life, but who didn't especially relish the search for the partner she would build it with. Erling was like that, too, I think now. But was I?

And was Bård? It's hard to imagine what my son might wish for his life, were he able to choose differently, but thinking about it,

I've always had the impression that there's something a little unsettled about him, as if he's wearing a sweater he's slightly outgrown, constantly pulling at the sides or tugging at the hem in an attempt to get it to fit the way he wants.

"Lots to do at work?" I ask Lise.

"Yes," she says. "And at home, too."

For a moment it seems she's about to say something, perhaps about being a PTA representative and the football team's manager and the handball team's coach. But she only rubs the skin around her eyes.

"You know how it is," she says.

Except that I don't.

"And how about Bård?" I say, trying to adopt a slightly conspiratorial tone – just between us girls. "Does he help out?"

"Oh, Bård," she sighs. "He's got so much on at work. It's total chaos on that front at the moment, but he's doing his best to keep things afloat."

I nod at this, affecting comprehension as I think: total chaos?

"That's why he asked you and Erling about the loan," Lise says. "I completely understand that you weren't able to help, and as I told him, it isn't your job to bail him out. But he didn't quite see it that way."

I nod again. I can trace the contours of what she's saying. So apparently Bård was at it, too.

"So now he's meeting with investors, here there and everywhere," Lise sighs. "Trying to pitch these property projects of his. *Live well in Havna Park.*"

She casts me a sideways glance.

"It's not that I don't support him," she says. "I always do, of course. But as I told him, maybe the time has come to just let this dream go. He's been operating at a loss for several years. It isn't sustainable in the long run. And it's starting to weigh on the entire family. It feels as if we'll never get the renovations finished."

She rubs her eyes, and when she looks up, she's pasted a friendly smile across her face.

"But listen to me, moaning on about my life," she says brightly. "What you're going through is far worse. How are you *really*, Evy?"

I'm standing on the street outside the surgery when Hanne calls.

"Hi, Mamma, how are you doing?" she asks.

I look about me. A tram rattles past and stops near the court-house; there are people dashing hither and thither, all of them busy, all of them in a rush. They all have places they need to be and things they need to take care of – presumably important things, because they speak loudly into their phones, take determined strides and seem to know where in the world they are and where they're going. I stand still among them and press the phone to my ear. I don't know where to go from here.

"You know," I say. "Fine."

It's eleven-thirty. I could go home. To the house in Montebello, with its empty kitchen cupboards. All the objects that might have been tampered with.

"Good," she says. "I heard you stopped by to see Ørjan the day before yesterday?"

Her voice is bright, but impatient. She doesn't get it. I've never been to see Ørjan before, so why am I doing so now?

"Yes," I say. "I just happened to be passing by the store, so I thought I'd pop in and see how he was."

"That's nice."

The line goes quiet for a moment. What Ørjan told me as we sat at the white counter hangs between us: the semi-detached house in Kjelsås. The money she evidently asked for. The loan Bård asked for, too – I know about that now. Both of them went to their father. Neither of them said anything to me. And Ørjan couldn't look me in the eye when I told him I didn't know.

There *is* something in all this. I'm fumbling at the fringes of it, trying to understand. The house – ownership of which has been transferred to me. The plots Erling acquired. Forget the gas leak at the cabin, forget the desk lamp, it all boils down to this: why did Erling give all his money to me? Why did he deny his children a loan? And why do I know nothing about it?

"By the way," Hanne says. "Ørjan said he mentioned the house we went to view, and that I spoke to Pappa about it."

"Yes," I say.

"Well, I just wanted to say – it was only a thought, something I sort of mentioned in passing. It wasn't a big deal. I just wanted to air the idea, see what he thought."

"Okay."

Why didn't you ask me, I think. We speak on the phone several times a week – about all kinds of trivialities. Why didn't she mention that she and Ørjan were house-hunting?

"It was only to say we were considering it, you know," Hanne says. "Mostly I just wanted Pappa's advice."

For a moment we both think back to the meeting at the lawyer's office. Neither of us says anything, but I know how her mind works. A pressure crushes my chest: Hanne and I so often end up saying the wrong thing to each other. It's not her fault. She tries her best, I know that. It isn't my fault, either. To tell the truth, I don't know why things always end up like that between us. When I've observed her with her friends, as an adult, I've seen how effortlessly their conversations flow. Something heavy and sad moved in me to see them laughing together, so freely and without any sting to it. No hidden meanings, nothing to decode.

I remember her on her wedding day in her bridal gown, her shoulders bare. Her best friend had given a speech. *Hanne really knows how to throw a party*, she had said, *but at the same time, there's nobody I'd rather speak to when things are tough, because Hanne always knows the right thing to say.* Hanne had smiled; wiped away a tear. Sitting there between her taciturn father-in-law and her brand-new husband, she looked so beautiful. So happy, too – so unreservedly happy. As the friend said: *Hanne always knows the right thing to say.*

But maybe we're too different. Maybe it's as simple as that. Once, when Max was a baby, she fell asleep on the pale blue sofa. I'd gone out to the kitchen to put the coffee on, and when I came back I saw her lying there, curled up in a ball, her head against the armrest. Her mouth was half open, her breathing heavy and even. I stroked her curls, the same colour my hair once was. I felt the ache in my heart: my daughter, the exhausted new mother. How I wish we could change the way things are between us, so we no longer hear an accusation or a reproach when a compliment or a confidence was intended.

"I haven't kept anything from you, or anything like that," she says. "If it seemed that way."

"No, not at all," I say, attempting to sound reassuring.

"I don't want you to think we're hiding something," she says.

But she is. So is Bård, and so was Erling. But what about Silje? I think for a moment. The two sisters in Erling's study, the appointment book on the desk.

As people hurry past me on the pavement, I try to conjure up Erling's face. It frightens me that I can't quite manage it – it's as if I can imagine him in passing, or as part of a group, but if I try to focus on him, remember him as he was to me alone, sitting at the kitchen table or in the living room, his features dissolve and he becomes fuzzy. Who was Erling? I lived with him for forty-five years, and now I'm no longer sure.

Hanne takes a deep breath.

"Actually," she says. "I was calling to see if you'd like to have lunch with me tomorrow. There's a cosy little café near my work."

*

When we hang up, it feels urgent that I speak to Silje. Hanne will probably call her. Maybe she already has. She'll call Bård, too, and perhaps Bård has already spoken to Lise, maybe he knows that his wife told me about the loan he asked for, and which Erling refused.

Now I'm the one with the assets. If they want money, they'll have to come to me. And they know it. It's beginning to dawn on me, too. I'm not sure what it will mean – will they become more or less open, will things get easier or harder between us? – but I know that it changes everything. It has to. Now I have power over them, and that's impossible for them to ignore.

She may well be out, I think, as the intercom chimes. It isn't a given, or even that likely, that I'll find her at home in the middle of the day on a Wednesday. For a while she had an atelier in Kværnerbyen, I'm not sure if she still does. I'm not expecting an answer, so when I hear her voice, I'm surprised.

"Yes?"

"It's Mamma," I say. "Is now a good time? Can I come in?"

"Sure."

The door buzzes, and I go up.

Silje lives on the second floor. She purchased the apartment with our help – we gave her a few hundred thousand kroner advance on her inheritance. Erling had an unshakeable belief in the importance of bricks and mortar, and Silje lives from grant to grant, doing the odd commission here, selling a few paintings there. With such an unpredictable income and no partner, there was little hope of her getting on the property ladder without our help. As I take the stairs to her apartment, I wonder how Bård and Hanne feel about the helping hand Silje received, and the fact that similar assistance was never offered to them. Whether they feel it unfair, and if so, whether it has affected the relationship between the three of them. I wonder how they see it now, after the meeting with Peter Bull-Clausen.

Erling must have been the one who said we'd help Silje out, but I was involved in the decision, it wasn't made behind my back. How long ago was that? Five years, perhaps? And I think: he involved me *then*, he asked for my opinion *then*.

*

She stands in the doorway. Her hair hangs messily down either side of her face, and she's wearing jogging bottoms and an oversized T-shirt. Her eyes are puffy, the skin around them slack.

"Are you sleeping okay?" I ask her after we've greeted one another.

"Yeah," she says. "I just had a bad night, that's all."

"Is it Pappa?"

She shrugs, doesn't reply. She looks so wounded. Silje – daddy's little girl.

The living room is the biggest room in the apartment, open and light. Three large canvases stretched over wooden frames lean against the walls. The room is furnished with a sofa, an armchair and a coffee table. There's a crumpled-up blanket on the sofa; she must have been dozing there when I rang the bell.

"You want coffee?" she asks.

"Yes, please."

As she pads out to the kitchen I study her canvases. The first depicts a woman with a grotesque, distorted face. The figure is embracing herself, and the colours and shapes are so blurred it takes a while for me to understand that it's her stomach she's holding. She's pregnant, embracing the child inside her. Silje has painted the foetus, too, as a bloody, dark-red lump in the transparent belly. The woman is surrounded by shadows, and I'm not entirely sure what they represent. Trees, perhaps; maybe people. I quickly move on to the next canvas.

Here there are several figures coiled together, all arms and legs. At first, I think they're standing, and then I realise they're lying down. The colour palette is the same as that used in the first painting, and the two faces that are visible are just as distorted as the face of the pregnant woman. I see breasts, something I understand to be a penis, and then I realise that the painting depicts a kind of orgy.

I'm not even sure how many of them there are. One of the faces belongs to a woman, and the more I study the canvas, the more I think I'm looking at an assault. I focus on her body, trying to distinguish it from the others, and see a dark-red nuance at her lower abdomen. Something swells in me: a gulp, a retch. Is this the child's conception?

In the last painting, the child is out. This is the least finished of the three, only the figures have been painted, but it's clear that they're the same people, and that the colours will correspond to the palette of the others. The child, a girl, stands in the middle of the room, her hands on her head. Behind her stands the mother, just as distorted, staring at her. The child is still attached to the mother by the umbilical cord, and she seems inconsolable. The mother cannot help her. Nor does she wish to, I think. The girl has to get away. My breathing feels constricted. Silje comes back into the room and sets the coffee pot on the table.

"It needs to brew for a few minutes," she says.

"Is this what you're working on at the moment?"

I try to keep my voice light, to sound pleasant and interested, but I can feel a spiky ball of pain in my stomach and my breath is still choked, as if something is squeezing my windpipe.

"Yeah," she says. "It's for an exhibition this autumn. Or at least, I hope so."

"It's . . ." I start.

Silje says nothing.

"Is it me?"

Before I can stop myself, the words have escaped.

My breathing is audible now, heavy, shallow.

"What?" she asks.

"Her."

I point to the last painting, the mother with the mean face, the little girl with her hands on her head.

"Am I the mother?"

Silje just looks at me.

"Is that what you think of me?" I ask, and now my voice is more afraid, more desperate.

She hands me a cup of coffee. Doesn't pour one for herself.

"No, it isn't you," she says. "Jesus, Mamma, not everything is about you."

"Then who is it?"

"That's actually quite a personal question."

"I'm your mother, Silje!" I shout. "So I'm within my rights to ask you a personal question!"

This makes her sigh, deeply. I stare at her, wondering how much I really know about this daughter of mine. Silje was different from the other children in the neighbourhood, even from a very young age. She sewed her own clothes, painted patterns onto her jeans, cut her hair herself and dyed it wild colours. She was popular regardless. There was something uncompromising about her. She was herself, she refused to conform, and the other children respected that.

I'm sure things weren't always easy for her, but I can't remember her ever coming home crying after arguing with friends, the way her siblings did. She spoke in a headstrong way, she was stubborn, refused to budge an inch. She was so unlike me – I remember thinking that – and I didn't understand this uncompromising strength, had no idea how to relate to it. And sometimes I would catch myself wondering whether she had inherited it from an unknown American in Paris.

And this image of her conception, as if she's painting something she can't possibly know anything about. No, it's impossible – I don't even know myself – and God knows I've never told her about it. And yet, it's as if she's sensed it somehow, and painted it. I look at the woman with the twisted face, lying there between the men who paw at her.

"It's me," Silje says after a while. "Or, not *me*-me. But a version of me. A possible version."

I stare at her.

"I want a baby," she says simply. "I've been thinking about it for a while. I'd like to be a mother."

I'm unable to reconcile this. I stand there, speechless, the untouched cup of coffee in my hand, trying to put the pieces together. There is silence between us for a long time.

"But do you have a partner?" I ask at last.

"I don't need a partner to have a child."

She crosses her thin, bony arms over her chest, her face taking on a defiant expression.

"Actually, I don't think there's much to be gained from men," she says. "Every boyfriend I've ever had has had so many damn opinions about how things have to be. I find it exhausting, living with someone who criticises me all the time."

She takes a deep breath, appearing to think for a moment, and then adds:

"And I dislike the smell of them. Men sweat so much – have you ever noticed that? The stench – it stinks up the whole house."

She runs her hands through her hair. Her expression is firm, eyebrows raised, chin thrust forward.

"So I've been thinking about how I'll probably end up single. But I'd still like to have a baby. That would be something else entirely."

It's as if the light in the apartment shifts then. As if everything that was dark and frightening about her paintings withdraws, and the sunlight from outside takes over. She looks like a child herself, standing there, acting all grown-up and determined. I have to force myself not to put my hand to her cheek.

But there's something else, too. I can see where this is going.

"You want to have a child alone," I say slowly, thinking on my feet. "And you might need to go to a clinic abroad. And that costs money?"

"At least fifty thousand," she says. "If you count all the medications and consultations. With flights to Denmark and accommodation and all the rest, you're soon looking at around seventy thousand, and that's assuming you're successful on the first try. So I'm probably going to need well over a hundred, perhaps a hundred and fifty."

"And you asked Pappa for a loan," I say.

Silje gives me that obstinate look of hers, as if to say that the world has a habit of serving up erroneous assumptions about her; that those of us who are close to her must be a little slow, seeing as we haven't yet understood that we don't know her.

"Of course not," she says. "This is my project. I don't expect him to finance it. I *told him about it*. But I didn't go running to Pappa for money."

She spits this last sentence with contempt. I wonder what her siblings have said about their own loan applications. Her tone seems to indicate that she knows about them, at any rate.

"And what did Pappa say?" I ask.

She shrugs.

"He wasn't exactly over the moon about it. You know what he was like – he thought overpopulation was a problem for the environment."

I nod slowly. Imagine a one-year-old toddling around in here. Slapping at Silje's paints and art supplies, putting its hands, covered in banana or liver pâté, all over her canvases. And then later, a defiant three-year-old, a hot-tempered six-year-old, a prepubescent child pulling a face at her. She doesn't want to live with someone who criticises her, she says? She thinks *that's* exhausting?

But is she telling the truth when she says she only told Erling about her desire for a child, that she didn't ask him for anything? Silje has been living from project to project for years. She's received a little grant money here and there and sold a few paintings. But as far as I know, she has no significant savings she can tap into should she be in need of a few hundred thousand kroner.

"Do you have the money to go ahead with this, then?" I ask her.

"That's my business," she says, lifting her chin.

I'm the only one standing here with a cup in my hand, it occurs to me now. I haven't even taken a sip. That same unpleasant feeling prickles at my neck, the feeling of sleepiness and shortness of breath from Tjøme. Is it safe for me to drink this? I set the cup on the coffee table.

Just behind her, on the wall above the sofa, hangs a small, framed image, a pencil drawing of a little girl with pigtails. I recognise this drawing. The lines, the big eyes, the signature: Bilal's portrait of Silje, drawn at the art table in the kindergarten, just before he made the first sketches of Martine. I frown. It's a long time since I last visited Silje, but I can't remember seeing it hanging there before.

"Silje," I say. "Why didn't you say anything about this to me?"

"I think you know why," she says.

Something in her tone surprises me – it's closed, distant. As if she's blaming me for something.

"I know nothing at all," I say. "None of you speak to me anymore. You go to Pappa with the things that are important to you, things you want advice about. And none of you, nor Pappa, ever mention them to me. And I don't understand why. I quite honestly do not understand it."

She narrows her eyes, looks at me.

"Well then think about it for a moment," she says.

"I'm thinking," I say. "And I'm at a total loss. I don't understand."

She sighs deeply again. As if it has fallen to her to inform me of something obvious, something everyone knows.

"You drink quite a lot, Mamma," she says then.

This leaves me speechless.

"You've been drunk almost every time I've seen you this past year," she says. "Sometimes, you've been shit-faced when I've spoken to you first thing in the morning. Either that, or high on those anxiety pills you take. You're actually pretty far gone. Pappa should have done something about it, but he didn't. Hanne and Bård don't think it's any of our business, but fuck that, we can't just keep tip-toeing around each other the way we do in this family."

She crosses her arms over her chest again, hugging herself. Regards me with that steady gaze.

"I think you need help, Mamma. And there is help out there. But first you have to admit you have a problem."

I suddenly have the feeling that the floor is turning liquid beneath my feet, that I'm sinking, floundering and fumbling around for something to hold on to, and I find something, a branch, skinny and small, but I grab it, and say: "But I don't understand, Silje. I really don't drink *that* much? And I haven't taken a single pill since Pappa died."

"It does seem to have been better over the past few weeks," she concedes. "Who knows, maybe the shock helped. Maybe this tragedy can help you to grow, or something."

Then she reaches out her hand, touches my arm.

"But Mamma. Very few people manage this alone. You should seek help. There's no shame in getting help."

Her hand on my arm weighs a tonne.

"I just want you to be okay," she says.

EIGHTEEN DAYS BEFORE

The daffodils stood in a white vase on the coffee table. Their yellow heads lit up the room, putting me in a cheerful mood. Out on the table on the terrace was the bowl of punch I had prepared, with orange juice, rum and vodka. I had tested it a little as I made it, because of course I had to, to make sure it tasted right. And I had a glass or two of wine while I was cooking, but no more than that. Although I did use the big glasses.

Olav and Bridget were the first to arrive; they had Mother with them.

"Oh, it looks so nice in here," Bridget said when she saw the daffodils.

I handed her a glass of punch, but she said no thank you, she'd prefer alcohol-free. Olav smiled at me, hugged me more lightly than he usually did.

"Kari," Mother said. "Is that you?"

"No, Mother," I said. "It's me, Evy."

I laughed, loudly and merrily. All at once Mother's dementia seemed to manifest itself in comical ways – as if anything about me is reminiscent of Mother's sister! I turned to face my brother, but he wasn't laughing. He merely cast a questioning look in my direction.

Hanne wore a stiff expression. Because Max had been screaming all the way here? She seemed embarrassed, hugged me lightly, didn't look me in the eye. Then came Lise and Bård. Lise could only stay for an hour, then she had to drive Henrik to a football game.

"On Easter Eve?" I asked, astonished.

Lise cast a despairing look in my direction.

"We've told you about this several times, Mamma," Bård said.

Hanne sighed. She and her brother exchanged glances. It irritated me: why did they have to be so pedantic, why so much fuss about forgetting the odd little thing now and then?

"Well then I suppose you'll just have to tell me one more time," I said.

I laughed, but no-one laughed with me. Erling gazed out across the garden, saying nothing.

Silje was the last to arrive. I handed her a glass of Easter punch. She looked at me, then at the glass, and then at me again.

"What's in it?"

Not you, too, I thought. Don't be so pernickety, stop sticking your nose into everything, criticising everything I do. Can't you see that it's yellow? The colour of Easter? Surely that's okay? Can't you understand that it's supposed to be a bit of fun?

"It's all organic," I said. "So really, you can just *relax*."

Erling tapped his glass with his knife.

"It's so nice that you all could be here today," he said. "Evy has almost worn herself out getting everything just right, and it seems the Easter lamb will be delicious as usual."

Nobody looked at me when he said this. I laughed. I was most definitely not worn out.

"It's a little delayed," he added, "but it'll be ready very soon, I think, so I hope everyone has time to stay to eat."

"I'd better go check on it then," I said, giving a military salute. "Since the boss says so."

Erling didn't laugh, and neither did any of the others.

But the lamb wasn't done. There must have been something wrong with the oven. Maybe I'd messed up the settings. The thermometer was stuck in the meat, but it hadn't reached the right temperature. I kept having to go out onto the terrace to say: "It just needs a bit longer, it'll be ready soon."

At least the mood is good, I thought. Olav was speaking loudly in a friendly voice, throwing out jokes all over the place. But weren't the smiles a little stiff? Now and then I went out and topped up people's glasses. I poured the odd glass for myself, too.

The sound of the doorbell cut through the air.

"I'll get it," I shouted.

No-one out on the terrace said anything. Synne stood on the doorstep with a bouquet of lilacs. Her hand shot out to grab my arm.

"Is everything okay, Evy?"

"Oh of course, of course," I said. "I'm just busy with the cooking."

She looked sceptical. And we used to have such fun together.

When I led Mother back out onto the terrace, she tripped on the threshold. Or was it me? Neither of us managed to stay on our feet. Bridget grabbed hold of us.

"Things can't go on like this, Evy," she sighed.

Stupid bloody stuck-up suburban housewife, I thought, but what else would I have expected of Bridget? I went back into the kitchen, checked the meat, then came out again.

"It's almost ready," I said.

"I'm not sure we'll have time to eat before we have to go, Henrik," Lise said.

"It doesn't matter," Bård said, his expression flat.

Hanne strode into the kitchen, taking firm, sharp steps. "I'll go take a look."

Later, we all gathered around the table, except for Lise and her son. I couldn't remember the words to the grace Mother used to say at Easter, *Our Father, who art in heaven, hallowed be thy name*, or was there something to do with a *kingdom*, ha ha, whatever, it makes no damn difference. I stumbled through it. Did the others laugh? I reached the end, raised my glass, and said cheers.

"Mamma," Hanne said, her voice high-pitched and firm. "You've been hard at it for a long time now. Maybe you want to go and have a little lie-down?"

"No," I said. "I'm not a child."

They didn't stay long. At least it was nice, I thought. I'm sure I said it, too, several times: hasn't it been nice, getting together as a family?

But Erling looked pensive. He seemed to be pondering something, and for the rest of the evening he said very little.

SIXTEEN DAYS AFTER

The grandfather clock ticks heavily as I text Edvard to tell him I won't be able to meet for dinner after all. In some ways, I would have liked to be with him now. It would have felt so good to surrender to his aura of calmness and kindness, where everything is okay and I have nothing to feel ashamed of. But I'm afraid he'll be able to tell. I don't want him to see me this way, can't bear to fall in his estimation.

Unless he already knows. How well have I managed to hide it? I'm not sure. I've never thought about it this way before. Of course, I'm well aware that I enjoy a drink or two. As I did when I was younger, when the children were teenagers. I remember Erling and I speaking about it – he felt it was becoming a little excessive. I thought he was being overly priggish, but I cut down, it was no big deal. And it's been fine since then. Absolutely fine.

But lately, maybe it has started to get a little out of hand. I can admit to that. Over the past couple of years, perhaps. We've become more isolated. After the argument with Erling, Synne stopped coming over, and only then did it hit me that she was pretty much the only friend I had left. Olav and Bridget stop by very rarely, and otherwise the children are the only people who visit us. And Erling was getting more bristly, increasingly irritable. Maybe I began topping up my wine glass a little more frequently. I probably needed that little buzz – to take the edge off, as it were. And I have to admit that it felt good, like having your back scratched in a place you're unable to reach yourself. Maybe I've needed to scratch that itch a little more often.

And when it comes to the pills – well, I got them from the doctor.

She assessed me and decided I needed them, in order to relax, in order to sleep. Who am I to question her expertise? I may have taken a few too many, upped my dosage slightly now and then. Taken a blister pack from Mother's medicine cabinet whenever the opportunity presented itself; told my GP that I lost a pack, or managed to wheedle another prescription out of a different doctor. But these are medicines. They're there to heal, to cure. How wrong can it be to feel that they're helping, that they're serving their intended purpose? Surely it's a good thing – to feel better? To sleep, to wake feeling refreshed and calm?

And I haven't taken a single pill since Erling died – I haven't so much as touched the little box in the bathroom cabinet.

Someone tampered with Erling's pills. Might they also have tampered with mine? And I don't want to feel groggy at night, I don't want to be intoxicated. I want to be able to get to my feet quickly. I've gone easy on the wine, too. No – I don't think Edvard can have noticed anything.

Unless he *knows*. Unless Erling told him something, poured his heart out during these dinners of theirs. Again – how I wish I had access to that appointment book, so I could flick back through the pages and see when Erling made a note of his meetings with Edvard. *If* he wrote them down. I think of the box in the calendar Miriam showed me: *Private appointment.*

Because he did meet up with Edvard, didn't he? Surely Edvard can't be lying? Surely he can't have fabricated a close friendship, now that Erling is no longer able to deny it? Edvard's kind eyes; the calmness I feel when I'm with him. No – none of this can be his fault. And yet I can't stop the doubts from spinning through my head: Edvard's flowers arrived four days after That Day, someone left them outside my front door. A florist, perhaps – or Edvard himself? The front door might have been unlocked. He might have gone into the study, snatched the appointment book from the desk.

And the person Mother saw on Easter Eve – was it necessarily a member of the family? Nothing in what she said establishes with any certainty that it was one of us. I don't think I locked the front door after speaking to Synne. The rest of the family was in the garden, on the other side of the house, and inside it was just Mother and me – one of us addled with dementia, the other decidedly well oiled.

But could Edvard have swapped out Erling's medicines? Could he have replaced the hose on the gas container at the cabin? It begins to sound a little far-fetched.

Part of me cannot believe I'm even thinking like this, that I have it in me to suspect Edvard Weimer. But it's so hard to get everything to add up. What happened at the cabin was nothing less than attempted murder. That's what I tell myself now, in a moment of unusual clarity: someone *must* have removed the recently inspected hose between the stove and the gas bottle, and installed an old, cracked one in its place. This was done to wreak havoc. And when you look at it that way, the next question becomes: was the hose replaced before or after Erling died? In other words: was the gas leak at the cabin an attempt to do away with Erling? Or to get me?

Almost as soon as I've sent the text to Edvard to cancel, my phone starts to buzz. At first I think it's Edvard calling to persuade me to come anyway. If it is, I won't be hard to convince, because a column of emotion rises from my belly to spread through me: maybe he was looking forward to seeing me. But the name on the screen is that of my brother.

"Hello," I say.

Almost immediately, I regret taking the call. I think back to the Easter dinner party. Mother calling me *Kari*, thinking I was her sister. Me turning to my brother and laughing. Olav looking me, his features a blank.

"Hello, Evy," he says. "How are you doing?"

"Oh, you know. And you?"

"Yes, fine."

He clears his throat. He has something on his mind.

"Evy," he says. "I've been speaking to Bård. And I gather that Erling, well . . . that he made some surprising arrangements concerning his assets before he died."

"Yes."

I glance at the dining table, where Bård and I sat the day he came over with the chicken stir-fry. I think: tomorrow, I'll go see my son. Before I meet up with Hanne, I'll drop in on Bård at work. See him with my own eyes, talk to him about all this.

"From what Bård says, the whole thing seems fairly nuts," Olav says. "And I understand you knew nothing about it?"

Olav waits, wanting me to affirm his statement. For a moment there is total silence. Can I trust my brother? And can I trust Bård? In spite of his far-too-wide smile, Peter Bull-Clausen seems to be my safest bet. The man Erling chose himself: a stranger, with no interest in or ties to the family.

"Erling got me to sign some papers," I say slowly. "Something about ownership of the cabin, he said, he thought it would be more practical. You know how things were between us. He managed those kinds of affairs. I just assumed he made the right decisions."

Olav is silent. I can hear him breathing heavily.

"Right, okay," he says. "Because your children were a little taken aback. After all, it's fairly unusual to have a separate property agreement on shared real estate. And the fact that you now own everything, when the house was inherited from Erling's family. It's enough to make you wonder."

"Yes," I say. "It is."

Olav breathes heavily again.

"Is everything okay with you, Evy?" he asks.

But he doesn't use my pet name. Little Sis – that's what he usually calls me when we speak in confidence.

"Well," I say, quickly, angrily. "I've just lost my husband, the police keep knocking on my door, and yesterday I was almost done in by a gas leak at the cabin on Tjøme. So what do you think?"

"What did you say?"

"I was at the cabin yesterday," I say, my voice hard. "And when we went into the living room, we started to feel woozy, and it turned out the contents of the gas bottle had been leaking into the room for weeks – the cabin was full to the brim with hazardous gas. Luckily, we got out in time. The man from the fire brigade said it could have ended in disaster."

"Wow, really?" Olav says. "When did you say this happened?"

"Yesterday. So I think I'm entitled to feel a little out of sorts."

"Jeez," Olav says. "This is the first I'm hearing about this, I . . . Do the children know about it?"

"No. But it's not as if they share much with me, either. Apparently, at least two of them have asked Erling for money, and none of them thought of mentioning it to me."

Olav clears his throat, as if in agreement, and I stop myself. It isn't a given that I should involve him in all this. He was here on Easter Eve, too. And the day after Erling died. He could have taken the boxes of pills, the bicycle, the appointment book. He's also been to the cabin many times. Wouldn't it have been easy for him to cause that leak?

"The thing is," Olav says. "Your children are considering contesting the transfer of the properties to you. It seems things might have been unravelling a little for Erling, there at the end. With his commitment to the environment and all that. And he did seem a little out of it in the period leading up to his death. So maybe he wasn't entirely in his right mind when he made these rash decisions. It might be worth checking."

I swallow a couple of times.

"And just how would we check that?" I ask.

"Well. There's the post-mortem report, of course. But maybe the simplest way is just to base our conclusions on his behaviour. You know, he did seem to be acting a little strangely at the Easter dinner. Bridget and I spoke about it in the car on the way home. He didn't really seem himself."

"And what did you think about my behaviour?"

He falls silent.

"Evy," he says finally.

And that's basically all the confirmation I need. Of course they talked about us in the car on the way home – but it wasn't Erling they discussed. Oh, no. They talked about me. About how drunk I'd been, how I'd made a fool of myself. Anything they said about Erling must have been in connection with me: how embarrassing the whole thing must have been for him, and so on.

Now, in retrospect, this has all been turned on its head. Because now it benefits them – the children, but perhaps Olav, too – to think that it was *Erling* who was the problem, that it was *Erling* who was out of it, who was losing his mind and acting rashly.

"Erling wasn't going crazy," I say. "What he did, he did with his eyes wide open, and he did it for a reason."

"I just can't understand what that reason might be," Olav says.

I think of what Edvard said in the French restaurant, about how it almost seemed Erling wanted to ensure his children wouldn't inherit his assets. But I take the thought no further.

"I'm not entirely sure myself," I say. "But I'm trying to figure it out."

"Right."

Something in Olav's tone tells me that he doesn't hold out much hope that my investigations will make us any the wiser.

278

"Anyway," he says, taking a breath. "It's within your power to reverse quite a bit of all this. By selling the cabin, for example, and dividing the proceeds between the children. You've never liked it there, Evy, and I can't imagine you'll use it much now that you're alone. Then the children will receive their inheritance from their father, and you can continue to live in Nordheimbakken."

The double doors are open, the dark hallway behind them indecently on show. I peer down it. The door to Erling's study is ajar.

"I understand that," I say. "But it's not what Erling wanted."

"What do you mean?"

"I mean," I say slowly, "that Erling went to fairly great lengths to give me complete control. And I'd very much like to know why he did that."

"But does it really matter?" Olav asks. "Isn't it more important that the family is taken care of? You, your children, your grandchildren?"

The dark hallway draws me towards it. The study, the stairs that lead to the cellar.

"You know, Olav," I say. "I find it curious that it's only *now* that I'm suddenly being asked about what I want. Only *now*, when I'm the one who gets to decide."

There is silence again between us. From his end I can hear a rushing sound, as if he's drawing breath deep into his huge body, permitting air to fill his lungs, his whole chest.

"Okay," he says finally. "I just wanted to tell you what Bård and I discussed. I thought it only right that you should know."

"Fine," I say. "Thank you."

As soon the words are out of my mouth, I regret them. What am I thanking *him* for? In what way was this conversation something he initiated for my sake, out of concern for me?

"By the way," he says then. "Who was with you? Out at the cabin?"

"What do you mean?"

"You said 'we'. You said 'we' got out in time."

"Oh yes."

I really shouldn't have mentioned it. I wish I could take back that "we", but it's too late, and there's no point in lying. It's probably in the fire brigade's report, anyway. It would come to light eventually.

"Edvard Weimer," I say.

"Ah."

But there is no surprise in Olav's response. The children must have told him about Edvard, too.

"Evy," he says. "If I could give you a piece of advice. Just watch yourself around Weimer."

"What do you mean?" I ask. "What's wrong with him?"

Silence again. I hear him breathing.

"There's always been something a little underhand about that one," Olav says. "And he seems extremely interested in all this. I think it's best we don't tell him too much. We should resolve this within the family. That's what I think."

"Thanks for the advice," I say, and hang up.

TWENTY-SIX YEARS BEFORE

It was no skin off my nose that Bilal's artwork could be seen everywhere you looked. I didn't care that the publisher had put him in touch with another author to produce the text to accompany his illustrations, or that the book had made it to the top of every bestseller list and was on display in the window of every bookshop. It was never about *that* for me. I had no great need to be an author. I just thought it was fun to do something different, to see that I could achieve something. I didn't let it get me down, I had other things to worry about. Jesus, I was mother to two teenagers and a seven-year-old – I had more than enough on my plate.

But the afternoons were long. The mornings were busy: the breakfast things needed to be cleared away, the housework done. After lunch it was quieter. The house was empty. The children didn't get home until around three, and they often went over to friends' houses after school. So I sat around twiddling my thumbs. Sometimes I poured myself a glass of wine. Nothing excessive, I was never drunk. Just enough for me to feel that life could be this way, too – that there was breathing space within the boredom. Sometimes I would get dressed up, take out a silk blouse and skirt, sheer stockings, high heels. The housework seemed more fun then. Sometimes I played music on the stereo I had bought following the publication of the second Martine book. Other than this, we didn't use it all that much.

I went into Bård's room, in my high heels and silk blouse, carrying a basket of clean laundry. The room was a mess, and it stank of dirty socks. The clean clothes I returned to the chest of drawers were neatly folded. Early the next morning, he would dig through them with his oversized paws, hunting blindly for something to wear, and crumple the lot. That's how the work was – futile and fleeting – but at least I was dressed up, at least I felt attractive. And I actually liked keeping the house in order, keeping the family's wheels turning. Pressure to deliver, nagging editors and libraries full of snotty-nosed children – I was done with all that. Classrooms full of noisy pupils likewise. I put away my son's folded underpants.

Atop the chest of drawers was the portable CD player Bård had bought with his confirmation money, surrounded by stacks of CDs. Metallica, Korn, Rage Against the Machine – I didn't know these bands. I would have liked to ask him about them, instead of just nagging him to put his dirty laundry in the basket. I would have liked to have discussed music with him, to show him that his mother did actually know a thing or two. Didn't it draw its inspiration from the music I had listened to in the seventies? Isn't that how it works? Everything's built on something else, taking it for inspiration and running with it, transforming it into something new while still carrying within it that which came before. I picked up one of the CDs. The cover featured a black-and-white image of a man engulfed in flames. I put it in the empty laundry basket.

Downstairs in the living room, I placed the CD in the stereo's tray, selected a track and pressed play. A guitar riff interrupted the ticking of the clock, and I turned up the volume, letting the music fill the living room. A male voice groaned, and then the rest of the band kicked in, creating a dense, clamorous sound. It had nothing in common with the music I listened to when I was young, but I liked it. *Now you do what they told ya*, the man taunted, over and over. *Now you do what they told ya.* I laughed at myself when I caught myself swinging my hips to it, because wasn't it actually quite heart-warming, that Bård and I could come together like this, across the decades that divided our youths?

The vocalist's words became a scream, nothing but pure protest and rage, and I kicked off my shoes, dancing around the living room and shouting with him: *Fuck you, I won't do what you tell me! Fuck you, I won't do what you tell me!* The words stomped through my body, vibrating through my legs and arms. Sixteen-year-old Evy would have loved this. She would have jumped up and down beside sixteen-year-old Bård, screaming at the top of her lungs. And wasn't this the sound of youthful abandon and revolt, and didn't it actually feel so fucking *good*?

Then I heard him above the music.

"Mamma!"

I turned around. He was standing there, flanked by two friends. One of them had covered his mouth with his hand; it looked as if he was smirking. But didn't he also seem just a tad impressed? Would *his* mother have done this, danced around to Rage Against the Machine? The second friend looked down at the floor. Bård stared at me, his eyes burning. I hurried across to the stereo and turned off the music.

"I found your CD," I said to him, laughing. "I like it."

My glass of wine was on the living-room table. The high-heeled shoes lay on the floor at the feet of the three boys.

"That's *mine*," Bård said. "Give it back!"

I pressed the button, and the tray containing the CD popped out of the stereo.

"I like the rhythm in it," I said.

I tried to say something insightful about the music, about the lyrics and the arrangement, but Bård wasn't listening. I handed him the CD, and he snatched it from me, turned on his heel and disappeared up the stairs. His friends followed him, and then they were gone. I tidied away the wine glass and the fancy shoes.

SEVENTEEN DAYS AFTER

He's sitting at his desk when I arrive. The receptionist let me in and pointed out his office. She can't possibly have had time to let him know that I'm here, but he doesn't appear surprised.

"Hi, Mamma," he says.

I close the door behind me. The office is small, little more than a cell, and his desk takes up half the room. Behind him is a window facing the rear courtyard and the building opposite. Before him is his computer and a cup of coffee. WORLD'S BEST DAD, it says on the mug.

"I was in the neighbourhood," I say.

"Yes," he says, with a faint smile. "I thought it might be my turn next."

I return his smile. He's attractive, my boy. Tall and slim, like his father, and he dresses well. But he has this tired look about him. Whenever I see him like this, the way he looks now, I think he must have been tired for years.

Or is it about me? Is his exhaustion primarily a response to my presence? This shudder of self-consciousness again: how does he see me, what have I done? Perhaps he's virile and animated otherwise – with his colleagues, with his family and friends.

I haven't often observed him with his friends, as an adult, I mean. I remember the young men at his wedding. He was young when he married – they still seemed fairly childish, almost boys. They had open, shiny faces; they laughed loudly and helped themselves to the wine. The speeches mentioned Bård's antics at parties. Something about jumping off a balcony at a ski resort in Hemsedal, something about a nightclub on Corfu, with some girls and some drinks. The boys laughed raucously. Lise smiled indulgently. Bård blushed. He laughed – because he had to, of course – but he seemed ill at ease. He cast a glance or two in my and Erling's direction. At his father especially. Bowed his head, like a little boy waiting for a scolding.

"Yes," he says as I take a seat. "I gather you've been doing the rounds, asking us all about the financial predicaments we've ended up in, so I may as well come clean from the get-go. The company isn't exactly doing well."

He rubs his face with his hands, looks tired again.

"We have two major projects underway. Havna Park and Røa Hageby. It's taken longer than we expected to make the necessary sales, and at Røa we've had to invest in some upgrades to get the site market ready. That's why I went to Pappa and asked for the loan."

I nod again, recalling how freely Lise spoke about the loan – she just assumed that I knew. Ørjan had been the same. This tells me something. It isn't my son- or daughter-in-law pulling the wool over my eyes. The concealment is being perpetrated by my own children.

"Well," he says, throwing his arms wide, grinning in the boyish way he used to as a child, when he had forgotten to do his home-work or pick up his dirty socks. "I need a few hundred thousand. Just to keep us afloat over the summer. We have some interested buyers, we're in negotiations, but these things take time. Right now, we have a liquidity problem. As I told Pappa, I'd be able to pay back the loan as soon as the sale of Havna Park is in the bag. And we *are* going to sell. If not before the summer, then immediately afterwards."

"But Pappa said no," I say.

Bård sighs.

"He thought I ought to be able to stand on my own two feet. And who knows, maybe he was right. Although I've never heard him say anything like that about Silje."

There's something bitter in his tone. The hard demands that were made of him and Hanne – not explicitly, but as abiding values they had to live up to: always be good, do well at school, build sturdy, respectable lives for themselves. These things were expected of them, but perhaps especially of him, the firstborn. The boy. Erling was old-fashioned, he didn't see the point of imaginative play and craft projects. Hanne and Bård constantly fished for praise, while he simply shrugged.

But wasn't I generous with the loving gestures and attention? Admittedly, I may have been a little distant for a few years, losing myself in the vacuum that arose after Paris. I can't quite imagine what it must have been like for Bård, or for Hanne, when the enthusiasm they so desperately craved from their father was so willingly served up to their little sister, who never even asked for it.

"But you didn't ask me," I say. "You never said you needed money."

He looks at me. He's assessing me, that's the impression I get. He narrows his eyes, considering me more carefully than he usually does.

"Pappa wouldn't have liked it," he says.

"You didn't think it would help," I say. "*That's* what you really mean. You thought I'd just tell you that you'd have to go speak to Pappa regardless."

"Yes," he says. "That did occur to me."

Bård is so capable, I've always thought that about him, he works so hard. I remember him as a child, sitting with his head bent towards his left hand as he wrote in his maths book, the curls that settled around his tiny fingers. Oh the ache in my chest – my boy, practising what life would come to demand of him.

I think I've always viewed him this way, as moving away from me, out into the world. A mother's love is disproportionate, given in amounts it is never intended that the child repay. But of course you hope they'll love you back. I look at him now, at his greying curls, which are starting to thin. Did I do enough for him? Might I have harmed him, without meaning to, in ways I'm unable to see?

"And you probably thought I drank a little too much," I say.

He tilts his head slightly, and a hint of concerned affection appears in his expression.

"Silje didn't mince her words, then."

"But why didn't *you* say anything, Bård?"

He shrugs.

"I thought you knew, Mamma. I mean, how long does it take you to put away a three-litre box? I didn't think it was something we had to *tell* you, that it isn't good to be drinking wine before noon."

Now sympathy wells up in me. That afternoon, when I was dancing to his music. I didn't think it was so bad at the time, but now I understand how humiliating it must have been. I was probably drunk, and far less glamorous than I imagined. I got myself all dolled up, in my shortest skirt, and then unwittingly danced in front of his friends. And I never said anything about it, never apologised. I just allowed it to be a thing we never spoke of. Can I really blame him for not speaking up, when keeping quiet is something I've taught him?

"It can't always have been easy, having me as a mother, Bård," I say. "I don't think I really understood that until now."

I think about Silje, who asked me to seek help. And Erling, at the Easter dinner, pensive with his furrowed brow. Erling never said anything to me. But maybe he didn't really see it. To him I was always the industrious schoolgirl from Røaveien.

"It's fine, Mamma," Bård says, his features stiff as he stares straight ahead. "I'm sure things weren't always that great for you, either."

Then we are quiet for a while. His phone lies there, silent on the desk, and it makes me sad. Shouldn't they be calling him, all these potential buyers? Shouldn't they be begging to buy his properties, outbidding one another? Or at least negotiating the price and hand-over date? Bård started this company, along with a friend he later bought out. I can still hear how he used to talk about his job over dinner at home in Nordheimbakken. Often addressing me, but casting tiny sideways glances at Erling.

Did he still crave his father's approval? And did Erling refuse to be impressed? The way he refused to get excited about their draw-ings, their skiing competitions, or their grades? Was it only Silje, who walked her own path and made choices that were almost the exact opposite of what Erling considered acceptable, who received her father's admiration?

"Olav called me yesterday," I say.

"I know," Bård says.

"So you want to contest the will?"

He sighs. The boyishness has vanished; all at once, he looks old.

"I don't know what else to do," he says. "It seems utterly insane, what Pappa has done. And Olav says you're not interested in put-ting it right. But you could, you know, Mamma. If you sold the cabin on Tjøme, you could make all of this right."

I nod, slowly, thinking of Bård sitting at Peter Bull-Clausen's table. The affection and tenderness I feel for my son blinds me when I look at him, and it always has. But now I understand: Bård came to the meeting at the lawyer's office thinking he was about to get rich. He thought he was going to get the house, to inherit his share of the millions he believed Erling had in the bank. He had counted on that money. He'd probably created spreadsheets and run calcu-lations, agreed with Lise how they might best use these new funds. He sat at that table in the meeting room and felt cheated. As if Erling had taken something that rightly belonged to him. Yes, there is a grasping side to my son. It's just so hard to see it, because I have such a soft spot for him.

"I really don't know what to do," I say. "But I have to try to understand why Pappa did what he did."

"But the clock is ticking," Bård says. "I need the money, and Hanne does, too. And so does Silje, for that matter. While you're trying to understand, doors are closing for us. Can't you see that?"

I look at him.

"An inheritance is a gift, Bård," I say. "This isn't your money."

Something in his face hardens then. Something dark veils his eyes, and he withdraws.

"Of course," he says formally. "You do as you wish. I'm just trying to explain the situation we're in."

Hanne is already sitting at the table when I arrive. I see her before she sees me, and I note the impatient glances she keeps casting towards the door. But there's also something serious and unfamiliar in her face, something grown-up. When I think about her, I see her as a young woman, but she turned forty this past winter.

She catches sight of me. A couple of hundredths of a second pass before she seems to react, and in this tiny instant she just stares at me. Then she puts on a smile and waves.

When I reach the table, I give her a hug, and as I hold her, I smell her perfume. She always has such shiny hair, such clean and freshly pressed clothes. I remember the first few months after Max was born, when he refused to sleep or eat and only screamed, how Hanne, in one of Ørjan's discarded sweaters, make-up free and with unwashed hair and red-rimmed eyes, stared grimly at me across their messy kitchen table and said: I'm climbing the walls, Mamma. But then the baby began to sleep better, and this version of Hanne, the unkempt primal woman, receded into the shadows.

"I only have half an hour," she says, glancing at her watch. "I have a meeting with a supplier at one, and I really ought to read through their offer first."

"That's okay," I say, taking a seat opposite her.

"Great," she says, her voice bright and breezy. "I ordered us some food, by the way, so we'll have time to eat. Is quiche okay?"

"Of course," I say, without even considering it. "How are you, honey?"

"Good. You know, sad about Pappa. But otherwise fine. And you've been to see Bård, I gather?"

The amount of time they must spend on their phones with each other, she and Bård and Silje, perhaps even Olav, too. At any given time, everyone knows precisely what I've said to the others. I suppose that isn't so strange, when it comes down to it, but I don't like it. Is any of what I tell any of them confidential? Can I say something now that will go no further than Hanne, or are they a many-headed monster, different versions of one and the same beast?

"Yes," I say. "I thought it best I speak with all of you."

"Yes. I'm sure that's true."

I consider her. She gives me a quick smile then looks around for the waiter. Hanne always seems to have her attention directed elsewhere. Our telephone conversations are generally initiated by her – she calls from the tram or from the car, as she hurries to the kindergarten or picks up what she needs to make dinner. It's easy to think she's not paying attention, but then you also risk underestimating her, because she's sharp.

"Well," she says, looking back at me. "Aren't you going to ask me?"

"About what?"

"About the money I asked Pappa for. Or *the loan*, if you will."

Her tone is ironic. She and Bård must have talked about this, too, about the words they should use when discussing the proposals they brought before Erling.

"Well," I say. "You've already told me, haven't you? On the telephone yesterday."

"Yes. But just so you know. I asked Pappa for help with some equity, so we'd be in a position to buy the semi-detached house in Kjelsås."

She sighs, and her eyes narrow.

"It would be just perfect for us," she says sincerely. "Max's best friend's parents bought the other side. We'd live next door. The boys would be able to run over to see each other without even bothering to put their shoes on. And it's such a lovely location, with a view of the lake. We can't stay in our tiny, dark apartment for all eternity. Max will be starting school next year, so now's the time to move. And this is about Max, about where he's going to grow up. Not *me* – it doesn't matter to me where I live. All I want is for my child to have the best possible start in life. I just don't understand how Pappa couldn't see that." She takes a breath, sighs.

"Things may have got a little heated the last time we spoke," she says. "I mean, we were on good terms when we hung up and every-thing, but you know how uncompromising he could be. And I was probably a little upset. This means a lot to me. To Max."

"And when was this?" I ask her. "The last time you spoke to Pappa, when was it?"

She looks at me, and something in her eyes changes. She's won-dering why I'm asking, suddenly wary.

"Oh, well, let's see," she says breezily. "When would it have been? About a week before he died, maybe? Plus or minus a few days. I don't remember exactly."

"Was it at home in Montebello?"

"Yes," she says. "I dropped by one day. The week before. You weren't home – I think you were with Grandma. And then I spoke to him on the phone a day or two after that."

"And how did he seem?" I ask.

"Pappa? Same as usual. Apart from refusing to help me, of course."

We look at each other, and then she gives a tense laugh and says:

"Or maybe that was exactly the same as usual, too."

"Hanne," I say. "Had you arranged to see him on the day he died?"

"No," she says.

Lightly. But she's on high alert. We're sizing one another up, and for a moment there is total silence between us.

"Am I being subjected to an interrogation here?" she asks.

She gives a sort of laugh, but it sounds forced.

"No, no," I say, my throat dry. "I was just wondering."

When I returned home from Paris, Hanne would hardly let go of me. For several weeks she clung to my legs; she wanted to be picked up, carried, held. She was a little too big for it. A little too heavy, and a little too old for it, too. But I tolerated it. I felt guilty about having left her. And yet, I was so distant. I let her climb all over me, but I was numb.

For a while they fought over me, Bård and Hanne. He became irritated at her for sitting on my lap all the time, so called her a brat. Hanne cried with her face pressed to my neck: *Mammaaaaa*.

I was generous with my affections, at least before Paris. But perhaps I showered Bård with these gestures a little more often than I did her. And if Erling was most attentive towards Silje, you might ask how this must have appeared to Hanne. It's tempting to think she didn't notice the imbalance – she's so brilliant, so robust. But you shouldn't underestimate her sensitivity – that's what I think as I look at her now.

Hanne looks back at me, as if assessing me across the café table. A young waitress comes with our plates, both bearing quiche and salad. We're silent as we are served, smile stiffly.

"So," Hanne says after she's swallowed her first bite. "Have you thought about what you're going to do with the cabin?"

This is playing to the gallery. She's spoken to Olav, and to Bård. She knows full well that I've refused to be pressured into saying I'm going to sell.

"No," I say.

"You haven't?"

I chew laboriously. The quiche isn't particularly good, the pastry is dry.

"I have to think about it."

"Of course," she says. "It's important that you don't do anything rash here. I mean, we have to find a solution everyone can live with, right?"

I think for a moment, tasting her phrasing.

"That everyone can live with," I repeat.

"Yes," she says. "After all, it's really rather odd, what Pappa has done. But of course, he could be a little odd. And we all loved him so much. We're a close-knit family, when it comes down to it. We have to stick together. We have to be generous with each other."

She's practised this little speech, I think. That word, *generous*. I can just imagine how she said it to Bård, to Silje. I take another bite of my quiche, feel how the crust dries out my mouth, crumbling and turning to dust.

"For me," Hanne says, "I think that if we could have a little help, Ørjan and I, with the equity we need for the house, then that's all I need, right? The rest of the inheritance comes when it comes. But it's vital we put in an offer *now*, before someone snatches the house out from under us. Surely you understand that, Mamma? Don't you want me to be able to give Max the kind of childhood we had? With a big bedroom and a garden and a safe walk to school?"

I chew and chew, neglect to answer her. Feel the refusal building in me. Feel, even now, the weight of the rage she will counter it with.

"So if we could just have a little help," she says. "Maybe five hundred thousand – seven at most. It isn't enough that you act as our guarantor, you see – the bank says we need actual capital. And Ørjan doesn't have very much he can contribute on that front, because his parents can't exactly sell the farm. So if you could just help us out, we'd be able to buy the house. And then I need nothing more. And I mean, of course I'll speak with Bård and Silje, too, so we can make sure we're in agreement, all four of us."

"Hanne," I say. "Is that how you think of your childhood? As something you want to pass on to Max?"

She looks at me, wide-eyed. The boxes of wine, I think. The dull sense of utter emptiness as her little hands patted me, fiddled with my hair, pulled up my arms, my chin, *look, Mamma, come on, Mamma.* But there's nothing wounded about her.

"Of course," she says. "We had a wonderful childhood. Plenty of space, no busy roads on our walk to school, friends in the neighbourhood. That's exactly what I want Max to have."

TWENTY-THREE YEARS BEFORE

The book's reception came as a shock to me. It shouldn't have, because there had been no shortage of hints, and afterwards, as I sat there at home in the middle of the day, with my feet up on the table and a glass in my hand, I asked myself whether deep down, I had known all along. Whether it had occurred to me, and whether something in me had been working to steel me for what was to come. As if my consciousness had been operating on two levels, so that I believed, entirely genuinely, that it was a fantastic idea, while at the same time I was preparing myself for defeat. I tried to ask myself these questions, but felt only hollow.

The first hint had been Bilal. I sought him out several times. I called his agent, because that's how things were now – you couldn't just get hold of him, you had to make it past the gatekeeper. The agent said she would ask him. Later, she called back and said that unfortunately, Bilal didn't have the capacity. I tried again; wrote letters, called again. In the end, I went to yet another vernissage. This time, I wasn't invited, but I'd found out the date and time. The exhibition was being held at the same gallery in Frogner, and I arrived late, security was lax. His paintings were more explicitly related to war this time: tanks and bombers, simultaneously impressive and appalling.

Bilal stood speaking to a small group over in a corner. I watched him from a distance. He was a few years older now, around thirty. His hair was shorter, cut in a more grown-up style; his curls had been sheared away. He'd filled out a little, too, some of the hardness in his face was gone, but he still appeared taciturn, with those around him doing the talking.

When I finally went over to him, it was almost eleven o'clock.

"Hi, Bilal," I said, smiling widely.

He frowned, as if he couldn't immediately place me. Then he nodded. His eyes still gave a sense of the depths that lay behind them, which he kept so hidden in conversation but seemingly poured into his paintings. I wondered if he was surprised that I'd been invited. He probably had people who compiled his guest lists for him now.

"The exhibition is wonderful," I said.

He nodded hesitantly, but said nothing. To fill the silence I gushed about the qualities I had observed in his work. The lines! The colours! The symbolism! I laid it on thick.

"But there was something I wanted to ask you about," I said finally. "I have an idea for a new Martine story, and I think this one could be really special. Martine is on a walk in the forest with her family when she gets lost and befriends a group of bears."

Bilal nodded slowly. He didn't exactly look enthusiastic, but nor did he interrupt me, and, fired up by the fact that he was letting me speak, I continued. I told him the entire story I had plotted out. I even made a few suggestions regarding the illustrations. Emphasised that of course it would be entirely up to him, but I thought the youngest bear could have the look of a teddy bear, all round and soft, with huge eyes.

As I prattled on, an authoritative young woman came over to us. She had bleached blonde hair and was wearing bright red lipstick. Maybe she was his agent, the dismissive woman I'd spoken to on the phone. The look she gave me was impatient, and she cast quick side glances at Bilal, but as long as he didn't say anything and nor did she, I kept going, talking and talking until I could think of no more to say.

"So that's that," I said at last. "I think it could be really great, but, well, what do you think?"

304

There was a long silence. Bilal seemed to be gathering his thoughts. It was as if he were looking within himself, as if his vacant gaze was a kind of standby expression he put on for the world. The young woman with the lipstick appeared to have something pressing on her mind, but she held back, waiting for the artist to speak. I wished she would leave; I wanted to be alone with him.

"I don't think so," Bilal said at last.

He looked at me. His gaze was steadfast, unwavering.

"Oh, come on," I said. "Those books mean so much to the children who read them, you have so many young fans."

"No, I'm done with all that."

I took a breath to mobilise a counterargument, but the woman with the lipstick beat me to it. I must respect Bilal's decision, she said, and this request of mine was in fact rather intrusive, he had said no to my invitation several times, what did I expect?

A tsunami of disappointment and anger surged within me, and I hit back: how dare she? And as for him, what right did he have to treat me like this? Wasn't I the one who had discovered him? If it hadn't been for me, he'd probably still be sitting at the art table in the kindergarten. The people standing nearby turned to look.

But Bilal looked away. His answer was final.

"Now I think you should leave," the woman said, and apparently there was nothing else for me to do.

Nobody looked me in the eye as I walked towards the exit, but I could feel their gazes boring into my back as I went.

It was the editor who provided the second hint. I went to the offices of the publishing house and had coffee with her a couple of times. She was tentatively interested – yes, she said, it might work, but what did Bilal say? When I was forced to admit that he had declined, her interest waned.

"The illustrations were one of the most important things about the books," she said. "And anyway, the kids who grew up with Martine are too old for these kinds of stories now."

So I went home with unfinished business, home to the big, dark rooms of the house in Montebello. Home to my children. Bård, who was nineteen and would soon begin his military service. Hanne, who was seventeen, and who believed that this or that aspect of her upcoming final exams was *crucial* to how her life would turn out. Silje, who illustrated her own books, drawing ghastly monsters in crayon and watercolours. The long, empty hours alone in the house; glass after glass of red wine.

A few months later I went back to the publisher. I had a new idea: Martine as a teenager! A book designed for the fans. Problems associated with the age group they were now in. Pressure to smoke! Pressure to fit in, to look a certain way! Broken hearts!

"Will people really want to read that Martine has taken up smoking?" the editor asked.

"These are problems young people of that age can relate to," I said with conviction. "And because it's for older readers, we won't need an illustrator."

She allowed herself to be persuaded – or, more precisely, she said that I could go home and write the book, and she would read the manuscript and give me feedback when I was done. In the end, she passed the text to a younger colleague – a girl in her twenties who wore crop tops that showed off her navel piercing – and she thought the idea was *really exciting*, but that the text needed work.

Getting it into shape required a great deal of me. The girl with the navel piercing became less enthusiastic with every draft. This was the third hint, which should have been all I needed to decide to shelve the project, but by then I had invested far too much.

*

So I couldn't say I was entirely unprepared for the book's critical reception. Besides, it was mostly non-existent – an insistent, deafening silence in response to all my hard work. The libraries didn't call, and nor did the schools, and I failed to find the book displayed in bookshops. This niggled at me for weeks: when would it cause a stir, when would the excitement take hold? But just as I was getting used to the idea that it was never going to happen, the only review the fourth Martine book received was published.

It was in a national newspaper, and it was merciless. *In order to milk a successful but limited concept, the author has written a tasteless and entirely unnecessary update to the Martine series,* the reviewer wrote. He used phrases like *cynical* and *absence of literary merit,* and insinuated throughout that the only reason I had written the book was a desire to make money. Finally, he wrote that Bilal's illustrations had been the best thing about the previous books in the series. Without Bilal, they were nothing.

I started getting up later. Bård and Hanne were often already out the door before I got out of bed, and I only just managed to give Silje a quick peck on the head and ask her whether she'd brushed her teeth before she had to leave, too. It became harder to go to bed – I stayed up late into the night, reading books, watching films on TV. In the evenings, before it got too late, I called Synne.

"Do you remember how we'd sit in my room listening to David Bowie?" I would say. Or: "Do you remember when I nearly left Erling at the altar and we almost drove to Stockholm? Do you remember when I went to Paris alone?"

"You have to put this behind you, Evy," she said.

"Do you remember when Håvard left you?" I asked. "How easy was it to put that behind you?"

She sighed, deeply and heavily.

"It wasn't easy. But I did it. You need something to keep you busy. Why don't you get yourself a job, or do some volunteering? And save the wine for the weekends."

"Do you remember when we used to go out clubbing in Bygdøy?" I asked.

"I think we went out together maybe once. Usually you just stayed home with Erling."

Two weeks after they printed the crushing review, the same newspaper ran a piece on Bilal's latest exhibition. *Colours of Spring*, it was titled. The journalist raved: the exhibition was *important* and *shocking*, Bilal had *a unique ability to communicate the deepest of human emotions*. I was furious. But at the same time, I knew there was nothing to be done about it. I should have realised at that very first vernissage. The fact that I failed to do so was my downfall.

EIGHTEEN DAYS AFTER

"Erling told me something on the day he died," I say. "At breakfast, he mentioned a problem he had finally tackled and solved."

Edvard nods. We're sitting opposite each other at the dining table in his apartment in Skillebekk. It has been refurbished and is so well maintained you could almost forget the building is a hundred years old. The lighting is subdued, and the furniture is modern and unobtrusive. The table we're sitting at is made of pale wood; the chairs feature comfortable cushions in soft pastel wool fabric.

"All this time, I've been thinking his problem was to do with Green Agents," I say. "But I don't think Erling actually ever *said* that. It could just as easily have been to do with the private appointment he had later in the day, the one Miriam showed me."

I've tried to go back to the morning of That Day. I sat at the kitchen table as recently as this morning and imagined it: we were sitting opposite one another, Erling and I. He had taken a cup from the cabinet. He wiped it, rubbing it free of dust and small flecks, because he thought I was doing a slovenly job with the washing-up – or that's what I thought then. But I no longer think that.

So there we sat, opposite each other. I stared at the polished pine of the kitchen table and attempted to push the nausea back down into my stomach. Erling spoke about the weekly meeting at Green Agents; they were supposed to discuss their media strategy that day. He snorted: *media strategy.*

"And then I'm going to meet someone afterwards," he said. "Do you remember how I told you there was something I needed to sort out? An irregularity I had discovered?"

Even now I struggle to grasp what he was saying. It's like those splotchy, daubed paintings you sometimes see in museums. Move too close, and everything appears muddled. But view the painting from a distance and relax your gaze, and the motif appears.

Erling told me about this irregularity. It was really quite concerning, he said. He couldn't fathom how it could have got so far out of hand. Frankly, it was downright dangerous. But only for him, luckily enough – and he had found a solution. He was going to sort it out. Had done so already, actually. Now he just had to meet with someone and inform them of what he had done. And that was what he was going take care of, right after the meeting at Green Agents.

"I know what I have to do," he said, adding: "When I get home, it will all be done with."

Edvard nods thoughtfully. Meet someone, inform them. An expression passes over his face, concern or unease, but he says nothing. Is he trying to protect me? Or is he holding something back?

For a while we eat in silence, and then he says: "I looked into what you told me about the pass. You said Miriam told you that Erling had let himself into the building after hours a few times, the week when the lamp blew? I managed to get hold of a printout, and it shows that the pass was used twice during the evening. The last time was the day before the lamp blew the fuse."

"Oh," I say.

"Right. Late in the evening, too. Just before midnight."

Erling likes to go to bed early. He's an early bird, always up at the crack of dawn. I used to go to bed late, but in recent years I've started feeling tired earlier and earlier. I've probably been a little woolly-headed, too, by the time evening rolls around. Say someone wanted to borrow the pass. Say they didn't want Erling to know about it. Could they have let themselves into our house and stolen it late that evening, then put it back at some point during the night? Wouldn't we have noticed?

"Edvard," I say as I continue to consider the pass. "How did you get hold of the list?"

"What list?"

"The list of people who entered the Green Agents premises."

It takes him a moment to answer, but when I look at him, he's smiling.

"I asked nicely," he says, before adding: "She's a nice young woman, Miriam."

We sit in silence for a while, listening to the music.

"You have a really nice place here," I say finally.

"This is my childhood home," he says. "Did I never mention that? My parents bought the apartment just after the war. I renovated it completely after my father died."

"Really? So you ran around on these very floorboards as a child?"

We both look at the floor.

"Yes," he says. "There was once the patter of my little baby feet right here."

I don't stay long. I'm afraid of drinking more than I should, becoming too intense – too much. I want things to be simple with Edvard. Before I go, he hugs me. He embraces me for a moment longer than is usual, and in those hundredths of a second it's as if there's something there. As if he's asking me again: would you like to join me?

But then he releases me and says the taxi is probably waiting, and I go out into the stairwell and make my way down the stairs. I hear that he doesn't close the door straight away. I can tell without turning round: he's holding the door open, watching me go.

*

As the city flickers past outside the car window, it occurs to me that I didn't see a single photo of Edvard's wife. No portraits of a woman of the right age, no images of them together, framed and hung on the wall or arranged on the mantelpiece. Judging by his apartment, you'd think she'd never existed.

When I get home, there's a police car parked on the drive. I approach it, taking rapid steps, alarmed at the sight of it. Gundersen is leaning against the vehicle's bonnet, his hands in his pockets.

"Hello," he says. "Have you been out on the town?"

"Is everything alright?" I ask.

"I thought it was about time we had a chat. Is now okay?"

Not really, I think. It's ten-thirty at night and I've had two glasses of wine – small ones, admittedly, which Edvard poured for me, but two all the same. And I'm tired, I just want to go and lie down. But there's something compelling about this man. He's straightened up now, all tall and dynamic. And I'm not actually sure I'm allowed to say no. His asking whether now is a good time is likely only for appearances' sake. I have no particular desire to make him disclose that he can force this conversation on me.

"Of course," I say. "Come on in."

We sit in the living room. It looks more disordered now than it did the last time he was here. The blanket I usually drape over the arm of the sofa where the fabric has worn thin has slipped onto the floor, where Erling's slippers are strewn untidily because I can't bring myself to move them, even though I'm constantly stumbling over them. I suspect that Gundersen registers all this. I wonder whether he's noticed this penchant I have for a drink or two. It wouldn't surprise me, though I was stone-cold sober when he was last here.

Just to be on the safe side, I say: "I've just had dinner with a friend, and I've had a couple of glasses of wine."

"That's no problem at all," he says, apparently unruffled.

He sits in the armchair, as he did last time. His knees still stick up and splay out either side of him. His legs are thin, I see, as are his arms. But I bet he's strong and tough, and probably stubborn. I bet he stands his ground, that he doesn't budge an inch. I assume all this based on a single fact: he has the same build as Erling.

He fishes something from his jacket pocket and sets it on the table.

"It's a Dictaphone," he says. "Is that okay?"

"Yes," I say helplessly.

He presses some buttons and some small numbers appear on the display, counting up or down, preserving the conversation for posterity.

"So," he says. "I understand you had an unpleasant experience a few days ago. On Tjøme?"

"Yes," I say. "Yes, I was out there with a friend. Edvard Weimer. Who I also just had dinner with this evening."

Without wishing to, I notice that I blush as I say this. Gundersen says nothing, but I'm sure it won't have escaped him.

"The fire brigade say the hose between the gas container and the stove was old and cracked," he says. "Despite the fact that the tank was inspected a year ago, and at that point the hose was brand new."

"Yes," I say. "They told me that when I was there."

"So how do you make sense of this?"

I shrug, feeling weary.

"I mean, it seems like sabotage."

"Indeed it does, to put it mildly," he says. "It certainly seems this might have been done to harm someone."

I make no reply to this. I look at the grandfather clock. How long is he going to keep this up, how much longer before I can go and lie down?

"When were you last at the cabin?" he asks.

"Oh," I say. "Last year, in the autumn, I think. We hadn't readied the cabin for the summer season yet."

"And Erling?"

"The same, I think."

Something flutters through my consciousness, as if I'm back in Peter Bull-Clausen's meeting room for a moment. I don't want to mention it, it will only make everything all the more complicated, but nor do I think I can simply ignore it.

"Apparently, Erling bought two plots of land out there," I say. "Just before he died. He may well have gone out there to view them. But if he did, I know nothing about it."

"Right," Gundersen says, nodding. "I gather there have been some testamentary surprises."

To my astonishment, he pursues the matter no further. Instead, he asks:

"Who else has keys to the cabin?"

"The two of us," I say. "And the children each have one."

"So your son- and daughter-in-law also have access?"

"Yes. And our keys hang on the hook over here, so yes, if you came into the house, you could just . . ."

I stop myself. This is what it's come to, this is the way I've started to think.

"So who do you think replaced the hose?" he asks, in an almost offhanded manner.

"I don't know," I say. "God, I have no idea. I just don't understand any of this."

My eyelids almost close, I'm so sleepy.

"When did you last speak with Bilal Zou?" Gundersen asks.

"What was that?"

"Bilal Zou? You published some children's books together, around twenty, thirty years ago?"

"Oh, that's right – yes, we did."

I blink several times, as if coming to.

"I'm sorry, I'm just a little surprised. I haven't thought about Bilal in, oh, I don't know, years."

"I just spoke to him earlier today, you see," Gundersen says, just as casually. "And he told me that the last time the two of you spoke was in 1995, in connection with an exhibition of some of his paintings."

"Yes, that may well be true."

"You attended the opening, Bilal said, even though you weren't invited. And you argued with him."

A pressure asserts itself between my eyes; a headache creeping up on me.

"Bilal says you threatened him," Gundersen says. "He says you told him that if he refused to illustrate your book, then he ought to watch his back. That he owed you that much, and that you usually made sure people paid you what they owed."

"That's taken out of context," I say. "I didn't mean it like that."

"Bilal was afraid," Gundersen says. "He perceived your threat to be extremely serious."

"I was just a bit disappointed. Yes, I may have said a few things I shouldn't have, but I never *threatened* him."

I close my eyes. Think of him standing there, in the gallery, among all the paintings of tanks and bombers. How many glasses of bubbly had I drunk before I finally plucked up the courage to go over to him? Two, three? More? The humiliation of it – I had gone there uninvited to beg him. And he had rejected me with so little kindness. After that they had shown me the door, he and his agent with the lipstick. I ran the gauntlet towards the exit while all the

318

other guests looked away. Yes, of course I was upset. But I wasn't threatening. I believe that absolutely.

"A few weeks later, someone threw a home-made firebomb through the window of the same gallery," Gundersen said. "Did you know that?"

"No," I say, my eyes closed.

I listen to the ticking, silently willing him to leave.

"One of his paintings was destroyed. The bomb wasn't particularly effective – a Molotov cocktail. They're fairly easy to make, but difficult to get any great effect out of. The scope of the damage wasn't extensive – a broken window, a singed curtain and the painting. But yes. It frightened him."

"I'm sure it did."

I feel strangely removed from all this. As if I'm standing beside the terrace door, looking over at us.

"The police didn't investigate the matter very thoroughly back then, so nobody was caught. Bilal was disappointed. He had a few theories about who might be behind the attack. Were you aware of that?"

"No."

"He mentioned your name, actually. When I spoke to him earlier today."

"That's absurd," I say. "What do I know about making firebombs?"

"You don't need to know much to make one like that," Gundersen says. "Especially one that functioned as poorly as this one did."

"You mean you think I attacked a former colleague?"

I don't ask this with any form of indignation. I enunciate slowly, lazily.

"I'm just saying that that's what your former colleague thinks," Gundersen says. "And so I'm giving you the opportunity to tell me what you know about this."

"I know nothing," I say quietly. "Absolutely nothing."

"Have the boxes of pills turned up?"

"What?"

"Erling's medications? The ones that disappeared. Have you found them?"

"No."

"What about the bicycle?"

"Are you accusing me of something here?" I ask. "Because if you are, you may as well just come straight out with it."

Gundersen leans forward, sets his elbows on his knees. He has a penetrating gaze. He can seem restless and agitated, with all the energy trapped in that long body, but when it counts, he has the patience and precision of a sharpshooter. Then he holds your gaze without looking away. Yes, I think, he's a little like Erling in that respect. It's easy to think you've got him all figured out. But equally easy to underestimate him.

"This is a dangerous business, Evy," Gundersen says. "Playing around with firebombs and medicines and gas. This isn't something to be taken lightly. If you know something, I think you ought to tell me about it, right now."

Erling that morning. The problem he had managed to sort out, the person he was going to meet that afternoon. But he never made it that far.

"I know nothing," I say with my eyes closed. "Can I go and lie down now?"

TWENTY-TWO YEARS BEFORE

COLOURS OF SPRING, the banner outside the gallery read. It was the middle of the night, nobody else was around. The good citizens of the neighbourhood must have all been tucked up in their beds. I felt a little unsteady. I'd taken a few swigs from Erling's bottle of whiskey, but at the same time I was fully aware of what I was doing. Perhaps I'd never been so clear-headed in my life.

So he wouldn't help me? So I wasn't good enough for him? *Him* – the man who was drawing for little kids in nappies when I came across him. Now he was too good for all that, was that it? He no longer needed me – people were queueing up to work with him. He no longer needed childish stories with *an absence of literary merit*. Not him, with his *unique ability to communicate the deepest of human emotions*. Colours of Spring? What a load of crap.

With a Molotov cocktail, you use a rag as a wick. You have to completely soak it in lighter fuel, then stuff it into the bottle and stopper it. I had read about this in a magazine, but it was also perfectly logical: if you don't seal the bottle, the fuel might spray out when the weapon is thrown. In many cases over you, setting you ablaze. Once you've stoppered the bottle above the soaking rag, you can light the wick. And then you throw your weapon. Only then. But you have to know where to throw it. Don't trust the bottle to do the job by itself.

The little path that ran through the front garden to the gallery entrance was flanked by small, square stones. They were loose, so all I had to do was pick one up and toss it through the window. Aim with precision, without hesitation. The window rang; half the glass fell away and the alarm howled. And then, at that very instant, the bottle could be thrown. The rag ignited without issue. I raised my right arm, swept it back in an arc. Threw the bottle properly, with confidence – this was no weak underarm effort. I aimed well, too. The bottle, with its burning wick, sailed soundlessly through the empty window frame.

Then I turned on my heel and walked away. Collected Erling's bicycle, which I had parked a few blocks from the gallery. I cycled home with great difficulty. If anyone stopped me, I'd simply tell them I'd had a little too much to drink at a party. But nobody did. I let myself into the house as quietly as I could. When I got into bed, I felt Erling move; he groaned, but he didn't speak. I lay still, counting his breaths. Waiting for him to wake up, to ask me where I'd been. But he never did.

The following day, it felt unreal. I almost couldn't believe I had done it. Yes, I was upset, it bothered me that Bilal was now lauded, and the rejection still stung, but surely I would never have taken it upon myself to do something like that. I read the newspaper that morning; made sure to be tidying the kitchen while Erling watched the news on TV. If I had started a major fire, I would hear about it soon enough. When I didn't hear anything, I presumed nothing had come of it.

I rewrote the incident for myself: one evening, when I'd had a little too much to drink, I took Erling's bicycle into the city, to the gallery. In frustration, I threw the bottle from which I was drinking. That was it – littering on someone else's property. Not a very nice thing to do, but not a crime, either. Then I cycled home again and became a better person.

NINETEEN DAYS AFTER

Mother is sitting in front of the TV when I walk in. This time she's watching the snooker, well-dressed men with focused expressions creeping around a table; they assess, measure and take aim. Mother is watching them intently. She's wearing jogging bottoms and a knitted cardigan. Her thin, matted hair sticks out from her skull in clumps. This isn't my usual day to visit her. Do the staff know? Do they make less of an effort with her on the days they don't expect to see me?

"Hello, Mother," I say.

She doesn't answer. Keeps her eyes fixed on the men on the screen and their game. I take hold of the plastic chair and pull it alongside hers. See the edge of her incontinence pad above the waistband of her trousers, the expression her face has taken on: sceptical, angry. It's often made me want to cry. It's ten years since she became ill, and I lost something then, a source of support in my life that I really could have used. Especially now.

But at the same time, in this moment, I'm also in way too deep. She couldn't have helped me with this, no more than Olav can, no more than Edvard.

"Mother," I say, looking at her earnestly. "Mother, listen to me. Do you remember the dinner party at Easter?"

A low sound comes from her throat; she mumbles something, but doesn't look at me. It could just as easily be the snooker game she's reacting to.

"Mother," I say again. "The dinner we had – you know. When we were all at the house in Nordheimbakken. Do you remember?"

She casts a glance at me. Her eyes are irritated, not her own.

"What a load of shit," she says.

"Mother. You don't remember?"

I pick up the remote control from where it lies on the table before her and turn off the TV. She wasn't expecting this, and she gives me a questioning look.

"We were all there together," I say urgently. "Erling, Olav, Bridget. My children and their families. Do you remember? We drank yellow punch?"

"Piss yellow?" she asks.

"Sort of," I say. "But someone went through the double doors into Erling's study."

She nods, pensively, and I feel a wave of satisfaction crest at my breastbone – she remembers, I'm getting through to her.

"Who went in there, Mother?"

"Kari," she says.

"Kari is dead, Mother. Who went into the study?"

"Oh, Kari, what are you saying?"

I bite my lip, change tack.

"I'm just wondering who went into the study," I say. "At Evy's house."

"Evy," Mother says, and then: "it was much better before those . . . Those . . ."

She turns her attention to the television. Watches the blank screen as if the snooker game is still unfolding on it.

"Piss yellow," she says again.

"Yes," I say. "Piss-yellow punch."

"Haakon should never have been King," she says loudly.

I'm not sure what I'm supposed to do with this. I grip her hands; they're small and hard, bony. They grip mine in return. They're surprisingly strong.

"It was Evy," she says. "Evy went in there."

I hold my breath.

"Evy?"

She looks at me, stares intently into my eyes, and says: "Evy. That tart."

"No," I say, a little too loudly, my voice trembling. "No, Mother, who was it?"

"Tart."

"Who was it?"

I'm shouting now. I hold her hands, just as hard as she's holding mine, and shout at her.

"Who went into that room? Who was it, Mother?"

Now she looks afraid. Her eyes are wide, her mouth tense. Then she lifts a hand and slaps me across the face.

It happens so fast that I don't understand at first; I was completely unaware of what was coming. She didn't hit me hard – she has neither the strength nor the precision for that. But it stings all the same. She's never hit me before. I put my hand to my cheek.

Mother looks at me, her eyes so wide that the whites are visible all the way around the iris, and then she shouts: "Help! Help!"

"Mother," I say, on the verge of tears. "Mother."

"Help!"

A nurse appears in the doorway almost instantly.

"Is everything okay in here?"

I turn to face him, with tears in my eyes.

"Yes, yes," I say breathlessly. "Everything is absolutely fine."

Synne calls while I'm sitting in the car with the engine off. The car park is almost empty. I rest my head against the steering wheel, feeling the sting of Mother's hand against my cheek, and cry so hard my shoulders shake, what have I done, what have I done? Screaming at a defenceless old woman with dementia? Throwing firebombs? Drinking, neglecting my children, suspecting everyone I know of murder? In my mind's eye I try to see Mother during the Easter dinner, in her leggings and nice wool sweater, clothes she no longer recognises, rattling around in my house. In from the terrace, into the living room. Past the door to the kitchen, where I stood knocking back drink after drink, through the double doors and into the hallway. Towards the study. The door is half open. And there's someone in there. There *is* someone there. Not Erling, but who?

I imagine that it's me. That I'm the one standing there, swabbing a cloth dipped in something dangerous, something poisonous, over the keyboard of his computer. I imagine standing in the upstairs bathroom, tampering with his pills. Or out in the garage, taking a pair of wire cutters to the cables that lead to the brake pads of his bike.

But he left all the money to *me*. He told me he had taken care of the problem. It wasn't me he suspected.

To him, I would always be the schoolgirl from Røaveien, the young bride with the lilac bouquet. Not too long ago, he told me he thought he might have been too hard on the children when they were growing up, so it was lucky that they'd had me. *A blessing*, he even said. He must have seen my drinking, but despite that he meant this, truly, right until the end. And that wasn't so many weeks ago. It may, in fact, have been just days before he died.

"How are you?" Synne asks.

I try to pull myself together.

"Yes. Good."

But I sniff. I hiccup, short of breath. My body is shaking, and I'm unable to keep the tears from my voice.

"Where are you?" she asks.

"At the nursing home. In the car park."

I whisper into the receiver.

"I think I'm about to fall apart."

"Stay where you are," Synne says sternly. "I'm coming."

She drives me back to her house. I sit beside her in the passenger seat, wracked with sobs, but that sort of thing doesn't faze Synne. She was the chief flight attendant on international flights for two decades – she's coped with flight phobias and drunken outbursts and breakdowns and air rage. She's wiped up vomit and tears, calmed the angry and the afraid, comforted the anxious and the panicked.

I haven't seen much of her since she and Karsten moved to the apartment in Røa. That was just before the dinner at our place, when Synne and Erling came to blows. I probably took his side – or, no, I don't know. I don't think I actually took a position. Perhaps Synne thought being caught in the middle would be too hard for me. Wasn't that also how I started drinking again? Slowly but surely, the lonelier we became in the dark house in Montebello?

Synne's apartment is light and warm. Karsten is away on a business trip, she says, he won't be home until tomorrow morning – would I like to stay overnight? It would be really nice to have me there. For a moment I imagine her on my front step at Easter, and it occurs to me that she knows where the key to the garage is kept, she knows where the cabin on Tjøme is, and so on, but then I bat the thoughts away, because I can't take any more of this, I'm exhausted.

She sends me upstairs to take a bath. Gives me a glass of iced tea to take with me, and orders me to relax while she makes dinner.

But what would she say if she knew what I'm really like? Erling made up his mind about me once and for all; to him I was the diligent girl he had married and made into a good wife, a warm and caring mother. But others would judge me differently. Who was Erling, I have asked myself, but an equally good question is: who am I? I was once an innocent trainee teacher in a cheap bridal gown. What have I become?

Synne has made a pasta salad. She has poured two glasses of white wine, and I grip mine tightly. I'm going to stay in control tonight. Silje thinks I should seek help, but I'm going to show her. I'm perfectly capable of cutting down, it's no problem at all.

"So. Tell me," Synne says.

I glance at her.

"Tell you what?"

She throws her arms wide.

"Everything."

"Surely it's not so strange that I've been a bit out of it since Erling died," I say.

"Of course it isn't," she says. "That's to be expected. But there's something going on with you."

She places her small hands on the table. They're adorned with rings; her nails are painted scarlet.

"Don't you think you need to speak to someone, Evy?" she asks. "Someone outside the family?"

And then I tell her all of it. I tell her about the police coming to my door, about the post-mortem report that revealed Erling wasn't taking his medications, about the bicycle with the faulty brakes. I tell her what Edvard said about Erling fearing for his life, and how Erling never told me about their friendship. I tell her about the defective gas hose and the meeting with the lawyer, all the surprising arrangements Erling made, and what Edvard thinks of them. I mention that Gundersen came back, but say nothing about the Molotov cocktail or Bilal's gallery, and I omit the part about my children asking for money and telling me I drink too much. But I tell her that Olav called, and that my children are planning to contest the will. The more I speak, the more I find myself opening up, and it does me good, because she's right, Synne: the more I say, the more I feel the weight lifting from my shoulders, the less tense I feel. As if talking about it has the same relaxing effect on my body as a crying fit.

"Jesus," Synne says.

She pours me another glass of wine. I think I ought to pass, but I say nothing, and when it comes to the crunch, I take a sip.

"Anyway," she says, leaning forward, setting her thin forearms against the tabletop and smiling. "Tell me a bit more about this Edvard, why don't you?"

Erling thought Synne was *foolish* – his harshest judgement. And it's true that she's both impulsive and vivacious, a combination that has led to two wrecked marriages and several abruptly ended relationships with live-in partners. I'm not sure I want to be like her, or, rather, I *know* I don't want to be like her, that kind of life just isn't for me. But just a touch of her personality – that I would have liked. I think this as I'm telling her about Edvard. If I were Synne, I would make a move on him. Not necessarily now, so soon after Erling's death. But nor would I have waited too long. And I wouldn't have desisted because I wasn't sure how he felt, or what he wanted or was hoping for. Of course, there is self-preservation in failing to act. The person who doesn't ask can never be rejected. But the person who doesn't ask may never hear a *yes*, either – and who knows what they might be missing out on?

"How often have you actually felt head over heels in love, Evy?" Synne asks. "If you were to be completely honest about it?"

And what can I say to that? When Erling kissed me for the first time, in my bedroom in Røaveien, I felt butterflies – but what if I had known it would be my only first kiss? On the day I married, with the white lilacs – was I head over heels in love then? And other than that, have I made do with crumbs? What loving gestures has Erling deigned to grant me? Just how close have we been?

What if, back then, I had chosen differently and said yes to Edvard? If I had gone along to the nightclub, joined the party, met some boys? For a moment I imagine an alternate reality: Edvard and me in our youth, or middle age, wandering hand in hand down Strøget in Copenhagen, deep in conversation. I blink, and then it's gone. It's always seemed as though life simply had to work out the way it did, but there were once other possibilities. And when I've met up with Edvard over these past few weeks, haven't I felt invigorated? Haven't I dressed up a little bit, checked my reflection in the mirror before leaving the house?

That moment, when I left him yesterday. When he hugged me, holding me for just a little longer than is usual. Was there an opportunity there? What would have happened if I had plucked up my courage, turned towards him and kissed him?

"You have to do it," Synne giggles.

We've finished the bottle of wine, but she's fetched another from the fridge.

"I don't know," I say, blushing and feeling suddenly unsure. "What would people say?"

"Who gives a shit about what people say?" Synne says. "Let the neighbours talk, who cares?"

"What if I've completely misunderstood?" I ask. "What if this isn't his intention at all?"

"If you've misunderstood, well then you've misunderstood," she says. "You'll have given him a confidence boost, and that will be the end of it. But you haven't. I can feel it. There's something there. Nobody is so attentive towards a friend's widow just because they feel sorry for her."

She fills up my glass.

"Okay," I say. "Screw it. I'll do it."

While Synne watches over my shoulder, I send Edvard a text: *Hi! Would you like to meet for dinner tomorrow?* We're still sitting at the table when he replies: *That would be lovely. I'll book us a table for around 7.*

"Oh, my dear Mr Weimer," Synne squeals. "You have no idea what's heading your way!"

TWENTY-FIVE DAYS AFTER

They're here. I stand in the hallway, listening to their footsteps crunching on the gravel. The crunching stops, just outside the front door. I can hear their voices – not what they're saying, but I can tell they're speaking to one another. Hastily, in hushed tones. As if they're conferring.

Soon they'll ring the doorbell. My hands are trembling slightly, and this surprises me, because I feel calm. I haven't had a single drink today, and I'm not going to drink wine with dinner. I have to remain clear-headed. If I'm going to manage this, I cannot waver.

It's so close now. I take a breath, and at the same moment the grandfather clock strikes eight. The chimes are drawn out, a lamentation. When they die down, there is total silence. I count one second, count two. Then the doorbell cuts through the air.

TWENTY DAYS AFTER

The walls of the restaurant are covered in expensive wallpaper. Golden borders follow the skirting boards, and thin, glittering metallic bands stretch towards the ceiling. The chairs look comfortable, and there are small lamps placed on the tables, as if each one, with its white damask tablecloth, is its own little island. There he is, sitting at one of them. Waiting for me.

He's well dressed. Not looking at his phone, the way people usually do. Just sitting there looking out of the window, with a glass of water on the table before him. I have time to study him for a moment before he turns and sees me, and there's something good about seeing him like this, a man waiting. It feels good to know that I'm the one he's waiting for. When he sees me, he smiles, and his face opens up. I walk over to the table, and he gets up and hugs me. He smells good. Aftershave and soap, and something else, something lightly spiced.

"It's good to see you," he says.

"And you," I say, and I mean it with all my heart.

But I'm also a little nervous. What I'm about to do is so far removed from the way I usually behave. I'm on unstable ground; it feels intense and dangerous. And, good God, it's only twenty days since Erling died – that's nothing, nothing at all.

It isn't as if I think something necessarily has to happen *now*. But there's something about being honest about one's feelings. Taking a chance. It pounds at my temples, hard and fast, the thought of doing something like this, of being so forward.

But I wait a little. First we eat, and I mention that the police came to see me again. I don't say much about what Gundersen said, other than that he agreed that what happened at the cabin was serious. Edvard nods thoughtfully. I tell him that the children might contest the arrangements Erling made before he died, and that Olav is involved. At this, Edvard raises his eyebrows.

"I see," he says. "So that's the path they've chosen."

"Apparently they need money, all three of them," I say.

A certain vigilance comes over his face; a tension in his brow, something in his eyes. I regret mentioning the dispute – regret bringing my children into it. Because I understand how it must look. Olav asked me not to say anything about this to Edvard, and now I've gone and done it. And he's taking it all in, I can see that.

"But Edvard," I say. "They're my children. I raised them. I can't suspect them of something like this."

"I understand," he says.

But the tension in his forehead is still there. He's pondering something.

Only when dessert is on the table do I finally pluck up the courage. I've only had a single glass of wine, and I've drunk it slowly. I'm absolutely compos mentis.

"There's something I wanted to tell you," I say.

I pick at my serviette. I hardly dare look at him, but I cast a tiny glance across the table and see that he's listening.

As my fingers tear the serviette in two, then twist the pieces together to create a kind of rope, I tell him how much I've appreciated him being there for me over the past few weeks. How he has cared for me, taken me out, joined me on the trip to Tjøme. Shown an interest in what has been bothering me – helped me. And more than that: how he has been my friend. Stepped up when I needed him most. I cast another glance at him and see that he's smiling.

"It's been a pleasure," he says.

We sit like this for a moment. The little lamp illuminates the table between us. My blood surges through my veins so I can almost hear it, and my stomach twists, am I really going to do this? Should I go for it? My mouth goes dry, my breathing is shallow and feverish at the base of my throat, and I look at him and think yes, I'm going to do it, okay, here we go.

"So, yes," I say, looking at my serviette rope again. "And there's one more thing. Because, you see, I've started to care about you. As a friend. But perhaps also as something more."

I look up at him.

"Do you understand?" I say.

But his smile is no longer so wide. He looks serious. Nods, slowly. The tension in his brow is there again. And from somewhere deep in my belly an icy feeling begins to spread, *oh no*, I've misread the situation entirely, *oh no*, I've misunderstood, I'm a fool, an idiot, and how could I ever believe he saw me as anything else?

His silence is unbearable. It can't last more than a few seconds, but the icy feeling is creeping beneath my skin to cover my entire body, to overpower me, so much so that I could pick up the fork from beside my plate and thrust it into my own hand, through the flesh and tissue so that it sticks deep into the tabletop, so the damask tablecloth turns red with blood, just so I can feel something else. Edvard takes a breath. He's about to answer me, but I don't want to hear what he has to say, I already know that nothing good will come of it. But now that I've set these wheels in motion, presumably I have to hear him out. I have no choice. So I simply sit there, staring intensely at the fork, steeling myself.

"That's such a compliment you've given me, Evy," he says, in his

345

soft, pleasant voice. "But unfortunately, I'm unable to reciprocate it. Because you see, I'm gay."

The world stops.

"I thought you knew," Edvard says. "I just presumed Erling would have told you."

And then the restaurant collapses around us. The golden-striped walls are reduced to dust. The guests vaporise, leaving only the two of us sitting there. And I would give anything – truly anything at all – to disappear with all the others. To turn to dust, to scatter on the air and vanish.

"No," I say, my voice unsteady. "Erling never mentioned it."

My hand trembles as I reach for my handbag; I see it, and he sees it, too. My knees are weak as I stand.

"Evy, wait."

He stretches a hand out towards me, but I've already got up, I'm already leaving, because I can't stay sitting there, no, I know that all too well, I cannot spend another minute in this restaurant. It feels like a matter of life and death, as it was at the cabin on Tjøme that day: get out, or go under.

"Can't we talk about this?" he asks.

But no, we can't. There's no more to say, and by Christ I don't want to hear any more. I manage to squeeze a *speak to you soon* from between my dry lips and stagger away, past the other lamplit tables and out of the restaurant, out onto the street. I look around blindly for a taxi to help me, to take me away, take me home.

And I think: there were no photographs of his wife in his apartment. But there was a photo of a man. It seemed so random, there on the sideboard in the living room between photographs of his parents. And I think, he never said *she*. Not a single word to convey the gender of the partner who died of cancer. I simply assumed.

And I think, as the taxi I finally find carries me away from the city centre, towards the gloomy house on the hill: that day in my room in Røaveien, in the early seventies, when he knocked on the door and asked if we wanted to join them. Was it *me* he was looking at then? Or was he actually looking over my shoulder, at Erling?

I have returned to that moment so many times. Probably given it too much weight, viewed it as more defining than it actually was, but that is indeed how I've thought of it – I believed it said something about my life.

But now it turns out I misunderstood the entire thing. This critical moment had nothing to do with me at all. The attractive young man I thought was asking me out was actually interested in my boyfriend. Not even *this* was mine. The invitation, with all the weight I gave it, was actually intended for someone else. I was just a bystander.

TWENTY-ONE, POSSIBLY
TWENTY-TWO DAYS AFTER

I'm lying on the baby-blue sofa. I've pulled the blanket I usually use to hide the worn armrest over my body, because what does it matter? I'm watching TV, what appears to be a soap opera. I have no idea what it's about. All these rich, attractive people on the screen seem to be deeply unhappy, but I don't understand why.

I have finally opened the box of pills. Now I doze my way through the days, cocooned in sweet indifference. Because what does any of this matter?

Hanne called. A few hours ago, I think, but it may have been yesterday, the days all merge into one. She just wanted to talk. Or maybe she had something on her mind. Her voice was brusque.

"Have you been drinking?" she asked.

I don't remember how I answered her, but I don't think I bothered to deny it. We didn't speak for long. The phone lines must be hot again by now – she's probably called Bård, and Silje, too. Bård has probably called Olav, who will have called Hanne, and so on. Let them carry on as they please. Why should I clean up my act? The children are grown up, they can look after themselves. Erling is gone – Edvard is gone, too – and Mother is in the process of disappearing. Nobody needs me anymore, and I need nothing but this: the TV, the sofa, my pills. The box of red wine. This soft intoxication, nothing matters anymore.

Edvard called. I didn't pick up the phone. He left a message, but I didn't listen to it, just deleted it straight away. I can still, even in this pit of indifference, feel the humiliation from the restaurant burning beneath my skin: what a wretched sight I must have been. What on earth was I thinking? Stupid woman, who has nothing to show for her life but an *absence of literary merit*. Who has never managed to hold down a job. Who is a drunkard, who has puffy skin from all the drinking, who has let life pass her by. I failed to take care of the husband I had, failed to take care of my possessions, failed to take care of my children. I didn't even manage to take care of myself. Why would someone as attractive as Edvard – so successful, so undoubtedly sought-after – have fallen for me? It would have been out of the question even if he were interested in women. I understand them now, my children. Understand why they smirked at the whole idea. Hanne, who presumed Edvard was after me for my money; Bård, who found the very thought that someone could fall for me uproariously funny. They were right. I was the only one who didn't see it.

Because I was sozzled, in all probability. All the drinking must have affected my brain; left me dull, self-obsessed.

So what else is there to do but drink even more? I've been so good since Erling died. Hardly drunk anything at all. I didn't even touch the pills. And what good has it done me? I've gone and got myself mixed up in things that are worse, more painful, than the situation I was already in. I may as well just throw in the towel. May as well just wallow in my own self-loathing. Isn't that my right?

Synne called, too. I didn't answer. I sent her a message: *Edvard is gay*. She called again, and when I still didn't pick up, she wrote: *Really?? But then it was nothing to do with you, at least*. Then she asked how I was doing, and told me to call her.

In the end, she turned up at the front door. I didn't open it, and I'd already brought in the spare key. She walked around to the terrace door and knocked on the window. I was lying on the sofa, as I am now – she saw me, saw that I saw her, and then I had no choice but to let her in. She talked, and I let her drone on. Dozed as she spoke. Refused to be tempted by her pseudo-feminism, *you don't need a man, what a fool to not be honest from the start.* What does it matter? It's all just empty words, just flattery and hollow self-delusion. I wanted to sleep. Wanted her to leave. In the end, I told her as much: Would you please just go? Could you just leave me in peace?

"I'm worried about you, Evy," she said.

"I'm doing fine," I said. "I just want to be alone."

In the end, she left. What else could she do?

Since then, it's been quiet. With the exception of Hanne, that is, who called. Was that before or after Synne came over, I'm not sure. She hasn't called again. The others haven't called, either.

Finally darkness begins to fall outside. I don't know what day it is, and I'm not entirely sure what time it is, either, but if it's starting to get dark, then it's evening. With the blanket around my shoulders, I drag my body up the stairs. Oh, these weary old bones, I'm so heavy, so slow. In my hand I clutch the box of pills. It makes no difference to me whether someone has tampered with my medications, too, no difference to me if I kick the bucket. Let me just die, let my children fight over what's left. Let my brother attempt to pacify them, if he's so righteous. I surrender, I can't take any more.

But it doesn't seem that there's anything wrong with my pills. They make me drowsy and indifferent. Permit me to sleep, permit me to slip away.

TWENTY-THREE DAYS AFTER

I wake, half-naked, and I know that I'm in the apartment in Paris. Someone's lying beside me, but I don't look at him. Still, I have the impression that I know who it is, and that it's not who I would expect it to be. But I don't turn my head to check. Instead, I fix my eyes on the open door. It leads out to the living room, and it's calling to me, pulling me towards it. I get up. On unsteady legs, I walk towards it, then through it and into the living room.

The room is larger, more open than I remember. Canvases stand propped up against the walls, I can just make out a figure on one of them, tall and straight, with muscular arms, or perhaps branches. There's no-one lying on the sofa. I turn back to the room from which I came, but it's gone, the door is no longer there, there's only a wall, and I understand that I can't go back.

But there is someone in the kitchen. I hear a voice say my name, and I think to myself: it's Edvard! I move towards the kitchen door. I want to find him, to throw myself into his arms. To let him save me.

To my surprise, I see that I'm in the kitchen of the house in Montebello. I see the old pine cabinets; my mother-in-law's tiles. A man is standing at the kitchen counter. He has his back to me. It's Edvard, I think, and I'm happy – now I'm saved. But then he turns around, and I see that it's Erling.

Erling stands there and looks at me with his steel-grey eyes. There's a generosity in them that I had completely forgotten. Kind Erling, who only wants the best for me. It makes me happy to see him. I want to say something to him, to tell him something, but then I see that his eyes are wide open and afraid. He looks at me.

"Run, Evy," he says.

"But don't you want to come with me?" I say.

He shakes his head, raises his voice. "Run!"

There's not a sound to be heard when I wake, nothing beeping or blaring, no alarm, and still I've been jolted from sleep, even in my drugged state. As if it really *was* Erling who woke me. And that's when the smell hits me.

The stench is hard, acrid. Like steel, I think. Not a smell I recognise, but I know instinctively that it's a warning, that this is dangerous. I sit up. I don't feel completely out of it, I must have forgotten to take the last pill, must have stopped drinking and gone to bed earlier than I thought.

I get to my feet. Nausea laps at the base of my throat, but I swallow it down, stagger out onto the landing, fumbling my way along the banister – and then I see it. An unfamiliar light flickers against the staircase wall. A stronger, heavier smell floats up from downstairs. There's a crackling, a cracking sound.

The stair treads are hard against my bare feet; after just a few steps, the heat hits me. My breathing becomes quick and shallow – this is really happening, this is serious. I take the stairs with rapid steps, running, as Erling urged me to in the dream. See something flickering through the study door which stands ajar. I look inside and see it, an intense glimpse from the corner of my eye: behind the desk the curtains are ablaze, the flames rising from the floor, sharp and orange.

But I do not stop. I don't hesitate for even a millisecond. No – I do as Erling told me to: I run. Through the double doors, past the kitchen, out into the living room. I grab my phone from where it lies on the coffee table beside the whiskey glass, unlock the terrace door and storm out into the garden.

I once read that poisoning is the most common cause of death in connection with fires. That it isn't usually the flames that kill you, but the gases that are released as the flames consume your home. I stand on the grass as if paralysed. I've called the fire brigade, they're on their way, will be here in a few minutes. They've asked me to wait, and what else is there to do? My breathing is quick and panicked. At the side of the house the light flickers, but otherwise the fire isn't easy to spot from out here. The flames crackle and spit, but other than that there is only silence, calm.

And then there's a rustling from the bushes behind me. It's coming from the path behind the house – someone is moving back there. The path travels between the gardens and hedges to Morgedalsveien, and now the foliage is trembling. Because someone is pushing branches aside. Because there's someone there. Because the person who was in my house is now fleeing down the path.

And then a furious rage surges up in me – how dare they! The house is mine, Erling was mine. And I refuse to stand here and take this.

Quick as a flash I cross the garden, running barefoot over the cold, damp grass. I see the study window hanging open on its hinges, the orange, flickering glimmer of the flames. As I reach the path, I see the figure.

It all happens so fast – all I see is a dark shadow that vanishes – but I *saw* him. Him or her. I take a deep breath and it hurts – I *saw* this person, they exist. This isn't just a theoretical presence, the product of a paranoid brain, Erling's or Edvard's or mine. An *actual* person. They were slipping away down the path, and they came from my property, from the garden around the house, where the open study window is dangling on its hinges. I'm shaking, I can feel the adrenaline in my arms and the tears that squeeze my throat – and then I set off after the intruder. The leaves are wet with dew, they slap against my arms, paw at my nightgown.

But Morgedalsveien is empty. I emerge from the path, mouth agape as I look up and down the road, but there's nobody here, the street is deserted. A short distance away I hear a car start. A dog barks up by Makrellbekken. I stand there panting in my night-dress, and it's so peaceful, so completely ordinary and calm, as my breath moves heavily and painfully up and down my throat. And then I hear the sirens.

It's called a Molotov cocktail, a handsome young firefighter informs me.

We're sitting on the terrace, where the family gathered for the Easter dinner party a few weeks before That Day. His colleagues are stomping around my house. But more calmly now, is the impression I get. The firefighter tells me that they've put out the fire, and that the damage isn't extensive, in spite of everything: Erling's study is a mess, the floor and walls are scorched and all the furniture is ruined, but the door was almost closed, so the damage to the hall-way outside is relatively modest. The rest of the house is apparently unscathed, and luckily there is nothing to indicate that the fire has managed to eat its way through to the load-bearing joists.

The police officers who come are younger than Gundersen. In uniform, too. The one who interviews me is intense, he leans for-ward eagerly when he speaks, and has a high, slightly nervous voice. I'm not sure I can really blame him for his enthusiasm. It's certainly inappropriate, but I'm sure he doesn't often come across firebombs on the west side of Oslo. He asks, as the firefighter predicted, whether I know of anyone who might want to harm me. I hesitate.

Then it occurs to me that Gundersen asked me the very same question the first time I met him, but at that time it was about Erling. Back then I had replied forthrightly, *there's nobody who would have anything against us.* The thought was ridiculous. That was only a couple of weeks ago.

I tell the intense policeman about Erling's death, and about the gas leak. I give him Gundersen's name, suggest he get in touch with him. I can feel it in my gut – Gundersen will tell him about what Bilal said, which Gundersen obviously believes: that I threw a Molotov cocktail into Bilal's exhibition in the nineties. Now someone has thrown a similar firebomb into my house. Will that ease their suspicions against me? Or strengthen them? Maybe it will look as if I did this myself.

And could I have? I've been out of it for several days. I'm unable to properly account for myself. If I close my eyes, I can still see that night outside the gallery in Frogner. Are there images in my mind from tonight? I collapsed into bed. Could I have got up again? Gone downstairs, opened the window to the study nice and wide? Taken a bottle of whiskey, found a dishcloth and soaked it in the spirits. Put a lighter in my pocket, gone out into the garden, round to the study window. Raised my arm, and thrown. Watched the burning bottle sail through the air and through the window, heard the jangling crash as it smashed against my father-in-law's desk. And then gone back upstairs and got back into bed?

Was that why the dream woke me? Did I know that I was in danger? Can I really have been so unaware? Have I drunk myself into oblivion, done things in my intoxicated state that have later vanished from my consciousness? Are there blanks in my memory?

But I *saw* someone. There on the path behind the house. I saw a person, a dark shadow running away. Surely I can't have imagined that?

And then I feel it, in the depths of my being – just how alone I am. I begin to sob uncontrollably, here, in front of the eager police-man. No-one is on my side. Not my brother, not my children, not my mother. Not Edvard, either – not anymore. Not Erling. Erling, who had been by my side since I was a teenager. I might not always have leaned on him, and perhaps he didn't always lean on me, either. Maybe it wasn't always so good, this marriage of ours. But he's been there. He hasn't always managed to do what was best for me, but he was never less than willing. Erling has always wished me well.

"I'm sorry," I gasp to the intense policeman between the sobs.

"It's okay," I hear him say as my vision wavers and I lean over and throw up onto the terrace floor.

The man who lets me back into my house ten hours later is an older firefighter. He speaks with a broad Eastern dialect, running a hand through his grey curls.

"The house is serviceable enough," he says. "With the exception of the room where the fire started. But I'm not sure I would stay here right now. You never know what kinds of gases might be lingering. Especially in an old house."

I ponder this. I've spent a few hours of the morning asleep in Synne and Karsten's guest room. The police drove me over there at around five o'clock. Synne came to the door in her dressing gown and let me sleep on their surprisingly comfortable sofa bed.

I haven't touched the pills. And I'm not going to drink anything today, that's for sure. Things are serious now. I can't afford to slip up.

"Thank you," I say to the firefighter. "But this is my house. This is where I live. Where else am I going to go?"

He nods, thoughtfully. He probably thinks I'm crazy, but he's polite enough not to show it.

"I'll wait here," he says. "The study is cordoned off, but otherwise you can go anywhere you please."

He goes out onto the front step, and I hear the door slam shut behind him.

There are no longer any pills in the bathroom upstairs. Erling's are gone; my box is in the bedroom. I pick up the photograph of the children that stands on the chest of drawers. Bård must be around ten, Hanne perhaps eight. Silje is sitting on Hanne's lap, a happy, chubby one-year-old. I want to hold on to this.

Then I go downstairs. I steel myself; I know what I have to do. I pass the police tape that cordons off the study. Walk over to the cellar stairs, stick the key into the lock and open it. Wrinkle my nose at the mouldy air that floats up to greet me. Then I turn on the light, and go down.

The steps are concrete, cast when the house was built, around eighty or ninety years ago. The entire cellar is damp – everything we store down here reeks of it when we bring it back up again, and that's why we use it for nothing but junk. The stench of rotten apples mixes with the burnt smell of the fire and I feel a gag making its way up my throat, but I pull myself together.

I remember when he brought us down here. It must have been two, maybe three years ago, and it was just us. No partners, no grandchildren. Just the five of us. He made us memorise everything, harping on and on. He was so intense. The children and I exchanged glances – Pappa must be losing his mind.

There are three storerooms down here. The first is full of furniture. The second contains empty apple crates and sports equipment. In the third are discarded household items Erling believed we should save, perhaps repair – maybe use one day. Broken electronics, old lamps. Sets of chipped cups and cracked dishes. And the safe.

I start in the second storeroom, as Erling instructed, picking my way between skis and old kids' bicycles – they're heavy and scratch me as I lift them. A spider darts out and disappears under some old sledges when I move the apple crates. At the very back, behind the stack of crates, I find the little tin box with its flowery pattern, which contains the key.

Erling's instructions state that you then have to go into the first storeroom. The key from the tin box is a perfect fit for the bottom drawer of my mother-in-law's old linen cupboard. The jewellery box that lies inside it is white with gold fittings, so delicate and old-fashioned, but its padlock is the kind people use on their lockers at gyms, with a numerical code. I turn the wheels to the numbers Erling impressed upon us: 1970. The year we met. In the jewellery box is yet another key. This one is larger, and looks more solid. I clutch it in my hand.

The safe doesn't become visible until you're some way into the third storeroom – it's hidden behind all the junk. To find it, you have to know it's there. On the door there's a lock with eight number wheels and a keyhole. First I set the wheels to the eight-digit code: the year each of our children was born, plus 70 again. Perhaps he considered it a birth year of sorts for us as a couple, or maybe for the family itself. It's a comforting thought. I stick the key from the linen cabinet into the keyhole and turn it. Something clicks in the lock, and then the door jumps out a little, so I can allow it to soundlessly swing open on its hinges.

Inside are the rows upon rows of canned foods – Erling believed they would be invaluable in the event of the upcoming and unavoidable climate apocalypse. There are the bottles of water, the gas burner and the dry goods. The old metal cash box – the kind of thing you use when selling coffee at handball games or manning a stall at a flea market. In a way I already know what's coming, but there's still the possibility that I'm wrong, and my hand shakes as I open the box.

The box is empty. Seventy thousand kroner in cash is missing.

Someone has been down here and taken it, perhaps leaving the cellar door ajar as they left. And it can't be anyone but one of the five of us. If Ørjan or Lise or Olav had been told about the safe, getting access would have required such comprehensive

365

instructions that one of us must have been in on it. And Erling is dead – there are only four of us left.

I lean against the safe as I get up. My knees are weak and I stagger for a moment. Reach out with my other hand, and use the handlebars of an old bicycle for support. I stand this way for a moment and breathe, regaining my balance. When I look down at my hand, at what I'm leaning against, there's something familiar about the handlebars. There's tape on them where you're supposed to put your hands. Then it dawns on me, slowly but somehow all at once: this is Erling's bicycle. The one he was riding when he died, the one that carried him down the hill on Sondrevegen and ended up lying there with one wheel off the ground. The bicycle that was standing outside my garage when I came home from the hospital That Day, and which then disappeared.

I let go. Simply stand there, staring at it. As if it's dangerous, as if I'm afraid that it acted of its own accord. It's been down here, hidden behind all the clutter. My breathing becomes more even again, and the bicycle stands there, utterly still. I crouch down, run my fingertips along the brake pads.

Beside the rear wheel of the bicycle there's a plastic bag from a supermarket. It isn't full, but nor is it empty – it bulges here and there. I pull it along the floor towards me. Open it with numb hands, white fingers. Peer into it, slowly, so slowly. There are several things inside: a couple of boxes and a bottle of pills with Erling's name on them. A kind of rubber hose, which may well be the kind used to supply gas, manufactured from some colourful, brand-new material. And an appointment book, with all its pages ripped out.

This time, he sees me the moment I arrive. He squints at the sun, then gets up and stands in front of the bench looking almost puzzled, his palms turned towards me, passive and a little awkward. The path up the slope is steep; my pulse is elevated, but it's a small price to pay, the view will be worth the effort. You can see all of Oslo from here. It was Synne who first showed me this place, more than forty years ago. A hilltop in Vettakollen, with unrivalled views of the city.

"My dear Evy," he says when I'm close enough to hear him. "I'm so glad you called."

I pause to get my breath back; turn to face the view. The weather is glorious today. A little hazy, but that will lift as the sun climbs higher. From here we can see the huge bowl in which Oslo sits, all the streets and buildings that make up this city of ours. The harbour basin, the islands, the deep green hills. The silver-blue arm of the fjord reaching for the sea, our artery to Copenhagen, to Paris, to the rest of the world. I smile at him. And it doesn't really hurt all that much. It feels okay.

We sit down. I open my bag, take out the thermos and cups. Pour coffee for each of us.

"I'd really like to explain," Edvard says.

"You don't have to," I say. "I think I understand."

"Still," he says. "If you have no objections."

He's almost always known, he tells me. But back in the sixties, of course, it was an altogether different matter. There weren't exactly

367

educational leaflets in schools, and let's not forget that he came from an extremely conservative family. He was expected to follow in his father's footsteps, so he thought he'd better just do the best he could under the circumstances. Qualify as a lawyer, find a nice girl, have a couple of kids. There were places you could go, to live out that other side of yourself. You could be discreet. He thought that was how it had to be.

But then, as a university student, he found new friends. Along came Erling Krogh: tall, dark and handsome. A little withdrawn, a little shy, but smart, and with the courage of his convictions. They became fast friends, and Edvard felt there was something more there, too. Something to do with how his friend occasionally held his gaze, or laughed at a joke only the two of them could understand. There was something there, Edvard had thought, and so he did what he knew, sooner or later, he would have to do: he tried to kiss Erling.

"Erling didn't take it well," he says with a flat, sad smile.

There's a trembling in his jaw. This rejection, now more than forty-five years past. He fled the country to get away from it, it changed the course of his life. It still affects him – I can see that – and I avert my eyes, as if I'm being presented with something so naked it's improper to continue to look.

"What I have understood in retrospect," he says after a little while, "after the evening at the restaurant, when it dawned on me that you truly didn't know, is that Erling kept my secret to such an extent that he didn't even share it with you."

Edvard looks out across the fjord. He passes a hand over his jaw, wipes away the tremor.

"But if you thought I knew, why didn't you just say something?" I ask. "After all, you told me about your . . . partner. But I'm fairly sure that you never said *him*."

A tiny uncertainty itches behind my ear: can I be certain, could I have been drinking?

"When you grow up the way I did, you develop a kind of sixth sense," Edvard says, and now he actually gives a little smile. "You learn to use neutral language in situations where you aren't entirely sure. So you can share what's on your mind, be entirely truthful. And at the same time, not disclose anything."

His name was Søren, Edvard says. He was seven years older than Edvard, also a lawyer, and he worked as a political activist. Søren was loud and charismatic – somewhat crude, but extremely funny. He helped Edvard to shake off his shame, to peel away the conservative ideas that had been forced upon him. Edvard was twenty-two when they met; he grew up alongside him.

"I was younger than you when I ended up alone," he says. "If I can put it that way. Not to belittle the immensity of the love we shared, but I wouldn't change anything – it taught me how to manage on my own."

And this I can understand. For a while we sit there, drinking our coffee, looking at the view.

"It took me a few years of being in Oslo to pluck up the courage to contact Erling," Edvard says finally. "I had no idea what I could expect from him, but I knew I didn't want to live with never having tried."

Erling accepted his invitation, and they began to meet up – not often, but regularly. They talked about work, first and foremost, but they also told one another about their lives. Edvard spoke about his father. Erling talked about me.

"What did he say?" I ask lamely.

"Oh," Edvard says with a laugh. "What do men like Erling say about their wives? Nothing but words of the utmost honour and praise, of course."

I smile. Erling boasted unrestrainedly about the kind of wife I was, the kind of mother. Because that was how our family life appeared to him. There's something beautiful about this, and at the same time, something a little sad: when it came to me, the old realist never could see clearly.

"Could I ask you something?" I say. "About you and Erling. These dinners of yours. Was there ever anything . . . you know. Anything more between you?"

For a moment he looks at me, astonished, and then he begins to laugh.

"I'm sorry," he says, still with laughter in his voice. "But Evy, can you really imagine Erling cheating on you? With *anyone*? Not to mention someone like me?"

"Okay," I say, smiling. "I'll take that as a no."

"You can do that with absolute confidence."

"But then I don't understand why you didn't just tell me," I say. "Or why he didn't."

"As for Erling, I can only guess. And at the risk of crossing a line here – I think if he thought you had, you know, any kinds of feelings for me when we were young, he would have preferred not to bring me up. I got the impression that he didn't feel entirely secure when it came to you. Didn't you leave him once? I think that still affected him."

I remember how hard Erling had embraced me when I came home from Paris. Erling, who was otherwise so sparing with his acts of love. He held me and held me, and wouldn't let go.

"And as for me," Edvard says, "I think I thought it was sort of up to you. That since you hadn't asked, maybe you just didn't want to talk about it. Apropos the somewhat strict treatment this kind of thing received when we were young."

"It wouldn't have bothered me in the slightest."

"Still," Edvard says. "And if you really didn't know, I wasn't sure how you would take it, so soon after Erling's death. I don't know. I thought I ought to give you a little time. I had no idea that you might . . ."

He casts a quick glance at me, then peers into his coffee cup again.

'. . . come to develop certain feelings."

The shame of the evening at the restaurant surges over me again. My hopeless declaration of love, which still makes me blush. Presumably this is just part and parcel of the experience when you accept the invitations life offers you, but nobody can say that it doesn't sting. Edvard clears his throat.

"The last time I met with Erling – it was in April, just a few weeks before he died, when he suspected that someone was out to get him – I asked him whether he thought it might be me. You know – I had to know for sure. And you should have seen him shake his head then, Evy. I've never seen anyone deny something more vehemently. No, I've never believed that I was the one he suspected. But he did have suspicions about *someone*. And by that point, they were limited to a single person. He believed he had come up with a cunning plan to disarm the individual in question, but first, he had to be certain he was right. What happened next we can only guess at. I felt a little uneasy when we parted ways on that last evening. And when Erling died a short time afterwards, I called a friend of mine on the police force. Gunnar Gundersen Dale, who you now know. I asked him to make a few enquiries. Not to open an investigation, necessarily, but just to do a little asking around. I explained to him that I had reason to suspect something."

"Yes," I say. "But I think Gundersen mainly suspects me."

Edvard thinks about this.

"Well, the police have to draw their own conclusions," he says. "And you could say that Gundersen is more impartial than me. But

I have complete belief in what Erling told me. He didn't suspect you, not for a moment. And therefore nor do I."

He takes a deep breath. Holds it in for a good while, then releases it in a long sigh. For a time we sit beside one another in silence, looking out over the city. The mist is lifting, the sun gaining ground.

"So now you know all there is to know about my role in the investigation, too," Edvard says. "And I'm sorry I didn't tell you all this until now."

"That's okay," I say. "But this isn't what I came here to talk about."

He turns to face me.

"It isn't?"

"No. I came because I need your help."

I clear my throat. Set down my cup of coffee.

"There's something I have to do," I say. "And I need you to help me do it."

TWENTY-FIVE DAYS AFTER

The grandfather clock has just sounded its eighth chime when the doorbell rings. I cast a final glance at the set table. I quickly run my finger over the envelope taped to the underside of the tabletop, and with the greatest of care, I touch the knife beside it. I brush invisible dust from my blouse and take a breath. And then I get up to go and open the door.

They're standing there on the doorstep, all three of them. They've arrived together, in the same car, and they're smiling. Hanne says it's so nice that we're doing this, just us. Then they embrace me in turn. Bård hugs me weakly, is the only thing – it's as if we hardly touch. But otherwise, an atmosphere of tolerance suffuses their arrival. As if none of us is aware that they're conspiring with my brother to take what Erling has left to me. Nobody would ever guess this to look at us. And none of them mention the smell of smoke, despite the fact that the air in the hallway remains thick with it. They hang up their coats, speaking in friendly voices.

"Is this where the fire started?" Silje says, once we've made it into the hallway.

"No," I say. "It was in Pappa's study."

I open the double doors. Now the acrid smell wafts towards us, sour and nauseating. Hanne coughs and puts a hand over her mouth. Bård pulls a face. Silje seems startled, but she goes in anyway. The other two follow after her; I bring up the rear. We stand there in the doorway to the ruins of the study. Peer inside, at the charred curtains, the remnants of the scorched rug. The ruined walls, floor and ceiling.

"Wow," Hanne says.

"Jesus," Bård says. "But hopefully the insurance will cover most of it?"

Silje says nothing. She simply stares. I imagine the ruined study appearing on one of her canvases.

"The police believe it was started intentionally," I say.

Nobody says anything to this.

"Shall we go sit down?" I say. "The food is ready. And thankfully, the smell isn't as strong in the dining room."

The table is covered with a damask tablecloth. Candles burn in the holders.

"How lovely, Mamma," Hanne says.

"Please, have a seat," I say.

I take my customary seat at the table; lay claim to it. And the children are obedient, each taking the place that was theirs when they were small. Hanne and Silje on one side, Bård on the other, Erling and I at either end. I've set a vase of flowers in front of Erling's empty chair. Lilacs. Maria Berger has a bush in her garden that is currently in bloom, and when I asked if I could pick a few, she enthusiastically agreed.

Hanne glances at Erling's chair. Bård sees this and does the same, and then we sit there, all four of us, looking at it.

"Uff," Hanne says. "It sort of feels as if we're waiting for Pappa."

"The flowers are nice, Mamma," Silje says. "As if he's still here."

I'm sure she means this to be a comforting thought, but for a tiny moment it hangs between us, as if Erling's ghost is walking slowly through the dining room. As if the ticking of the grandfather clock is actually his footsteps. It lasts for just a moment, but the eeriness lingers on their faces.

"So," I say, as lightly as I can. "I'll go get the food. I hope you're hungry."

I let the meal unfold, saying nothing regarding what's about to happen. The chicken I serve has been carefully prepared. It is properly cooked through, but still juicy. Everyone helps themselves, but nobody takes much. The conversation falters a little, limping along. I stay quiet, listening carefully to what they say, taking everything in. But there's no denying that I'm nervous. I'm preparing myself, one could say.

Hanne takes charge of the situation. She tells us about something that's going on at work, a conflict with one of the employees who has been on sick leave for a long time, and who is now demanding this and that from the organisation. Bård permits himself to be lured into the conversation, because this is the kind of thing he has no patience for – employers must be able to make certain demands. Silje, as is her wont, takes the opposite stance: has anyone considered that what the employee is demanding may actually be entirely reasonable? Glances are exchanged between my two eldest children, and Hanne puts on her most charming voice as she attempts to explain the particulars of the matter to her little sister. Silje refuses to be enlightened, and Hanne, who probably wants the dinner to proceed peacefully, lets the subject drop. Then there is silence.

"It's nice and warm this evening," Hanne says finally.

From the living room we hear the grandfather clock strike nine.

"Oh," Silje says. "That sound always reminds me of when we were young."

"I've always found it rather gloomy," Bård says.

I serve cloudberries and cream for dessert, the dish I would produce as a special treat when they were small. The dessert mother usually served on the major occasions: Christmas, Easter, anniversaries. But I can't see Hanne or Bård dishing it up for their offspring. Some traditions die out, and maybe that's just how it has to be.

It's fairly quiet around the table now; all that can be heard is the scraping of spoons against the glass bowls. As it begins to die down, I clear my throat. They turn towards me, all three of them. As if they suspected something was coming.

And I see each of them so clearly. I see every strand of hair in Silje's tousled mane, the flecks of paint on her strong, mannish hands. See the glow of the candles reflected in Hanne's glossy, neatly blow-dried hair, which is the colour my own once was. I see how the draught from the half-open terrace door causes goose pimples to rise on the skin of Bård's neck, beneath his greying curls. I see the fine, blonde hairs that cover his hands, all the way up to the watch around his wrist, the one Erling and I gave him as a graduation gift.

"So," I say.

My voice is surprisingly level. I might be nervous, but I'm also ready. I know what I have to do.

"There's something we have to talk about."

"Just before Pappa died," I say, "he told a good friend he was afraid someone was trying to harm him. On the day he died, he told me over breakfast that he had found a solution to a difficult problem, and that he was going to inform the person concerned later that day. Unfortunately, he never got that far. Now he's dead, and under circumstances that are suspicious enough to make one think the person who was out to get him beat him to it."

"But this is . . ." Bård starts.

"I'd like to finish what I have to say," I say. "You'll have the opportunity to ask questions afterwards, but I'd appreciate it if you could listen for a minute first."

This is teaching technique 101: let your students know what you expect of them, provide certainty. My son closes his mouth. He raises his eyebrows and shakes his head, but he holds his tongue and listens.

"A little over three weeks has passed since Pappa died," I say. "And in that time, a lot has happened."

I close my eyes for a moment. Think of the restaurant with the gold-striped wallpaper, where I shamelessly threw myself at the first man to show me a little attention. I replay Silje's voice that day in her apartment: *You're actually pretty far gone.*

"We've all learned what Pappa chose to do with his assets," I say. "And in addition to this, there have been what I believe to be two attempts on my life."

Every one of them draws a sharp breath; it creates a unified sound.

"The gas leak at the cabin *may* have been directed at Pappa,"

I say. "But if that were the case, I imagine that the person who was out to get him would have put everything back to normal as quickly as possible. So I regard it as probable that I was the target. And the firebomb that was thrown through my window on Thursday – *that* wasn't intended for Pappa. That was an attempt to murder me. And it might have worked. It's only by chance that I woke up that night and got out of the house."

I think of Erling in my dream: *Run, Evy.*

"I think Pappa suspected one of you," I say. "I think he believed that one of you was trying to kill him."

Hanne inhales sharply. I cast a strict glance in her direction and she composes herself, says nothing.

"You're in need of money, all three of you. And Pappa believed the person he suspected was willing to do away with him in order to get their hands on their inheritance."

"But Mamma," Hanne says – she can no longer hold her tongue.

"But you're his children," I say. "And parents protect their children. Pappa couldn't go to the police, and he wouldn't wish to do anything that might harm one of you in order to save himself. I believe the solution he had come to was the one his lawyer presented to us: he made arrangements to ensure that none of you would have anything to gain from his death. This, I believe, was his way of neutralising the threat posed by the person he suspected. Had he managed to inform them, they would have known that there was no longer anything to gain from killing him. I don't think it occurred to him that they might try to harm *me*. He probably believed you were closer to me than to him, and presumed the person he suspected posed a danger to no-one but himself. But I see it differently. I think they've also attempted to take my life."

I look at each of them in turn. They're speechless now. Bård has an expression of disbelief in his eyes. Silje's mouth is half open and her cheeks are hollow; she stares at me, entirely uncomprehending.

Hanne considers me with wrinkled brow and narrowed eyes, as if she thinks I'm losing my mind.

"I believe he had arranged to meet this person on the afternoon of the day he died," I say. "To tell them about the arrangements he had made. This, I think, was the final stage of his plan to ensure his safety. But as we know, he never got that far. And that is terribly sad."

The weight of this settles around my heart for a moment: Erling's attempt to protect himself while simultaneously taking care of his family. And just how unsuccessful it was. The soles of his trainers, the bicycle on the asphalt, the plastic clip under his chin.

"But I don't intend to make the same mistake."

I take a breath.

"It has occurred to me that your childhoods might have been harder than I realised. That I haven't been the mother I should have been. It makes me sad to think about this, because you are my children. I love you, all three of you, no matter what."

Here I give a serious look to each of them in turn. None of them reacts to this, it's as if their faces are masks, as if they are simply waiting for what is to come.

"And I will therefore never mention what I'm telling you now to the police. Just like Pappa, I want to protect you. I want that with all of my heart. But I do not intend to sit here in silence and wait to be bumped off. So the way I see it, there are two options. The first is that the person responsible comes forward."

I fall silent. I look at each of them in turn. At first they remain immobile, and then it's as if Silje comes to life. She looks at me, then casts a confused glance at her siblings. This awakens the other two.

"But," Bård says. "Do you expect . . .?"

"I expect," I say, "the person who killed Pappa to speak up."

"Oh my God," he says. "Surely you don't mean . . . it's insane!"

"Bård," Hanne says.

Then there is silence again. I count the ticking of the clock, the heavy, dragging seconds. One. Two. Three. Four. I allow fifteen seconds to pass. I had actually decided on twenty, but until now it hadn't occurred to me just how long that might feel under the weight of such an oppressive silence.

Nobody says anything. Nobody moves. No glass is lifted, no spoon scrapes against a bowl. It's as if we're hardly breathing.

"I see," I say.

I take out my phone, noticing that my fingers are trembling as I tap the screen. I don't have to do much – the message is ready, all I have to do is tap send, but it seems to take an eternity regardless. None of the children interrupt me. They wait as I send the message, and when I look up, the three of them are staring at me.

"Just as I thought," I say. "And therefore, I have no choice but to do this."

I feel beneath the tabletop with my fingertips. Trail them across the knife and onto the smooth envelope. I take hold of it and tug it loose. Set it on the table.

"Here," I say, "in this envelope, is documentation regarding the establishment of the Erling Krogh Memorial Fund. Right now, my lawyer is reading the text I just sent, in which I have confirmed that I wish to transfer all my assets to the fund, with immediate effect. The purpose of the fund is to award an annual prize to a person or organisation that has undertaken significant efforts *to preserve bio-diversity, counteract climate change and . . .* what was the last one again? I don't remember – but regardless, you can read it, it's all in there."

I nod at the envelope.

"The house will be sold," I say. "As will the apartment above the garage, the apartment in the city centre and the cabin and the plots on Tjøme. From the sale of these assets, the fund will award me an amount sufficient to enable me to purchase an apartment of my choosing, which I will be free to use for the rest of my life, and provide me with an annual salary, which will supplement my pension. I am only in receipt of the minimum state pension, as you well know. Beyond this, the fund will manage my assets, with one exception: a separate fund will be established for my grandchildren. Two million kroner will go to Henrik and Fredrik, to be shared between them; two million will go to Max, either alone or, in the event of any future siblings, to be shared with them; and two million will go to any children Silje may have, minus the advance she received when purchasing her apartment. The grandchildren will obtain access to these funds when they turn twenty-one. Should Silje have no children, she herself will receive the money intended for her descendants on the day Max turns twenty-one."

I turn and look at each of them again. Then say, slowly, earnestly:

"Whether I die tonight or in twenty years' time, it will make absolutely no difference to what you receive. You no longer have anything to gain from my death."

The three faces are stiff as masks. I can practically see the cogs turning behind their wax-like foreheads as they attempt to make sense of what I'm saying.

"But," Hanne says finally, "I don't understand. I just don't get how you can do this."

"It's already done," I say. "It's all in there."

I point at the envelope that lies there on the tablecloth, so white and virginal. None of them takes it, not even now, as if they think it might burst into flames should they touch it.

"This is madness," Bård says. "You're disinheriting us?"

"No," I say. "That isn't possible – it's against the law. No – I'm giving away my assets. Which I'm perfectly within my rights to do. And to be honest, it feels pretty good. I'm trying to use these funds to do something *good* in the world. As Pappa would have wanted."

"As Pappa would have wanted," Bård repeats, impotently.

A few seconds pass, the clock ticks. Then Bård slams his fist against the table, causing the rest of us to jump in our seats. The empty dessert bowls also jump, the clatter resounding off the walls.

"No," he shouts. "I refuse to accept this. Have you completely lost it, Mamma? Do *you* think someone is after you, too? Shit, what the hell do I know – but that any of *us* would want to kill you? I mean . . ."

He looks at his sisters.

"That's just utterly *insane*."

Hanne attempts to pull herself together. She moves her bowl, adjusts the angle of her spoon.

"This friend who Pappa confided in," she says. "Mamma – is it that Edvard guy?"

"Yes."

"Because if so, I think we ought to take a moment to think about this," she says. "And ask ourselves what *he* might be looking to gain from all this."

She looks at me. Calculating how best to approach this, is the impression I get.

"Have you, for example, considered that *he* might be after your money?" she says. "Or after you, Mamma. Because you have to agree that it's pretty crazy to come here and claim that any of us would want to kill you. Maybe we should ask ourselves what this guy has to gain?"

"Edvard has nothing to gain," I say calmly. "He's on the board of the memorial fund, but Peter Bull-Clausen is the CEO, and the award recipient will be selected by an independent committee."

Bård's face is white; the mask he has turned on me is bloodless and hard. I watch him closing himself off from me. Slowly. Terribly.

"This is just utterly . . ." he says. "I have no words. *Paranoia* is putting it far too mildly. You're talking about attempted murder here. What *is* this? Have you drunk so much you've given yourself brain damage, or what?"

The hardness in his words, in his tone, settles in my gut, heavy and painful. *Him* – my favourite. I was prepared for this, but it still stings. Some things can never be restored.

"I am sorry for that," I say. "I'm going to do something about my drinking, but I know it's impossible for me to make it up to you. I've been a bad mother."

Bård sniffs.

"And I will carry that with me for the rest of my life," I say. "But I don't intend to allow myself to be murdered over it."

"*Murdered*," he says, giving a hollow laugh. "This is just too much."

"Someone did actually throw a firebomb through my window a few nights ago," I say.

"Maybe it was this Edvard guy," Bård says scornfully. "He seems reasonably enterprising."

"Bård," Hanne says. "I don't think that's particularly helpful."

She turns to face me; she has that hyper-adult look in her eye. As if she's the mother. As if I'm the child.

"Mamma," she says. "How could you think one of us would throw a firebomb into the house? Jesus, I don't even know how to *make* a firebomb."

"It's very easy," I say. "Especially these days, when you can simply look it up online."

For a moment we stare deep into each other's eyes. She's sizing me up, while I do the same to her. She *knows*, I think. They know, all three of them. Gundersen has spoken to them. He must have told them about Bilal's suspicions; asked them what they think.

But I already knew that. The person who started the fire must have known about Bilal. There are far more effective ways to commit arson — especially if you have access to the house. The Molotov cocktail was chosen because it so clearly pointed to me. Almost as if the arsonist was communicating with me: *Just look, see what I'm capable of. The police can't help you, because I know your secrets.* I think the same is true of the evidence I found in the cellar — that those items were put there to cast suspicion on me. And that's why I got rid of them. After we finished our coffee yesterday morning, Edvard drove me into Sørkedalen. I wheeled the bicycle several kilometres into the forest and dumped it in a lake. I threw the other items into another. Peeled the labels off the boxes and bottle of pills first, just to be on the safe side. Disposing of these items wasn't without risk, but the risk of keeping them was greater.

Silje clears her throat. All three of us turn to face her. She has set her hands on the table, palms down, and she's staring intently at her empty bowl. Seems to be scrutinising the remnants of her cloudberries and cream.

"I think," she says, "that we just have to understand that this is what Mamma wants."

Hanne and Bård protest in unison – you can't be serious, shouts Hanne; but it's fucking incomprehensible, shouts Bård. Silje only sits there, unperturbed, considering her bowl.

"It's true that someone threw a firebomb at her," she says. "And there really was a gas leak at the cabin – that policeman said as much. So it makes sense for her to protect herself."

Then she looks up. She looks first at her siblings and then she turns to me. Sets her candid eyes on me, appearing both familiar and strange.

"It wasn't me, Mamma," she says gravely. "I would never want to hurt either you or Pappa. I think it's a shame that you're doing this, but I understand."

She thinks for a moment.

"And I think the fund is a good idea."

"It most certainly is not a fucking good idea," Bård shouts.

He gets up, toppling his chair.

"This is sheer lunacy. So you think it was me? You think it was Hanne? Jesus, Mamma, it wasn't any of us. I just hope you understand what you're doing. Because if you do this – if you actually go through with this – then I want nothing more to do with you. Do you understand that? You'll never see the boys, ever again. Is that what you want?"

I'm prepared for this, too. I had thought it might be Hanne, rather than Bård, who would come out with this, but I also know that I have a soft spot for him, and that I'm therefore a little blind. My throat feels thick and tight.

"It's already done, Bård," I say. "I did it when I sent the text. It's irreversible, and I couldn't change it now, even if I wanted to. But I hope we can stay on good terms regardless."

"Like hell we can," he shouts. "What do you think is going to happen? That you can just rob us of our entire inheritance, of everything that's – shit, everything that's *ours*? And that we'll just continue to come here and fritter away Sunday afternoons? While you get shit-faced in the kitchen instead of cooking the dinner?"

My fingertips fumble beneath the tabletop again; find the end of the piece of tape that holds the knife in place.

"Because you can just forget it," he says. "Do this, and you lose us. You'll no longer mean anything to me."

I carefully loosen the piece of tape from around the handle of the knife.

"Bård," Hanne says again, and he turns to look at her.

"Don't tell me you're not thinking the same thing, Hanne," he says. "Don't even try to pretend you're not thinking *exactly* the same thing I am."

"Of course," she says. "But I think we ought to drop it now. Look at this again a little later, right?"

She nods towards the envelope. Bård reaches out to snatch it. He looks at me.

"I'm going to get my lawyers on this," he says. "Just so you know. This isn't over."

We hear him stomping out into the hallway. I let go of the piece of tape, allow the knife to hang there.

The girls leave shortly afterwards. Hanne's expression is closed, too, but in a way that is different from her brother's. She's put on that know-it-all look, the one that says she knows best, that she's enduring my ridiculous notions thanks to patience that is now wearing extremely thin. Not much more is said between us. They hug me, both of them. Hanne's embrace is loose and mechanical,

388

but Silje hugs me properly. Afterwards, she cups my cheek with her palm.

I stand there at the window in the hallway. Watch them walk down the drive to their brother, who stands leaning against the bonnet of the car, typing away on his phone. The three of them stand there for a moment. Words are exchanged. Bård throws his hands into the air. Hanne ushers them into the car and gets behind the wheel. Then they drive away.

When they're gone, I go back into the dining room. I take the knife from where it hangs beneath the tabletop and put it away. I tidy away the bowls, too, and all the glasses. Blow out the candles. Put everything back in its usual place. Stand there between the living room and the dining room and look around me. For the first time in a very long while I feel total peace of mind, completely safe. I'm home.

ONE YEAR AFTER

The asphalt in Sondrevegen is freshly swept and clean. Just as it was a year ago today – the day Erling came cycling down this hill and collapsed. Now, apart from me, the road is empty as I walk up the hill from the station, a bouquet of lilacs in my hands. I have cut the flowers from a bush in the grounds of my new housing cooperative. These ones are purple. As they should be.

Erling collapsed towards the top of the hill. I remember there was damage to the edge of the pavement just next to where he lay That Day, and it was never repaired, so it's easy to spot the right place. I stop. There's no trace of him here now. To anyone else this is just a mark on the road, a place you pass. Very few people know that this is where Erling Krogh died.

Because his body wasn't getting the medicine it needed? Because the pills in the jar had been replaced with a placebo? Or for some other reason? Poison, for example, which didn't show up in the post-mortem tests? I close my eyes and take a deep breath, all the way down into my stomach. Then I bend my knees and place the bouquet of lilacs on the ground.

For a moment I stand there, my eyes focused on the flowers on the asphalt. I try to bring to mind that morning: Maria Berger in her yellow running jacket on the road ahead of me; the people standing in a ring around him. The soles of Erling's worn trainers, the plastic clip on the strap beneath his chin. I remember all this, but it no longer hurts to think about it. These days I suffer from a different ache, the dull pain that resides in my abdomen: life without him.

It was only once I had sold the house and moved into the light and airy modern apartment in Røa that the slow trickle of grief began. I stood making dinner in my new kitchen, and refrained from putting salt in the food because Erling's doctor had said he should cut down. There was an article about recycling in the newspaper, and I began to rip it out to save it for him. I went to the housing cooperative's annual general meeting, and imagined how it would be to have him by my side. To walk home together afterwards, discussing what was said. I still catch myself wanting to show him this new life I've built.

During the summer, I checked myself into rehab and spent a few weeks at an institution. Ate my meals around a table with other addicts, chewing sliced bread that I spread with butter and jam from single-portion packets. I attended groups, shared the worst sides of myself with others. Learned the twelve steps: *We admitted we were powerless over alcohol – that our lives had become unmanageable.* I confessed my sins to the other patients, to the staff, to a young psychologist who appeared not to have experienced a single rainy day in her life. Didn't touch a drop of alcohol for the six subsequent months. I currently have strict rules: never alone, never more than two glasses, and never on weekdays. I still attend the clinic once a month.

I have also finally accepted the twelve steps. I no longer attempt to minimise my problem. No longer believe that *my* drinking is a mere trifle, compared to the full-blown alcoholism others struggle with. Realise that I will carry this vulnerability with me for the rest of my life. I also recognise what it has cost my family. As the steps state: *We made a list of all persons we had harmed, and became willing to make amends to them all. We made direct amends to such people wherever possible, except when to do so would injure them or others. These steps aren't so easy to complete.*

With Silje, it's been possible. She comes to visit me once or twice a week. We make dinner, and as we eat, we talk about Erling.

What was Pappa like when he was young, Silje might ask, or, what do you think his home life was like when he was growing up?

Between us, we cobble together his life. I don't know whether she still desires a child of her own, but it has occurred to me that she might want to hold on to Erling's memory so she can pass it on to her children. It may also be that she wishes to use it in her art. But maybe it's mostly something she does for herself. I don't ask. I'm just happy to be able to talk about it.

Whether it is possible to make amends with Hanne, I don't know. She and I still speak on the phone, but less frequently than before. Apparently, she doesn't speak with Silje very often, either. Sometimes she comes over for dinner, generally without Max and Ørjan. The unintentional accusations – this tendency she and I both have to say the wrong thing to each other – have almost ceased. I find this surprisingly painful, because it has only dawned on me now, far too late, that this tendency was benign after all. It was about our attempts to get closer to one another, in spite of our differences. Now, whenever she's here, it feels as if she's logged off. She vanishes from her eyes; only the shell of her remains.

I've asked her to forgive me for drinking so much when she was young.

"Don't dwell on it, Mamma," she said to me, batting my words away.

But perhaps things will come right again. In the winter, she finally convinced the bank to pre-approve her and Ørjan for a mortgage, so they were able to buy the house in Kjelsås after all. She seems to have thawed a little after that.

Bård no longer speaks to me. I pull my jacket around me as I stand here looking at the bouquet of lilacs on the asphalt, because this still hurts: the fact that he, my firstborn, cut all contact. He's angry, Lise says, and terribly bitter. Lise calls me every now and then, so I get to hear how they're doing. She told me that Bård dissolved his company and took a job at a property development agency. He's relatively happy, his wife says.

I don't ask many questions. Tell myself things might get better with time. And yet, I see Erling's stubbornness in my boy, and he may well cling to his rage until his dying day. This is the price I must pay, because I was not willing to die in order for Bård to get what he wanted, but of course it hurts. I inhale deeply. Exhale and try to release the ache from my body, to let it out with my breath. This is something I learned at the clinic. It's surprisingly effective.

Edvard I see, if not weekly, then at least every other week. We go out to eat at restaurants he's heard about. He keeps statistics on how happy we are with the food. I send our top recommendations on to Synne, who thanks me enthusiastically, although I have no idea if she ever follows up on our suggestions. Every three months there's a board meeting of the Erling Krogh Memorial Fund, and three times during the autumn I met with Miriam and two others to discuss the nominees for the Erling Krogh Memorial Prize. Working with the fund brings me more joy than I ever thought possible. I considered it something I had to do to disarm my children – I had no idea just how meaningful it would be, how life-giving. I enjoy hearing experts argue their case, and I like forming my own opinions, being heard. And being contradicted, too, when appropriate, because criticism is important, and more even than this: I enjoy being taken seriously.

I've begun to understand Erling's commitment to the environment, too. For years he tried to get me to see what he saw, peppering me with statistics and dark prophecies, asking me to read scores of books and pamphlets. Now I've finally read them. And he was right, I think now: the world is in a lamentable state. The challenges we face are immense – impossible to overcome, almost. There is little an individual can do, but we have to try all the same. The fund feels important, it's a contribution I can make. Just before Christmas we awarded 200,000 kroner to an organisation in Østfold.

I think less about what happened in May last year, too. Recognise that I'll have ups and downs, that in some periods I will have difficult thoughts. But not all the time, not anymore. And I've almost stopped waking in the middle of the night and sniffing the air for a hint of smoke.

Yes, I have built a life for myself. Quite a different life from the one Erling and I shared. Strictly speaking, it's one that suits me better. But I catch myself missing him more and more often. His sounds, his possessions, the smell of him in the house. Erling, who was always there.

In August, Gundersen stopped by one last time. I was in the garden, weeding the flower beds to prepare the house for sale. An unfamiliar Toyota parked down the road, and I heard his rhythmic footsteps on the gravel as he approached.

"Hello," he called to me as he came into view beside the garage.

I looked up. He was standing exactly where Erling had stood the last time I saw him alive.

We sat on the terrace. Gundersen told me the case surrounding Erling's death had been shelved. No punishable offence had been committed, was the conclusion, because they hadn't found enough evidence to indicate that it was murder. Gundersen said this with a certain amount of regret in his voice. The attempts on my life were still active cases, but he warned me that when so much time has passed without a breakthrough, the prospects for a conviction aren't great. Unfortunately, as he said.

He seemed genuine, too. Maybe he thought I was afraid, that I feared a stranger was lurking in the bushes at night, with a bag full of leaky gas bottles and Molotov cocktails. Or he may have taken the calmness with which I received his apology as evidence that I faked the entire thing. For a while we sat in silence, drinking our coffee in the afternoon sun.

"So you're selling up?" he asked.

"Yes, I don't want to live here anymore," I said, before adding, as an afterthought: "I never really liked this house."

He smiled. Looked a little preoccupied. I presumed he was thinking about something else, perhaps something he had to do afterwards: stop by the police station first, then on to the supermarket and then home. I imagined he probably had a partner waiting for him, a woman around his age or perhaps a couple of years younger, who had made dinner, or whom he would make dinner for. I could just imagine them at the kitchen table in a dusty apartment. But then he turned to face me with those sharp eyes, the ones that registered every movement, every quiver of the hand, every twitch of the mouth.

"But you're not afraid, Evy," he said, with the weight of a statement. "And why is that, do you think?"

I shrugged, looked down into my cup.

"I can't live the rest of my life running scared."

He looked at me – I counted four seconds – and then he said: "No – there's something else. You know something, don't you?"

For a moment we simply sat there. He narrowed his eyes.

"You know who was after you."

An overwhelming desire to confess bubbled up in me: just imagine, to be able to tell this intelligent man just how smart I've been! How I made all the arrangements, how cleverly I disarmed my children. But I swallowed it down. This is my penance: I will protect them from themselves, from the consequences of what they have done. As the steps say: I am willing to make amends. I will make direct amends with them, wherever possible.

"There's no more to say than what I've already told you," I said. "But I know how to take care of myself."

He considered me with his narrowed eyes.

"What we're talking about here is an extremely dangerous person," he said. "Someone who has killed, and who has tried to kill again."

The graveness of his voice made me uneasy, and I looked away. His gaze was penetrating, and I feared that if I met it, I would confess in spite of myself.

"When dealing with dangerous people, you need the help of the police," Gundersen stressed then. "Many people believe they can handle things themselves. But sadly, many of them are wrong."

Still, I said no more. Not long after, I sold the house. I haven't been back there since.

And this was actually the only thing I was supposed to do here in Montebello: find the place where Erling died and lay the flowers. Now I turn around. It's a beautiful spring day. I could take a walk in the forest, take along a flask of coffee. Perhaps sit out on my new veranda with a book. Because there's actually nothing more to do here, not for me. But then I just can't help myself. I simply have to go up to Nordheimbakken. I have to see my old house one last time.

There it lies, towering on its hilltop. The new garage is modern; the couple who bought the house have set up a trampoline beside the terrace, and I can see plastic toys in vivid colours strewn across the steep slope of the garden, but even these cheery props are no match for the house's inherent bleakness. When I came here for the first time, the property had seemed awe-inspiring. An awe with more fear to it, I have since thought, than wonder. The hill that must be climbed in order to enter it; all the dark rooms. It's a relief that I will never have to set foot in it again.

And it is as I'm standing there like this that I catch sight of her. My heart sinks. She's already seen me, waving exaggeratedly and wildly in my direction. On any other day I wouldn't have had anything against catching up, having a chat, but today I would have preferred to have been spared it. At least she isn't wearing that yellow running jacket.

"Well here's a sight for sore eyes," she says as she comes striding towards me.

She smiles broadly. She must have bleached her teeth, because they're far whiter than is natural, and Maria Berger has always been one to keep up appearances. Her shoulder pads and bouffant hair disappeared with the eighties, but she remains true to type. As we all do, in one way or another.

"Yes," I say wearily. "I suppose I am."

"It must be around a year ago that Erling died," she says. "Isn't it?"

"Around that, yes."

"I was just thinking about it earlier today. About how awful it was."

I nod. I'd prefer not to go into the details.

"So how are you doing?" I ask instead.

She embarks on a long and complicated story about how her gym was forced to move. As I half-listen I glance at the flower beds that once were mine. Yes – I should have gone straight to the T-bane station after laying the lilacs. I should never have come up here.

"And your family?" Maria asks.

I hesitate. To say that everything is fine feels dishonest, and to tell the truth feels excessively frank.

"Oh, you know," is all I say. "Well enough."

A brief gust of wind causes the leaves on the bushes in the garden to tremble. I notice this. Otherwise, there's complete silence around us. Not a car, not a sound. Only this faint rustling. And then Maria says: "I mean, what happened to Ørjan's parents, though. I heard about it."

The breeze is chill; the skin of my neck becomes goosepimpled.

"Such a terrible business," she says. "I gather that Hanne and Ørjan were there when it happened?"

Everything seems to happen so slowly as I turn to face her, so infinitely slowly. The features of Maria's friendly face are arranged into serious creases, and I see every detail of this: the lipstick that has smudged a little at the right-hand corner of her mouth, the blonde hairs on her upper lip, a tiny chip to her left front tooth. Indeed – I now see everything.

"My cousin lives on the neighbouring farm, you see," Maria says. "She's the one who told me. It was some bad seafood, apparently. What's it called again – botulism. It affects the nervous system, causes paralysis. Absolutely awful. And it can be deadly – as it turned out to be for Ørjan's parents. What were their names again? Tom and Eva? Lovely people, my cousin says."

Utter silence around us. As if no sound other than her voice exists.

Tom and Eva. They had stood outside the church at my daughter's wedding: Tom in a suit, red-faced with a pride he wasn't quite able to express. *Oh, my dear son*, he said, several times, giving Ørjan a companionable punch to the shoulder. Eva, small and plump, in her pale-blue silk dress with glittering clips in her grizzled curls. She smiled constantly, seemed so genuinely happy. I remember how they stood hand in hand when the priest declared our children man and wife. The way Eva leaned her head against her husband's shoulder; how he rested his cheek against her brow. And then in my mind's eye I see Hanne, in the white dress of her dreams.

"Poor Ørjan," Maria says. "It must be awful, to lose both one's parents so suddenly."

Hanne's bridal gown was purchased from an exclusive boutique in the city; her hair was pinned up with white flowers. She smiled beautifully for the camera, hugged her in-laws outside the church. As Gundersen said: we're talking about an extremely dangerous person.

"Apparently Ørjan is an only child, too," Maria says. "He inherited the entire farm. But I gather they sold it right away?"

As Gundersen also said: many people believe they can handle things themselves. And sadly, many of them are wrong.

Erling was wrong in thinking she would never pose a threat to me. And have I now made the same mistake? A disease that affects the nervous system. The smiling, grey-haired Tom and Eva, lifeless in their beds.

"Is everything okay, Evy?" Maria Berger asks. "You look a little pale."

The semi-detached property in Kjelsås, which she was suddenly able to buy after all. Erling at the kitchen table, just before he cycled to his death: it was quite concerning, he had said then, really quite concerning. The person he was supposed to speak to, the private appointment. *When I get home, it will all be done with.*

I lift my gaze to the brown house on the hill. Imagine that I'm standing inside it, in the hallway outside the kitchen. Where Mother had stood during the Easter dinner party. Mother, who no longer understands the passing of time, who can no longer distinguish what's happening now from what happened forty years ago. Mother, who thinks that I'm her sister.

I imagine how it would have looked, had it been Hanne who walked through those double doors, down the hallway and into the study. Her figure would have been tall and slim, because she has the same build I had when I was young. Who went into the study? Evy.

But Hanne looks like me – she looks just the way I did when I was her age. And not least: the colour of her hair is the exact same shade that mine once was.

HELENE FLOOD is a psychologist who lives in Oslo with her husband and two children. *The Therapist*, her first novel for adults, was the winner of Norway's Best Crime Debut Prize and Iceland's award for Best Translated Crime Novel. Film rights have been sold, as well as translation rights in twenty-nine languages.

ALISON MCCULLOUGH is a Norwegian-to-English translator based in Stavanger, Norway. Previous translations include *The Therapist* by Helene Flood, *The Wolf Age* by Tore Skeie and *Lean Your Loneliness Slowly Against Mine* by Klara Hveberg, which was longlisted for the PEN Translation Prize 2022.